The Land of Afternoon

A Satire

Gilbert Knox

Alpha Editions

This edition published in 2022

ISBN : 9789356701922

Design and Setting By
Alpha Editions
www.alphaedis.com
Email - info@alphaedis.com

Contents

Foreword

However this novel may be classified by readers or librarians, it is frankly intended to be a satire upon some phases of social and political life in Canada. Satire is properly a criticism of human folly or unworthiness in a class or in the mass, and the exact limning of people in real life is no part of its metier. When it makes such an attempt, it ceases to be satire and tends to become biography seasoned with defamation—a sad misuse of what is broadly regarded as a medium for the regeneration of society.

But however satire is regarded in the abstract by his readers, the author desires it to be clearly understood that all the characters upon his stage are purely imaginary. While he thought it necessary to occupy himself with some unpleasant minor types, on the other hand, he felt an optimistic joy in the creation of his protagonist. He feels that "Raymond Dilling" is no false start with the practical ethics of Superman. On the contrary, he believes that there are many men with whom we mingle in every-day contact, who, if put to the test, would react with a moral firmness and fineness quite measurable with "Dilling's" conduct.

THEY CAME

CHAPTER 1.

*B*yward Market had been freshened during the night by a heavy fall of powdery snow, that knew no peace from a bitter wind which drove it, in stinging clouds, up and down the street. The thermometer had made its record drop of the season.

Marjorie Dilling stood on the outskirts of a tight-packed group and shivered. The strangeness of the scene struck her afresh; the sense of loneliness was almost overpowering. She simply could not bring herself to push and jostle as the other women did—and a few men, too!—consequently she was always thrust away from the curb and prevented from seeing what lay beneath the furs and blankets and odd bits of cloth in the carts. Only now and again could she catch a glimpse of a tower of frozen beef, or rigid hogs which were trundled by their hind legs through the thronged streets, in a manner strongly suggestive of a wheelbarrow. Or, as the crowds broke and parted, she could occasionally see a stiff fringe of poultry and rabbits strung across the ends of the wagons. Eggs, butter, vegetables and cream were well covered, and spared in so far as possible, the rigours of the morning.

Byward was an open market which attracted farmers from districts as remote as the Upper Gatineau—across the river, in the Province of Quebec. Behind the line of carts or sleighs—automobiles, now!—there ran a row of nondescript buildings that rarely claimed the attention of the marketers; a confusion of second-hand stores, an occasional produce shop, and third-rate public houses, whose broad windows revealed a cluster of dilapidated chairs flanked by battered *crachoirs*, which had seen many years of unspeakable service. Behind these, a narrow passage led to the abode of spirits, of the kind latterly and peculiarly called departed. Here, the farmers gathered for warmth in winter and coolness in summer, and to slake—or intensify—their thirst in either season, while their women-folk remained in discomfort outside, and attended to the practical issues of the day.

The sigh that fluttered from Marjorie's lips took form like a ghostly balloon and floated away on the frosty air. Her basket was light and her spirits were heavy. She found it incredibly difficult to shop in the Ottawa market. She simply dreaded Saturday mornings.

At the corner, where the wind whipped down the street and few people cared to linger, she found herself standing before an ancient crone, who sat amid an assortment of roughly-cured hides, and under a huge, weather-stained umbrella. At her feet lay a rusty pail overflowing with a curious mass that looked like bloated sausages in the last stages of decay.

"What—what is that?" asked Marjorie, in her soft timid voice.

The old woman made unintelligible sounds from between toothless gums.

"I beg your pardon?"

"I tol' you, it is *sang pouding.* 'Ow much you want?"

"I don't want any, thank you," answered Marjorie. "I was looking for some sweetbreads. Have you any?"

"Sweet *bread?*" echoed the ancient, grumpily. "Well, why you don' look on de store, hein? W'at you t'ink I am—de baker's cart?"

Although unaware of the complexities of the French tongue and the French character, Marjorie perceived a rebuff in the old woman's words. She apologised hastily and moved away. What, she kept asking herself, could she substitute for sweetbreads? Chickens were expensive and eggs, a fabulous price. Nobody in Ottawa seemed to keep hens . . .

"Have *you* any sweetbreads?"

She began to feel a little hysterical. It *was* a funny question! No wonder the old woman answered her crossly. Have you any sweetbreads? *How* many times had she asked it? She thought of the game the children played—*Black sheep, black sheep, have you any wool?* And what on earth should she get in place of sweetbreads? Raymond was so difficult about his food. He had such a tiny and pernickety appetite . . .

By wriggling, she gained the curb before another cart.

"Have *you* any sweetbreads?"

No one paid her the slightest heed. The centre of the stage was held by a tall, spare woman with a stridulous voice. Marjorie knew her slightly. Two weeks ago she had called—not as people called at home, in Pinto Plains— but sternly and coldly, neither giving nor receiving pleasure by the visit, save when she had laid three bits of pasteboard on the corner of the table and left the house. Mrs. Pratt was the wife of a cheerfully ineffectual professional man with political aspirations, and she felt her position keenly. So did Marjorie; and she backed away while summoning her courage to speak.

"A dollar and a half?" Mrs. Pratt was saying. "Outrageous! I can't think what you people are coming to! I'll give you a dollar and a quarter, and not one penny more." She indicated a pair of frozen chickens, each with a large mauve face, that lay exposed on an old red blanket.

"Can't do it, lady," said the farmer, with chattering teeth, "it cost me mor'n that to feed them this three year," and he winked heavily at the surrounding circle.

"Oh, they're fowl! Well then, of course, they're not worth that much! There's a woman across the road,"—Mrs. Pratt swept her muff vaguely towards the horizon and unconsciously disarranged Marjorie's hat,—"who is selling her fowl for eighty cents!"

"*I'll* take them," cried a woman at this juncture. "It's too cold to haggle over a few cents. Giv'um to me!" She thrust a dollar and a half into the man's hand, seized the chickens and started off.

"Those are mine!" called Mrs. Pratt, in a tone that rivalled the sharpness of the atmosphere.

"You take the others at eighty cents," returned the woman, amid a ripple of laughter.

"Impertinence!" snapped Mrs. Pratt, as she turned away.

Marjorie drifted on, her basket still empty. These awful Saturday mornings! They seemed to accentuate her loneliness. Of course, the cold discouraged long conversations and the exchange of tittle-tattle that makes shopping, to some people, so delightful, but she was aware of the greetings that passed between women as they met—a tip, perhaps, as to some bargain, or a brief reference to some impending social function—and she would have been grateful for even the smallest sign of friendly recognition. Frequently, she saw people who had called upon her, but evidently she had made too little impression to be remembered. How different from Pinto Plains, where everybody knew her and cordiality was mutual!

She noticed that many of the ladies who came into church richly dressed on Sundays, wore the most dreadfully shabby clothes at market, but it was not until long afterwards, she understood that this was part of a scheme for economy—for beating the farmers at their own game. They disguised themselves that they might give no hint as to the fatness of their bank account, thus implying that well-to-do shoppers were asked a higher price than those of obviously modest means. These same shabbily-clad ladies never seemed to buy very much, and Marjorie often wondered how it was worth their while to spend the morning with so little result. In those days, she didn't realise that they had left their motors round the corner, and that their parcels were transferred, two or three at a time, to a liveried chauffeur who sat in a heated car and read stimulating items from the *Eye-Opener*.

Others, she learned, dragged overflowing baskets into one of the "Market Stores," whose prices were known to be a few cents in excess of those demanded by the owners of the carts. Here, they made an insignificant purchase, thereby placing the onus of free delivery on the shoulders of the management. The degree to which this practice was employed varied with the temperament of the shopper. Those of a less sensitive nature, felt no hesitation in asking Lavalee, the aristocratic Purveyor of Sea Food and Game, to send home six dollars' worth of marketing with a pound of smelts. Likewise, Smithson suffered the exigencies of trade, not only delivering the type of foodstuffs that he didn't keep, but every week of the year he was asked to send home the very things that were purchasable in his own store and which had been bought for a few cents less, half a block away. Seeing the baskets of produce that were piled high on the sidewalk every Saturday morning, Marjorie wondered how it was worth while for him to carry on his business or maintain his livery, at all!

Having made a few purchases, she set off down Mosgrove Street for the tram as fast as her burden would permit, when she came for the second time upon Mrs. Pratt, still searching for a bargain in chickens.

"One seventy-five?" she was saying. "Sheer piracy! I refused a much better pair for a dollar fifty!"

"Call it a dollar fifty, ma'am," agreed the farmer, between spasms of coughing. "The wife'll give me the devil, but I'm 'most dead with cold, and I wanta go home."

Pity for the man, coupled with a touch of innocent curiosity, tempted Marjorie to linger close at hand and see the end of the transaction.

"But that's what I'm telling you," cried Mrs. Pratt. "They're not worth a dollar fifty. They're miserable things. Half fed ..." Her eyes rested upon the owner resentfully, as though emphasising a definite resemblance between him and his produce. "I'll give you a dollar and a quarter and not one penny more!"

"Oh, lady! I've gotta live!"

Something in the man's tone told the astute lady that he was weakening, that he needed the money, that the chickens were hers. She pushed a dollar and a quarter into his hand, seized her purchase, and disappeared round the corner, into a waiting limousine.

A little later that same morning, Marjorie, finding that the children were all right in the care of Mrs. Plum, who "charred" her on Saturdays, went down town to The Ancient Chattellarium. Her errand was simple. She wished to have a piece of furniture repaired. It had been broken in the moving, and one of her callers had given her this address.

The Chattellarium could not, even by the most vulgar, be called a shop. It was an opulent apartment where elegant furniture was displayed—and sold—at dignified prices. Marjorie Dilling paused uncertainly on the threshold, feeling that she must, through error, have strayed into someone's residence.

But she hadn't! A lady glanced over the rim of a lampshade she was making, and invited her to enter.

"Just looking around?" she asked, with the instinct of one who recognises the difference between a shopper and a buyer. "I've got some rather nice things just unpacked," and she went on sticking pins into the dull-rose silk with which she was covering a huge wire frame.

"Thank you, very much," answered Marjorie, stealing a timid glance over her shoulder, "but I haven't a great deal of time, and I really came to see—if—if—to ask about getting a piece of furniture repaired. I was told that I might have it done, here."

The young lady took several pins from her mouth and looked up. She was quite pretty and had a pleasant manner in spite of her way of addressing most people as though they were her inferiors, and a few very prominent people as though they were her equals. She talked incessantly, and it had become her custom to illumine her speech with Glittering Personalities.

She discovered Marjorie's name and that her husband was a recently-elected Back Bencher from an obscure little Western town, as well as the nature of the repairs required, so cleverly, that she seemed to be answering questions instead of asking them, and she was ever so kind in promising to help.

"Of course, I *don't* do this sort of thing as a rule," she explained, "I simply *couldn't!* My men are dreadfully overworked as it is, and we are three months behind in our orders. But because I have just recently repaired a dressing-table for Government House, and repolished a china cabinet for Lady Elton, at Rockcliffe, I haven't the conscience to refuse *you.*"

Marjorie was rather uncomfortable after this speech. She had no earthly wish to ask a favour, and felt unduly exalted by "being repaired" in such impressive company. She tried to make this clear, and urged the young lady to suggest some much more humble establishment or person.

"I feel at such a loss," she explained, "not knowing where to turn . . ." and then, when Miss Brant had insisted upon helping her out of the difficulty, she said, "I wouldn't dare trust it to just anyone, you know. It's such a lovely thing! Solid mahogany, a sort of what-not design, with some of the little compartments enclosed in glass, and mirrors at the back—and each shelf ending in a decoration like a wee, little carved steeple. It's one of the steeple things that is broken, and one of the glass doors. I told Mr. Dilling,"—the young lady winced when she spoke of her husband as "Mr. Dilling"—"that it reminded me of a beautiful doll's house, and that we would have to collect heaps of souvenir spoons and things to fill it."

"How interesting," observed the other.

"And the association counts for so much, you see. The townspeople—our friends—gave it to us when we left Pinto Plains; a kind of testimonial it was, in the church. They said such beautiful things, I'll never forget it." Her voice was husky.

"Charming," murmured the young lady, wondering how such a pretty woman could be so plain.

Marjorie asked to be given some idea of the price, but her enquiry was waved airily aside. "Oh, don't bother about that," she was told. "It will only be a matter of my workman's time—" an implication that translated itself to Mrs. Dilling in the terms of cents, but which to the young lady resolved itself into about fifteen dollars.

Marjorie's thanks were cut short by the entrance of two Arresting Personalities.

One of them was Lady Fanshawe, the wife of a retired lumber magnate, and the other—Mrs. Blaine—assisted her husband to discharge his social duties as a Minister of the Crown.

"Well, well," cried Miss Brant, assuming her other manner, "this *is* a surprise! I'm simply *thrilled!* Only yesterday, I was saying to Lady Elton that I hadn't seen you since the House opened. I'm *dying* to tell you all about my trip in England, and my *dear*, such things as I've brought back! That's one!" She indicated a red lacquer table. "Isn't it a perfect *dream?* And there's another—no, no—not the mirror, the table! It was positively and absolutely taken from Bleakshire Castle where Disraeli used to visit, and there he sat to write some of his marvellous speeches! Isn't it *thrilling?*"

The ladies agreed that she had done very well, and moved about the apartment under the spur of her constant direction. Marjorie, feeling that she ought to go, but not knowing whether to slip away unnoticed or to shake hands and say goodbye, had just decided upon the former course, when Mrs. Pratt made a flamboyant entrance.

Seeing the group at the farther end of the room, she bewildered Marjorie with a nod that was like a rap over the knuckles, and rustled self-consciously forward.

"Good morning," she cried, so graciously that Marjorie could scarcely recognise her voice. "Cold, isn't it? I've just come from market. It was simply perishing down there—perishing!" She left an entire syllable out of this word, pronouncing it as though speaking the name of a famous American General, then continued, "I'm a perfect martyr when it comes to marketing! I can't overcome a sense of duty towards the *fermers*, who depend on us for encouragement and support; and when all's said and done, the only char'ty worth while is the kind that helps people to help themselves. Don't you agree with me, Lady Fanshawe?"

Lady Fanshawe supposed so, and turned to the examination of a Meissen bowl. Mrs. Blaine caught sight of an old French print on the far wall and appeared to lose interest in all else. Miss Brant discovered a blemish of some sort on the red lacquer table and bent anxiously over it, using the corner of her handkerchief in lieu of a duster.

No one considered Marjorie at all. Each was engrossed in her part, playing a little scene in the successful *Comédie Malice* which has been running without a break since June 8th, 1866, in the Capital.

If Mrs. Pratt was conscious of any lack of cordiality in the attitude of the others, she gave no sign. Hers was an ebullient part. All she had to do was to gush over the people who snubbed her, and to inveigle them into her house (making sure that their visits were chronicled in the Press). Incidentally, she had to provide them with as much as they wished to drink, and more than they wished to eat, and to acquire the reputation for liberal spending when and where her extravagance would be noted and commented upon.

Lady Fanshawe and Mrs. Blaine were cast in simpler parts. They had merely to preserve an air of well-bred disdain, merging now and again into restrained amazement.

Miss Brant, on the other hand, had a very difficult role to play. Marjorie scarcely realised how difficult. It devolved upon her to take advantage of Mrs. Pratt's effort to impress the others, to sell her the most expensive and unsaleable articles in the establishment, and, at the same time, to convey subtly to Lady Fanshawe and Mrs. Blaine, her contempt for this monied upstart.

The conversation progressed in this vein:

MRS. PRATT.—Now, *do* help me pick up some odds and ends for my new home.

MISS BRANT.—Oh, have you moved?

MRS. PRATT.—Dear me, yes! Our old house was much too cramped for entertaining.

MISS BRANT (*Half confidentially to Lady Fanshawe*).—Speaking of entertaining, shall I see you, by any chance, at the Country Club, tomorrow?

LADY FANSHAWE (*Distantly*).—I am going to Mrs. Long's luncheon, if that is what you mean.

MISS BRANT (*Burbling*).—It's *exactly* what I mean! I'm *so thrilled* at being asked—humble little me—with all you impressive personages.

Mrs. Long was the wife of the owner of THE CHRONICLE and it was suspected that she found the columns—both social and political—of her husband's paper a convenient medium for the maintaining of discipline and the administration of justice. She was naturally held in very high esteem, and persons of astuteness made much of her.

"I never know what's going on," she was fond of saying, "for I can't endure the sight of a newspaper. It's so much easier to blame than to read them," she said, paraphrasing Dr. Johnson.

Notwithstanding her professed disinterestedness, however, the arm of coincidence seemed longer than usual when it was observed that the recently-distinguished Lady Elton, who had overlooked her when issuing invitations to a reception in honour of her husband's knighthood, appeared on the following day as "Mrs. Elton". And, furthermore, that on the day succeeding this, her letter of protest, which was never intended for other than editorial eyes, was published under the heading "REGRETTABLE ERROR in ignoring a NEW TITTLE!" This was only one of many such incidents that entertained the subscribers and suggested that there might be a subtle influence behind the typographical errors which occurred in the composing room.

Mrs. Pratt's voice rolled like a relentless sea over that of the others, as she announced: "We've bought the Tillington place."

MISS BRANT.—Oh, that charming old house! Tudor, isn't it? I used to go there as a child. They had some *wonderful* things. I recall the bookcase especially, that stood opposite the bow-window in the library. Er—er—something like that one, it was. And one knob was off the drawer—I remember it distinctly.

MRS. PRATT (*examining the piece indicated*).—I think I'll take this one.

MISS BRANT (*evidently much embarrassed*).—Oh, *really* now—I didn't mean to suggest—this is really *too* dreadful! I assure you, I was only reminiscencing.

MRS. PRATT.—Well, I'll take it. It's much more suitable than my old one. Do *you* like it, Lady Fanshawe?

LADY FANSHAWE (*as though not having heard the question*).—Delightful!

MISS BRANT.—Well, you're awfully good, I'm sure! I'm really ever so glad you've got it. It's rather a good thing, you know—only, I don't want you to think . . . However, if you change your mind after you get it home, of course, I'll take it back. I mean, you *may* find it out of tune with your old—er—er—your *own* things.

MRS. PRATT.—What would you suggest in the way of a chair, and a table, perhaps?

MISS BRANT (*tearing herself from a whispered pæon on the subject of Mrs. Blaine's hat*).—Well, of course, if you want something good, that's rather nice! A little heavy for the modern home, but *the* thing for the Tillington library. And there's rather a decent chair—see, Lady Fanshawe? Isn't that cross-stitch adorable?—that harmonises perfectly with the other two pieces. I don't deny that it would be a bit stiff for the tired business man to sit in, but for the person who can *afford* to have a well-balanced room . . .

MRS. PRATT (*promptly*).—I'll take the chair!

Quietly, Marjorie left the room, and as the door closed behind her, Mrs. Pratt was saying in an attempt at playful graciousness.

"A hundred and seventy-five? Vurry reasonable! And it's such a satisfaction to get the best! I hope, Lady Fanshawe, and you, too, Mrs. Blaine, that you'll drop in on Tuesday afternoon for a cuppa-tea, and tell me how you like my new home!"

CHAPTER 2.

*T*he Dillings had come to Ottawa joyously, eager to accept its invitation and to become identified with its interests. They were less flattered by the call than elated by it. Neither of them expected merely to skim the pleasures offered by life in the Capital; they were acutely alive to their responsibilities, and were ready to assume them. They hoped to gain something from the great city, it is true, but equally did they long to give. Everyone who was privileged to live in Ottawa must, they imagined, have something of value to contribute to their country, and the Dillings welcomed the opportunity to serve rather than be served.

But when Marjorie thought of Pinto Plains, of its gay simplicity and warm friendliness, the three months that marked her absence from it, stretched themselves out like years. On the other hand, when she considered how little progress she had made in adapting herself to the formal ways of the Capital, they shrank into so many days; hours, indeed. So far as happy transplanting was concerned, she might even now be stepping off the train, a stranger.

Raymond Dilling, a country schoolmaster still in his thirties, had strong predilections towards politics, and saw in this move a coveted opportunity for the furtherance of his ambitions. Yet the idealist who shared his mortal envelope believed with Spencer: "None can be happy until all are happy; none can be free until all are free," and he fought sternly to crush a budding and dangerous individualism. With a little less ambition and response to the altruistic urge—public service—he would have remained a country schoolmaster to the end of his days. As it was, he heard the evocation of Destiny for higher things, read law as an avenue to what seemed to him the primrose path of politics, and grasped the hand of opportunity before it was definitely thrust towards him. He lived in the West during its most provocative period—provocative, that is, for a man of imagination—but he never caught the true spirit of the land, he never felt his soul respond to the lure of its fecundity, its spaciousness, its poignant beauty. The sun always set for him behind the grain elevators, and it never occurred to him to lift his eyes to the eternal hills . . .

Dilling was scarcely conscious of his soul. Had he been, he would have set about supplying it with what he conceived to be its requirements. Of his mind, on the other hand, he was acutely aware, and he fed it freely on Shakespeare, Milton, and the King James' Bible, copies of which were always to be found on the parlour table save between the hours of six and seven in the morning, when he held them in his abnormally long, thin hands. By following the example of those two great figures, Daniel Webster and Rufus Choate, Dilling hoped to acquire a similarly spacious vocabulary and oratorical persuasiveness.

He was a bit of a dreamer, too, believing in Party as the expression of the British theory of Government. He was simply dazed when he heard the ante-bellum ideas of group government, the talk of Economic Democracy and the Gospel of the I.W.W., which was merely Prudhon's epigram—*"La Propriété c'est vol,"* writ large.

He had secured nomination for Parliament through the finesse of the Hon. Godfrey Gough, who recognised his dialectical supremacy over that of any other man in the West. Gough was the *âme damnée* of the vested interests, and so clever was his advocacy that it captivated Dilling into whole-hearted support of their political stratagems, and made it easy for him to bring them into alignment with his conscience. But he did so without hope of pecuniary reward. He was honest. During his entire career, he held temptation by the throat, as it were, determined that no selfish advantage or gain should deflect him from unremitting endeavour for the Nation's good. No parliamentary success attained, nor honours received, should be less than a meed for a faithful adherence to high principles.

He had never talked much with politicians, but he had been talked to by them. On these occasions, it was not apparent to him that they were striving to maintain politics on its lowest plane, rather than to achieve the ideal commonwealth that is supposed to be the end and aim of their profession. He read into their speeches and conversations the doctrine with which he, himself, was impregnated, and the thought of working side by side with these men, aroused in him an emotion akin to consecration . . .

For years Marjorie had pictured Ottawa much as she had pictured Bagdad—The City of Mystery and a Thousand Delights—a place of gracious boulevards and noble architecture, where highly intelligent people occupied themselves with the performance of inspired tasks. And she thought of it as the Heart of the Great Dominion, as necessary to the national body as the human heart is essential to the physical body, transmitting the tide of national life to the very finger-tips of civilisation.

And often, down in the secret places of her self, she had even a more solemn thought—that Ottawa was the Chalice of a Nation's Hopes, and that merely to look upon it would produce an effect like that of entering some Holy Temple. Sin and sadness would disappear, and even the most degenerate must be led there to spiritual refreshment and transfiguration.

Nor did she stand alone; most of her friends were of the same opinion. They linked themselves to the Capital as closely as they were able, and informed themselves minutely concerning its activities, by careful study of the daily press. They read the Parliamentary news first—this was a sacred duty; they wrote papers on politicians and politics for their clubs, and spoke with a certain reverent intimacy of the People in the Public Eye. But most of all they enjoyed the social notes, the description of the gowns, and the tidbits of gossip that crept into the columns of their papers! Even the accidents, the obscure births and deaths that occurred in Ottawa, were invested with a stupendous importance in their eyes.

To them, it was The Land of Afternoon.

And now, as she sat in her tiny drawing-room, denuded of its handsome what-not, and waiting for possible callers, Marjorie tried to stifle a sense of depression, a conviction that all was not right with the world.

She reproached herself for this attitude of mind, trying to remove the trouble without searching for its origin or cause. The house was very still. The children were outside, playing. Her thoughts were filled with Pinto Plains and longing for her friends there.

She could almost guess what they were doing, especially Genevieve Woodside, whose turn it would be, to-day, to entertain the Ladies' Missionary Circle. A mist filled her eyes, and before she could control herself, she was sobbing.

"I've just got to put an end to this nonsense," she scolded herself. "They'd be ashamed of me, at home. I'm ashamed of myself, big baby! Whatever would Raymond say? I really am *very happy*. This is a *nice* little house, and the people *are* kind! A person couldn't expect to feel perfectly at home, even in Pinto Plains, all at once. They simply couldn't—and to think we are really living in Ottawa! Why, it's too wonderful to be true!"

The door-bell rang.

With a nervous glance at the tea table, covered with the handsome white cloth embroidered in pink roses and edged with home-made lace that had been such a work of love for her trousseau, Marjorie went into the tiny hall and opened the door.

"Is Mrs. Dilling at home?" asked a frail, little person, in purple velvet and ermine.

"I'm Mrs. Dilling, and I'm ever so glad to see you. Won't you come in, please?"

"Lady Denby," murmured the other, stepping daintily past her.

Marjorie closed the door, feeling very small and very frightened. This was the wife of the great Sir Eric Denby, the most perdurable public figure of our time. The soundest of sound statesmen, he stood, to Raymond Dilling, just a shade lower than God, Himself.

And the Dillings were profoundly religious people.

"Won't you take off your things?" she asked, timidly, and upon receiving a refusal, tinctured with a suggestion of reproach, excused herself and went into the kitchen to make tea.

When she returned, Lady Denby and Althea were staring unsympathetically at one another across the table.

"Why, darling," Marjorie exclaimed, setting down the teapot, and forgetting her social obligations in the pride of motherhood, "I didn't hear you come in. Dear, dear, what a very untidy little girl, with her tam all crooked and her ribbon untied! This is Althea, Lady Denby. You've no idea how helpful she can be—Go and shake hands, precious!"

Althea was obedient on this occasion. She marched round the table and offered a grimy, wet mitten—the left one—from which the visitor shrank with a movement of alarm.

"How do you do?" said Lady Denby, discovering, after an embarrassing search, a spot upon the shoulder, dry enough, and clean enough, to be touched by her white-gloved hand.

"Having a good time, darling?" asked Marjorie, glowing with joy in the child's loveliness. "Not playing too rough a game?"

"Cream, but no sugar," said Lady Denby, significantly.

For a few awkward moments, Marjorie gave herself up entirely to the duties of hostess, then turned again to her daughter.

"Where is Sylvester, and Baby? Are they all right, my pet?"

Althea nodded.

"Baby's all covered with snow," she explained. "Besser's playing she's a egg and he's a hen, and he's sitting on her!"

"Oh, mercy!" exclaimed Marjorie. "What a naughty boy! Bring them both home at once, Althea—he'll hurt Baby. Quick, now!"

Althea rushed off, leaving the front door open. Marjorie excused herself to close it. She was surprised that Lady Denby exhibited neither amusement nor concern in the family affairs. Indeed, she wondered if deafness might not account for her curious austerity of manner. Old Mrs. Kettlewell, at home, was like that, but everybody knew it was because she couldn't hear half of what was going on.

"Do let me give you some more tea," she urged, her voice slightly raised. Anxiety distracted her. She scarcely knew what she was doing. Suppose the baby should be smothered in the snow? Suppose the children couldn't dig her out? She felt that she should go to the door, at least, to make sure that Althea was successful in her mission. But something in Lady Denby's manner prevented her. She couldn't explain it, yet she simply couldn't find an excuse to leave the room.

Her hands fluttered nervously over the table and her eyes haunted the door.

"Cream, and no sugar, I think you said, Mrs.—er—er—"

"*Lady Denby*," corrected the other, with gentle reproof.

Apologies. Increased nervousness. Desperate effort at self-control. Where could they be, those children of hers? Sipping tea like this, when anything might be happening out there in the snow! It was cruel, cruel!

"How many children have you?" The calm voice trickled over her consciousness like a stream of ice-cold water.

"Three," she answered, hurriedly. "Althea's five, and Sylvester's nearly four—Besser, we call him, you know—and Baby, her name is really Eulalie, is two and a half and simply huge for her age. Have you any children?"

"No," said Lady Denby, implying by her tone that the propagation of the species was, in her opinion, a degraded and vulgar performance.

Marjorie tried other topics; church work, conundrums, Sir Eric's health and gastronomic peculiarities. She offered her favourite recipes, and patterns for crocheted lace, interrupted, thank Heaven, by the entrance of the snow-covered children and the consequent confusion that they caused.

In her domestic activities she was perfectly at ease, hanging damp garments on radiators to dry, wiping tear stains from ruddy cheeks, and even arranging a juvenile tea-party in a corner of the room.

She chattered happily all the while, never for a moment realising that in the Upper Social Circles, the last task in the world a woman should undertake cheerfully is the care of her children; that even allowing them to stay in the same room and breathe the rarified air with which the exalted adults have finished, is a confession of eccentricity, if not *bourgeoisisme*. She had no ideas that there were mothers, outside of books—or possibly New York—who not only considered their children a nuisance, but were ashamed to be surprised in any act of maternal solicitude.

Had Ottawa been Pinto Plains, and Lady Denby one of her neighbours there, she would have been helping to change the children's clothing, then she would have joined the juvenile tea-party, and later, would have heard Althea count up to twenty, prompted Baby to recite "Hickory, Dickory, Dock," and would have played "Pease Porridge Hot," with Sylvester until her palms smarted painfully.

As it was, Lady Denby did none of these things. She sipped tea and nibbled toast as though vast distances separated her from the rest of them, distances that she had no wish to bridge. Marjorie came to the conclusion that she was not only deaf, but suffering the frailties of extreme age, her contradictory appearance notwithstanding. In this kindly way did she account for her guest's indifference. That her visitor was a great and powerful lady, Marjorie well knew, but she had no idea that it was necessary for the great and powerful to assume this manner, as a means whereby they might display their superiority. According to her simple philosophy, the more exalted the person, the readier the graciousness. For what was greatness but goodness, and what was goodness but love of humanity? Was not Queen Victoria sociability itself, when she visited the humbler subjects of her Kingdom?

Other callers came; Mrs. Gullep, whose mission it was to visit newcomers to the church; Mrs. Haynes, whose husband was also a Member from the West, and two or three of the neighbours, with whose children Marjorie's children played. She had a somewhat confused recollection of the late afternoon, but certain features of Lady Denby's conversation recurred with disturbing vividness.

She was amazed to learn that opening her own door was, in future, quite out of the question. If she could not, or would not, engage the permanent services of a domestic, she must, at least, have someone on Wednesday afternoons to admit her callers. Furthermore, she must be relieved—relieved was Lady Denby's word—of all bother—(also Lady Denby's) with the children.

"They will stand between you and the possibility of making friends of the right sort," she warned, a viewpoint which was in direct opposition to the theory Marjorie had always held. "At least once a week, social duties demand your undivided attention."

Again, without in the least having said so, Lady Denby managed to convey the fact that she considered Marjorie a very pretty woman, and that it would be wise, in view of her husband's position, to make the most of her good looks. In the Capital, she observed, much weight attached to one's appearance, and Marjorie would find herself repaid for dressing a little more—another interesting word of Lady Denby's—"definitely". The word was puzzling. Marjorie made all her own and the children's clothes, her husband's shirts, his pyjamas and summer underwear, and she was humbly proud of her accomplishment. She had no doubt as to her ability to make more "definite" clothes, could she but understand exactly what Lady Denby meant. There wasn't anything very striking in a purple velvet suit, even though it had a collar and cuffs of ermine. Besides, Marjorie couldn't wear purple velvet, it was too elderly.

Her own crepe-de-chine blouse was a definite pink. There could be no possibility of mistaking it for green or blue. She had embroidered it profusely in a black poppy design (copied from a pattern in the needlework section of a fashion magazine) to harmonise with her black velveteen skirt, the flaps of which were faced with pink crepe-de-chine to harmonise with the blouse. Feminine Pinto Plains, calling singly and in groups to inspect her "trousseau," agreed that it was more than a costume—it was a creation—and they prophesied that it would dazzle Ottawa.

"So rich looking," they said, "with all that hand-work!" Pinto Plains set a great deal of store by hand-work. "With your lovely colour, Marjorie, in that bright pink you'll be charming!" And yet Lady Denby thought that she should have more definite clothes!

Then there was another thing—and on this point Lady Denby spoke with greater lucidity.

"I am sure you will find it convenient, my dear," she had said, in a whispered colloquy that took place in the hall, "to know some young girl who would be flattered by your patronage, and gratified to be of service to you. There are so many things the right sort of person could do—pour tea, and have a general eye to the arrangements when you receive; give you valuable hints as to the connections you should, or should not, form; advise you as to tradesmen, and a dozen other minor matters that must, for a stranger, be exceedingly confusing. It is quite the thing to encourage such an association in the Capital, and I might add that it lends an air of *empressement* to Members of the Party. One must always consider the Party, my dear."

Lady Denby saw no difficulty in the fact that Marjorie knew of no such person. "Leave it to me," she said, with an air of brilliant finality, "I have just such a girl in mind. Not pretty enough to be attractive, and too clever to be popular; so her time is pretty much her own. She would welcome the opportunity, I know, of shining in your reflected glory. I'll send her to you. Her name is Azalea Deane. And remember always, in your associations, to maintain the dignity that is due to your husband's position. I would almost go so far as to say that indiscriminate intimacies should be discouraged; they are so apt to be embarrassing—in politics, you know ..." Without exactly forming the words, her lips seemed to pronounce Mrs. Gullep's name. "Very estimable people, I am sure, the very vertebræ of Church

Societies, but in a small *ménage* like this, my dear, you must not waste your chairs!"

Marjorie lay awake that night reviewing the events of the day. Some cog in the well-ordered machinery of her existence had slipped out of place, and was causing unaccustomed friction. She didn't know what was the matter. Neither analytical nor introspective, she never got down to fundamentals, and the results that showed on the surface were apt to bewilder her. Consequently, she refused to admit disappointment with her surroundings, and did not even remotely suspect that she was experiencing the first, faint stirrings of disillusionment. She was a little depressed, that she admitted, but the fault was hers; of that she was thoroughly convinced, not only at the moment but throughout the months and years that stretched ahead. Always she blamed herself for failing to attain the state of mental and spiritual growth that would enable her to fit comfortably into her environment.

Of course, she couldn't put all this into words. She never could make her feelings clear to other people—not even to Raymond. So, when, somewhat impatient at her restlessness, he asked what was the matter, she answered, with a little sigh.

"Oh, nothing, dearie . . . nothing that's awfully important, I ought to say. Only—only—I sometimes wonder . . . do *you* ever feel that Ottawa's a difficult place to get acquainted?"

CHAPTER 3.

*D*illing adapted himself to his new environment much more readily than did his wife. He had not anticipated that the House of Commons would be a glorified Municipal Council such as he had left in Pinto Plains, and that his associations and activities would be virtually the same save on a magnificent scale; whereas Marjorie had deluded herself—subconsciously, it may be—with the thought that Ottawa would be an idealised prairie town, and that she would live a beatified extension of her old life, there. Differences in customs, in social and moral codes, ever remained for her a hopeless enigma, just as Euclid's problems evade solution for some people. She never could master them because she never could understand them. Black was black and white was white, and neither sunshine nor shadow could convert either into gray. No leopard ever possessed more changeless spots.

While, therefore, her husband was joyously engrossed in his work, finding novelty and stimulation in every smallest detail, remodelling himself to fit the mantle he had been called upon to adorn, Marjorie was confronted with unexpected obstacles, bewildered by inexplicable ways, homesick for familiar standards and people, and groping for something stable to which she could cling and upon which she could build her present life.

Of the nature of Dilling's work, she had but the sketchiest idea. His conversation was becoming almost unintelligible to her, try as she would to follow it. When, in the old days, they sat at the table or drew their chairs around the fire, and he told her of Jimmy Woodside's stupidity or Elvira Mumford's high average, she could take a vital interest in his daily pursuits, but now, when he referred to Motions, and Amendments, and Divisions, she had no idea of what he was talking about. He was seldom at home, and upon those rare occasions he fortressed himself behind a palisade of Blue Books and Financial Returns.

He abandoned himself to reading almost as a man abandons himself to physical debauch, and Marjorie, furtively watching him, could scarcely believe that the stranger occupying that frail, familiar shell was, in reality, her husband. There was about him a suggestion of emotional pleasure, an expression of ecstacy, as when a man gazes deep into his beloved's eyes.

"Ah," he would murmur, "three thousand, six hundred and forty-two . . . annually! Seventy-nine thousand less than . . . well, well!"

His cheeks would flush, his breathing would thicken, his forehead would gleam with a crown of moisture, and he would lose his temper shockingly if the children spoke to him or played noisily in the room.

Long afterwards, a rural wag observed that Prohibition touched few persons less than Raymond Dilling, who could get drunk on Blue Books and Trade Journals, any day in the year!

Marjorie got into the way of keeping the little ones shut up in the kitchen with her. The house was too small to allow Dilling the privacy of a library or study, and the three bedrooms were cold and cheerless. So he appropriated the tiny drawing-room and converted it into what seemed to her, a literary rubbish heap. Books, pamphlets, Hansards, and more books . . . she was nearly crazy with them!

She had never been to the House of Commons save once, when Raymond took the entire family on a tour of inspection. She had never seen Parliament in Session, and had no idea that many of the women who accompanied their husbands to Ottawa, spent all the time they could spare from bridge, in the Gallery; not profiting by the progress of the Debates, but carrying on mimic battles amongst themselves. Here was the cockpit, from which arose the causes of bitter though bloodless conflicts—conflicts which embroiled both the innocent and the guilty, and formed the base of continuous social warfare.

However, on the afternoon that Dilling was expected to deliver his maiden speech, she found her way to the Ladies' Gallery with the aid of a courteous official, and ingenuously presented her card of admission. Without appearing to glance at it, the doorkeeper grasped the information it bore.

"This way, please, Mrs. Dilling," he said, with just the proper shade of cordiality tempering his authority. "Here's a seat—in the second row. They are just clearing the Orders for your husband's speech," he added, in an officious whisper.

Marjorie sank unobtrusively into the place he indicated and thanked him. She wondered how he knew her name, not realising that he had held his position for forty years by the exercise of that very faculty which so amazed her. It was his duty to know not only all those who sought an entrance through the particular portal that he guarded, but also to know where to place them. Should he fail to recognise an applicant, he never betrayed himself. She was presently to learn that as her husband progressed nearer the front benches downstairs, she would be advanced to the front, upstairs.

Her first sensation—could she have singled one out of the medley that overwhelmed her—was not of exaltation at having entered into the sanctuary of the Canadian Temple of Politics, and being in a position to look down upon one of the clumsiest and most complex institutions that ever failed to maintain the delusion of democracy, but of the immensity of the place. The Green Chamber was at least four times as large as the Arena in Pinto Plains! Its sombreness discomfited her. Although she had read descriptions of the Commons, she never visualised the dullness of the green with which it was carpeted and upholstered; she had rather taken clusters of glittering candelabra for granted; indeed, it would not have surprised her to find golden festoons catching dust from the whirlwind of oratory which rose from the floor beneath. The unregality of the place made her want to cry. She felt like a child standing before a fairy king without his crown.

Directly opposite her sat the Speaker on his Throne—the chair which the late King Edward had used when visiting the Colonies in 1860. Above the Speaker, in a shallow gallery suspended below that reserved for the Proletariat, several men were languidly trailing their pencils across the stationery provided them by the generous taxpayers of the country. These were the scribes of the Press, profundite scriveners, whose golden words she had absorbed so often in her far-away prairie home.

On the floor of the House, at a long table in front of the Speaker, sat the Clerk. At the other end of the table lay the Mace, the massive bauble that aroused Oliver Cromwell's choler, and which symbolises, by its position, the functioning of the House. In splendid isolation sat the Sergeant-at-Arms, an incumbent of the office for forty-three years, during which time, it is said, he never changed the colour of his overcoat, or his dog.

On the Speaker's left sat His Majesty's loyal Opposition, led by that illustrious tribune of the people, the Right Honourable Sir Wilfrid Laurier. Facing him, across the table, was the Right Honourable Sir Robert Borden and the Members of his Cabinet, prominent among whom was Sir Eric Denby, who dreamed of a Saharan drought for Canada, and affirmed his stand on the Temperance question with the zeal of a Hebrew prophet. Then, as a counterpoise to Sir Eric, there was the Honourable Godfrey Gough, who sought to mould a policy for his Party that would have made Machiavelli blush!

These were the notables; the rest were a jumble of tailenders.

Marjorie could not locate her husband, immediately, but after a little she recognised the top of his head. He was sitting in a dim corner, in the very last row under the Gallery that was devoted to the accommodation of the ruck of our splendid democracy.

Then, before she was quite prepared for it, she saw him rise to his feet. Her eyes filled with tears of terror, and for a moment he seemed to stand alone—like a splendid column, islanded in a rolling sea. Marjorie could not resist the impulse to inform the impassive lady sitting beside her, that the speaker was her husband.

The lady looked surprised at being addressed.

"Indeed?" she replied, and her eyebrows added, "Well, what of it?"

Marjorie kept her hand pressed tightly over her heart. It thumped so heavily, she could scarcely hear what Raymond was saying. If he should forget his speech! If he should fail!

Gradually, the blur before her cleared, and she saw that he was standing quite at ease, one hand resting on his hip—a favourite and familiar attitude—and the other negligently grasping the back of his chair. His flat voice, carrying well for all its lack of resonancy, was perfectly steady, and his words were unhurried, clear; in fine, she realised that Raymond had no dread of what to her, was a scarifying experience, and, unimaginative though she was, there was borne upon her a strange, new consciousness of her husband's power.

For the formal test of his ability to command the attention of the House, he had seized upon the Motion of a Representative from the West, calling upon the Government to adopt a vigourous policy in the construction of grain elevators and facilities for the transportation of wheat—Canada's prime commodity in the markets of the world.

". . . As I stand here, enveloped by the traditions of the past," she heard him say, "listening to the echoes in this Chamber of the noble words and sound policies that have builded this great structure that is our Country, I am awed by the privilege that has come to me of taking a part, however small, in directing the national welfare of this Dominion. I seek not at this moment, Mr. Speaker, merely the glory of the Party to which I have the honour to belong, but I am ambitious to maintain a principle, to be worthy of the men who fashioned a nation out of chaos, out of a wilderness of local and parochial interests. I shall strive to be the force for good that such men would wish to see in every member in this legislative body to-day . . ."

Although he had known that Marjorie would be in the Gallery that afternoon, it was typical of Dilling to ignore the fact. Small acts of pretty gallantry were utterly foreign to his nature. He could no more have raised a woman's glove to his lips before returning it to her, than he could have manicured his fingernails. To himself he termed such graces "*la-di-da*", by which he probably meant foppish. If his personal vanity revealed itself in any one direction it was that he might appear superlatively masculine—even to the verge of brutality.

". . . The cause I plead," he continued, "is that which must appeal to every thinking man, to-day. I plead an economical policy for the guarding of our grain . . ."

". . . Wheat!" she heard him say. "The West is crying for elevators, and for freighting facilities in order that she may distribute her vast resources. The East is crying for food. The world needs wheat. *Wheat!* The very word rings with a strange magic, flares with a golden gleam of prosperity."

His eyes were fixed on his Chief's profile, save when they leaped across the aisle to the "White Plume" of the grand Old Man who bent over his desk and scribbled with a slender yellow pencil, apparently quite oblivious to Dilling's existence. Marjorie saw him through brimming eyes. She did not know that in the corridor men were saying, "Come on in! Dilling's got the floor. He's talking a good deal of rhetorical rot—as must be expected from an amateur—but the making of an orator is there. . . Come on in!" She was too nervous to notice that the empty benches which comprise the flattering audience usually accorded to a new speaker, were rapidly filling, that Members who discovered some trifling business to keep them in the Chamber, had stopped sorting the collection of visiting cards, forgotten appointments, and notes with which their pockets were stuffed. Laryngitical gentlemen forbore to snap their fingers at the bob-tailed pages for glasses of water—in short, Raymond was making an impression. He was receiving the attention of the House.

His concluding words were,

"I have come amongst you, a stranger, unversed in the ways of this great assembly of a young, ardent and democratic people—of members whose experience has been so much richer than my own. I trust that none of you—even those whose views may be at variance with mine—will have cause to resent my coming. I realise that a profound responsibility devolves upon each and every one of us who steps across the threshold of this Chamber, and that although our creeds may be translated differently, their actuating principles are identical.

"I know, Mr. Speaker, that life lies in the struggle, that work—and not its wage—brings us joy. The game is the important thing, not the score. To gain the peak of the mountain is the climber's ambition. If he be a true man, a man who rejoices in service for others, he has no wish to possess the summit. To serve the Empire at the cost of ease and leisure, to expend one's strength in the solving of her myriad problems, is the sum total of an honest man's desire.

"I submit that it is possible to spread peace and plenty throughout our Dominion. The Government has but to build treasure-houses for the grain, and lend assistance in the way of subsidies for transportation. A hungry people make poor citizens, and will inevitably bring desolation to any land, for, as Ruskin has said, 'There is no wealth but life, and that nation is the richest that breeds the greatest number of noble and happy homes and beings'."

His speech was short and admirably delivered. It hit the temper of the House, and Dilling sat down amid a storm of applause.

Through a mist of tears Marjorie noted that Sir Robert was bending over her husband with an air that was more than perfunctorily gracious. Several other men also left their desks and offered him congratulations. She felt a little faint with pride and the reaction of it all.

"A real triumph," said the voice of the lady sitting next to her, suddenly. "Your husband's quite a speaker, isn't he?" and Marjorie was too grateful for these words of friendliness to sense that the lady (who was Mrs. Bedford, wife of the Whip of the Liberal Party) would have been much more gratified had Raymond Dilling made of his speech a bleak failure.

CHAPTER 4.

*T*he Hon. Member for Morroway did not wait for the adjournment of the afternoon Session. With a gesture that the thirsty never fail to recognise, he signalled two colleagues who occupied adjacent benches, and led the way from the Green Chamber.

The Hon. Member was more than a little piqued at Marjorie Dilling's insensibility to his persistent Gallery-gazing. It was almost unprecedented in his experience that a young woman should find the sparsely-covered crown of her husband's head more magnetic an objective than his own luxuriant growth of silver hair. Looked at from above, the leonine mane of Mr. Rufus Sullivan was in the midst of such hirsute barrenness, as conspicuous as a spot of moonlight on a drab, gray wall.

The Hon. Member for Morroway disliked many things: work, religion, temperance, ugly women, clever men, home cooking, cotton stockings, and male stenographers, to mention only a few. But more than any of these, he disliked being ignored by a girl upon whom he had focussed his attention. Such occasions (happily rare!) always induced extreme warmth that was like a scorching rash upon Mr. Sullivan's sensitive soul, and this, in turn, promoted an intense dryness of the throat. Mr. Sullivan disliked being dry.

So, with admirable directness of movement, he led the way to his room, unlocked a drawer marked "Unfinished Business," and set a bottle upon the desk at the same time waving hospitality towards his two companions.

For a space the silence was broken only by the ring of glass upon glass and the cooling hiss of a syphon. Then, three voices pronounced, "Here's how!" and there followed an appreciative click of the tongue and a slight gurgling.

"Ah . . ." breathed the trio.

The Hon. Member for Morroway closed one limpid brown eye and examined his glass against the light. Although an incomparable picture stood framed in the small Gothic window of his room, it did not occur to Mr. Sullivan to look at the distant Laurentians slipping into the purple haze of evening, to feast his soul upon the glory of soft river tones and forest shades; to note the slender spire of silver that glowed like a long-drawn-out star on a back-drop of pastel sky.

Mr. Sullivan was concerned only with the amber fluid in his glass, where tiny bubbles climbed hurriedly to the surface and clung to the sides of the tumbler. If he looked out of the window at all, it was to investigate the possible charms of unattached maidens who strolled towards Nepean Point ostentatiously enjoying the view. Sometimes, Mr. Sullivan found the outlook enchanting, himself. This was when he was stimulated by the enthusiasm of a pretty girl who invariably remarked that it was a sin "to spoil the river shore with those hideous mills, and poison good air with the reek of sulphite."

Mr. Sullivan vehemently agreed, for he called himself an ardent Nature-lover, unwilling to admit that Nature, for him, was always feminine and young.

"Not much doubt as to the direction the wind blows from Pinto Plains," he observed, still intent upon his glass.

"Not a shadow," agreed Howarth, sombrely. "Eastlake and Donahue have certainly got that lad buffaloed to a standstill."

"Railroaded, you mean," amended Turner, essaying a wan jest. "I wonder what his price was." He drained his glass, set it on the table with a thud, and cried, "I never saw their equal—that pair! Time after time, we've thought they were down and out. Their subsidies were discounted, banks closed down on 'em, credit was exhausted—you remember the contractors we've fixed so that they wouldn't operate?—even their own supporters got weak in the knees . . . and they manage to find some inspired spell-binder, who pours the floods of his forensic eloquence on the sterile territory, so that first thing we know, a stream of currency begins to trickle from the banks, subsidies are renewed . . . God! how do they pull it off, boys? In a case like this, where do they get the cash to pay Dilling, and what do they promise him? What's his price, I'm asking you, eh?"

Rufus Sullivan, feeling that two pairs of eyes were upon him, spoke.

"Do you know," he said, slowly, "it wouldn't surprise me much to learn that young Dilling hasn't been bought at all, that he gave himself to the cause, and that all of that grandiose bunk he talked was truth to him?"

"Good God!" breathed Howarth, and gulped loudly.

" 'S a fact! I listened hard all the time he talked, and I watched him some, and it struck me he wasn't speaking a part he had learned at the Company's dictation, nor for a price . . ."

"—which means," interrupted Turner, "that he's another of those damned nuisances with principles, and ideas about making politics clean and uplifting for the man in the street."

"Worse than that," corrected Howarth. "It means that he'll be a damsite harder to handle, and more expensive to buy than a fellow who has no definite convictions and finds mere money acceptable."

"That's right!" Sullivan set down his empty glass and spread his elbows on the desk, facing them. "I don't anticipate that Dilling will be any bargain, but," he thundered, "we've got to have him. Fortunately, we can rely upon the incontrovertible fact that like every other man, he *has* a price. It's up to us to find out what it is!"

"But, damn it all, Sullivan," cried Howarth, "I'm sick of paying prices! Surely we can find some means of muzzling this altruistic western stripling."

"Nothing simpler," returned the older man, with heavy sarcasm. "We've only got to go to the country, defeat the Government, assassinate Eastlake and Donahue, deport Gough as an undesirable ... Godfrey happens to be backing Dilling in his constituency don't you forget..."

"What?" asked Turner.

"What for?" from Howarth.

Sullivan spread out his large, fat hands. "For some dark purpose of his own that is yet to be revealed ... and then, we must squash the vested interests. Suppose you take on this trifling job, Bill. I'm going to be busy this evening."

"Just the same," cut in Turner, "I think Billy's right. He ought to be intimidated—Dilling, of course, I mean—not bought. These Young Lochinvars ought not to be allowed to think they can run the country."

"Buying or intimidating, it's much the same thing in the end," said Sullivan. "You've got to find a price or a weapon." He corked the bottle, locked it away and strolled across the office to examine his features in a heavy gilt mirror that hung on the wall. "Did either of you remark Mrs. Dilling?" he enquired, attacking his mass of hair with a small pocket comb.

"Mrs. Dilling?" echoed the others.

"Why not? She sat in the Gallery all afternoon."

"How did you know her?" demanded Howarth.

"Why, I saw her come in, and noting that she was a stranger—"

"—and extremely pretty," suggested Turner, "you took the trouble to find out."

"Well, she is pretty," said the Member for Morroway, reflectively. "A fair, childish face, like a wild, unplucked prairie flower."

"Humph," observed Turner, exchanging a significant look with Howarth behind his host's back.

"Beauty is an amazingly compelling force," Sullivan continued, sententiously. "I have a theory—shared by very few people, it is true, but convincing to me, nevertheless—that Beauty wields a more powerful influence than Fear. What do you think?"

"Never thought about it at all," confessed Howarth, bluntly. "But what has all this to do with Dilling's price?"

"Oh, nothing, my dear fellow," said Sullivan, airily, "nothing at all! I was merely indulging in a moment's reflection, inspired, as it were, by Mrs. Dilling's loveliness. You must meet her . . . We must see to it that Ottawa treats her with cordiality and friendliness."

"Do you know her, yourself . . . already?" asked Turner.

"Er—no. I have not been through the formality of an introduction, but I know her sufficiently well to wager that she is the sort of little woman who responds to the sympathetic word; who is lonely, and searching for warmth rather than grandeur in her associations and who can be relied upon to work for her husband's advancement . . . when that good time comes."

A new light gleamed in the eyes of his two listeners. They gave up trying to think of ways in which the new Member might be intimidated— discredited with his constituents or sponsors; and waited for the master mind to reveal itself. But Rufus Sullivan, M.P., was not the man to discuss half-formulated plans. He changed the subject adroitly, jotted down the Dilling's address and excused himself on the plea that he was dining with the Pratts for the purpose of laying the foundations for a successful campaign.

"There's an interesting type," he declared. "Useful—most useful!"

"Pratt?" cried Turner. "Why, he's a jolly old ass, in my opinion!"

"I mean Mrs. Pratt, of course," was Sullivan's mild reproof. "Don't you realise, my dear chap, that the women of our day are the chief factors in our Government? We are harking back to the piping times of the 'Merry Monarch'."

"Oh, rot!" contradicted Howarth, who was a married man.

"*Régime du cotillon* . . . petticoat Government, eh?" Turner laughed. Both he and Sullivan had evaded the snares of feminine hunters. "I don't know the lady, but take it that she, also, is easy on the eye."

Sullivan shook his great white head. Mrs. Pratt, he explained, had not been born to adorn life, but to emphasise it. Nature, in her wisdom, had given to some women determination, and the callousness that must accompany it.

"Purposeful," said Mr. Sullivan, "grimly purposeful, with about as much sensitiveness as you would find in a piece of rock crystal. She's got her mind set on having Gus in Parliament, and if Queen Victoria and her attendant lion got off the pedestal outside there, they wouldn't be able to prevent her. She would repeal the B.N.A. Act if it stood in her way. A very useful woman," he repeated, and insinuated himself into his overcoat.

"What's he up to?" Howarth asked his companion as they bent their steps towards the restaurant and dinner.

"God knows!" answered Turner. "But there's a load taken off my mind by the knowledge that he's got something up his sleeve. And it won't be all laughter either, if I know him."

Howarth paused in the corridor. His dulled conscience was trying to shake off its political opiate and prompt him to play the man in this thing, but its small voice was speedily hushed by the animated scene about him. Pages were scurrying around; Members, released from the tension of debate, were greeting each other noisily; the *omnium gatherum* of the Galleries was debouching upon the Main lobby, so that the very air he breathed was vibrant with a *scherzo* of human voices.

"I say," he cried, "let's ask Dilling to feed with us. Under the intoxication of triumph, he may loosen up a bit—become loquacious. You get a table. I'll get him!"

CHAPTER 5.

*"I*t isn't the thing, my dear!" Or, "It's quite the thing, you know!"

The thing! THE THING! What on earth did it mean?

Marjorie first heard the phrase on the lips of Lady Denby, and gradually she recognised it as a social influence that was as powerful as it was mysterious. It was one of the most elusive of her problems, for, while she understood vaguely, the significance of the term, she failed entirely to apply its principles to the exigencies of her new life. "Besides," she said to herself, "one discovers what *is* the thing, only to find presently, that it isn't . . . or the other way round. There doesn't seem to be any fixed rule."

It was hers to learn in the hard school of experience, that Ottawa in the twentieth century, was controlled by a social code quite as remorseless in its way as the tribal etiquette which governed the Algonquins when Champlain visited its site, three hundred years before. Wherever she went, the attitude of the people from Government House down to those who moved on the very periphery of its circle, was such as to repress and chill the frank and unquestioning impulse for friendliness that lent much charm to her character. She developed a curious sort of nervousness—an inner quaking, that disconcerted her, and made her feel unnatural. She became so fearful of offending people, that her manner was frequently described as obsequious. Now and then, she knew she was being criticised, but could not, for the life of her, fathom the reason.

The Thing . . . of course, but what *was* The Thing?

She had tried to break the children of saying "ma'am". Lady Denby told her it wasn't *the thing*.

"No nice people speak like that, Althea, darling," Marjorie declared. "You should say, 'Yes, mother,' or 'No, Lady Denby,' or 'I don't know, Miss Deane,'—as the case may be, but please, darling, don't say 'ma'am'!" And yet to her astonishment, she heard Miss Leila Brant address no less a personage than the Lady of Government House in this ill-bred manner!

"This, ma'am," said she, "is one of the forks used at the Carlyle table. It's really rather a good thing, and I was *thrilled* at having picked it up."

"You have some very interesting bits," observed The Lady, graciously.

"Oh, *ma'am*! How can I ever thank you for those words," cried Miss Brant. "Even the slightest breath of praise from you, means—well, it means more than you can possibly realise."

Ma'am ... ma'am ... Why, Marjorie could scarcely believe that she wasn't dreaming.

She left the Ancient Chattellarium in a despondent frame of mind. Why, in Ottawa, must she appear so stupid? Why could she not make friends? Would she be humiliated forever, by the lifted eyebrow and the open reproof ... "It isn't the thing, my dear?"

It was not her nature, however, to be melancholy, so she thrust dark thoughts away and gave herself up to ingenuous excitement in anticipation of her first party at Rideau Hall.

The Skating Parties held at Government House on Saturday afternoons during January and February were very much THE THING; in fact, geographically speaking, Rideau Hall was its very source, its essence, the spot from which it emanated and seeped into virtually every other residence in the Capital. Scarcely a person from a master plumber down, but felt and yielded to its malison.

Owing to the intense and protracted cold, there was excellent ice as late as the middle of March, and Their Royal Highnesses extended the hospitality of the rink considerably beyond the date specified on the original invitations.

Not that the majority of the people went to the Skating Parties to skate, or even to toboggan—the thoughtful alternative suggested on the large, square card—about two inches below the Royal Coat of Arms. Sufficiently difficult were the performances already expected of them—the curvettings, gyrations and genuflexions demanded at the moment of their presentation to the Vice-Regal party. Sebaceous dowagers teetered dangerously in their endeavour to achieve a court curtsey, occasionally passing the centre of bouyancy and plunging headlong between the two pairs of august feet.

A crowd larger than usual massed in the skating pavilion and fought politely for the mulled claret, tea, coffee, cake and sandwiches that were being served from long, narrow trestles. His Royal Highness, the Duke of Connaught, and the picturesque Princess Pat had come in from the open-air rink below, and without removing their skates, had led the way to the tea-room, whereupon several hundred people unleashed their appetites, sampled the various refreshments, and disposed of the vessels from which they had eaten on the floor, window-sills or chairs, if any, that had been vacated.

In a corner, removed as far as possible from the disordered tea-tables sat three ladies, eating, drinking and conversing as though they were spectators at some bizarre entertainment. They stared with frank insolence about them, looking through many persons who came hopefully within their vicinage, and warning a few by the manner of their salutation that they must approach no nearer. They had been distinguished by receiving a welcome from the Duke and Duchess, who called each by name and hoped that their health was good. After this distinction, the ladies withdrew from the commonalty into their corner, exalted and envied.

"Who in the world *are* all these people?" asked Lady Elton. She spoke fretfully, with an edge of desperation on her voice. A stranger might have imagined that she was required by the statutes to learn the name and history of each member of the throng, and that she found the task inexpressibly irksome.

Of course, such was not the case. It didn't matter whether she knew any of these people or not—at least, it only mattered to the people themselves, many of whom would have been glad to be known by her or any other titled person. She asked the question because it was the thing *to* ask at Government House, because it was one of those intellectual insipidities that have supplanted conversation and made it possible for a group of persons without visible qualifications, according to the standards of yesterday, to exchange an absence of ideas, and form themselves into a close corporation known as Society.

Mrs. Chesley shook her head. "Isn't it amazing?" she breathed. "Only a few years ago it was such a pleasure to come down here—one knew everybody—and now . . ."

"Sessional people, I suppose?" interrupted Miss de Latour, with just the faintest movement of her nose as though she was speaking of a drain-digger, or some other useful class of citizen who, by reason of necessity, moved in the effluvia occasioned by his work.

Captain the Honourable Teddy Dodson approached at this moment to ask if the ladies were satisfactorily served.

"Do let me get you some more tea," he begged. "I'm afraid no one's looking after you—this awful mob, you know." He pushed a collection of discarded cups aside and seated himself on the edge of a chair, leaning forward with an air of flattering confidence. "Cross your hearts and hope you may die," he whispered, "and I'll tell you what we call these beastly tea fights."

The trio playfully followed his instructions and encouraged him to reveal the limit of his naughtiness.

"We call them 'slum parties'," confided the young Aide, and while the ladies shrieked their appreciation of his wicked wit, he clumped away on his expensive skates, balancing three cups quite cleverly as he elbowed a passage to the table.

"How do you suppose these people get invitations?" Miss de Latour demanded, indignantly. "Look at that woman over there—no, no, the one in the purple hat. Isn't that the awful Pratt creature who's pushing herself into everything?"

"My husband," said Mrs. Chesley, "calls her the Virginia Creeper. However, she'll get on. They say she's been left a disgusting lot of money, and that her husband's going to run for Parliament."

"That's no reason why she should be here," said the other. "Are there no impregnable bulwarks left to protect Society?"

"Why, Pamela," cried Mrs. Chesley, "how clever of you to remember that! I read it, too, in Lady Dunstan's Memoirs, but I've no memory—I can't quote things . . ."

". . . as though they were your own!" finished Lady Elton, and laughed at the neatness of her thrust.

Miss de Latour's question as to how people secured their invitations was merely an echo of her friend's banality. There was no secret about the matter; no bribery or corruption. Anyone—almost anyone—desiring to be insulted by the Lady Eltons, Mrs. Chesleys, and Miss de Latours of Ottawa, or to be snubbed of their acquaintances, had only to proceed to the Main Entrance of Rideau Hall, pass beneath the new facade—so symbolic of fronts, both physical and architectural, that had suddenly been acquired all over the City in honour of the Royal Governor-General—and there, in the white marble, red-carpeted hall, sign a huge register, under the eye of two supercilious, scarlet-coated flunkeys, who regarded each newcomer with all the antagonism of their class. This unique procedure was known as "calling at Government House," and within a few days of the delightful and friendly visit, His Majesty's Mails conveyed a large, rich-looking card to the door and one learned that "Their Royal Highnessess had desired the A.D.C. in Waiting to invite Mr. and Mrs. Van Custard and the Misses Van Custard for Skating and Tobogganing between the hours, etc., etc.". Thereupon, one wrote to rural relations or foreigners of one kind and another, and mentioned carelessly that one had been "entertained at Government House".

"There's Mrs. Long," announced Lady Elton. "Who's the man?"

"Oh, some newspaper person, I think—an American," volunteered Miss de Latour. Obviously it was bad enough in her opinion to be any kind of a newspaper person, but to be an American newspaper person offered an affront to Society that was difficult to condone. Pamela de Latour was intensely proud of her father's legendary patrician lineage, her capacity for avoiding friendships, and her mother's wealth. She was well aware of the fact that she was regarded as a person whom "one should know."

"He's not bad looking," murmured Lady Elton, charitably, "and he must be rather worth while, Pam. She's introducing him to everyone. Let's wander over and see what we can see."

But Mrs. Long, watching them from the corner of her very alert brown eyes, and anticipating this move, beat a strategic retreat, and soon lost herself and her newspaper man in the dense crowd. Lady Elton, Mrs. Chesley and Miss de Latour looked significantly at one another as though to say,

"Ah-ha! What do you think of that? Something queer about this affair, if you ask me!"

An expression of their thoughts was denied them, however, for the moment they left the shelter of their corner they were like the Romans advancing across the Danube—a target for the surrounding barbarian hordes.

Almost immediately they were attacked by the Angus-McCallums, two sisters with generous, florid cheeks and rotund figures, who, to quote Azalea Deane, seemed to lie fatly on the surface of every function, rather like cream on a pan of milk.

Their grandfather was a Bytown pioneer whose first task, after complying with the formalities imposed upon all immigrants by the various government officials, had been to find a house—a house, that is to say, requiring the services of a stone mason.

Now Masonry, whether Free or Stone, has always offered signal advantages to those who labour in its interests, and the present case was no exception to the rule. Not only did prosperity attend the twilight years of old Thaddeus McCallum, but especial privileges descended to his progeny, the most conspicuous being the Freedom of Government House grounds which the Misses Angus-McCallum enjoyed. That is to say, the young ladies were at liberty to pass unchallenged within the sacrosanct limits of this estate, whenever whim or convenience dictated . . . an inconceivably rich reward for the excellence of the fine old man's chisel-drafting and hammer-dressing! They seemed, however, to lose sight of the patriotic service he had rendered to the nation, in an unremitting search for families on whom, without demeaning themselves, they could call.

"Who is . . .," dominated their every conscious thought.

"Ah, Effie," cried the elder sister, addressing Lady Elton, "I thought you would be skating."

"For Heaven's sake, hush!" warned Lady Elton, severely. "Weren't you here last week to see me crash to the ice with H.R.H.? I dared not risk another such fall!"

"But with the uncle of a King," murmured Miss Mabel Angus-McCallum, "such an honour, my dear!"

Helena Chesley laughed.

"That's not bad for you, Mabel. It's a pity Mrs. Long didn't overhear it," she said.

Between her and the Angus-McCallums there existed an almost perceptible antagonism which was regarded variously as a source of amusement and uneasiness by their friends. Such traditional antipathy was not at all unusual, and marked the relation between many of the "old" families in the Capital.

Before her marriage to the scholarly young man, whose nimble wit and charm of manner had won him a permanent place in the Vice-Regal entourage, Helena Chesley had been a Halstead, and the Halsteads had owned the estate upon which such discomfiting evidences of Thaddeus McCallum's craftsmanship rose up to confound his descendants. Whether they imagined it or not, is difficult to state, but the Angus-McCallums always felt the condescension of the landed proprietor to the day labourer in Helena Chesley's cynical smile, while the latter resented the patronising air which the others assumed as a cloak for the inherited resentfulness of Industry towards Capital.

Miss Mabel Angus-McCallum's retort was cut short by the arrival of Mrs. Hudson, who, metaphorically speaking, embraced the ladies as Crusoe might have taken Friday to his bosom.

"My dears," she breathed, "I'm so glad to find you! Did anyone ever see such a mob, and *such* people? Who do you suppose brought me my tea?" and without waiting for an answer to the question, she continued, "That awful Lennox man! You remember, he used to be the stenographer in Sir Mortimer Fanshawe's office!"

"Did you drink it?" asked Mrs. Chesley.

Mrs. Hudson's social position was triumphant and secure. She could sit on the top rung of the steep and slippery ladder (if one finds an apt metaphor in so comfortless a recreation) and look down upon a mass of struggling, straining, pushing microcosms who clutched, and climbed, and slid and fell in an effort to reach the pinnacle she had attained; for just what reason or by what right, no one was prepared to explain. True, she was a frank snob, which was partially accountable. Also, she was wealthy, and "entertained" in a pleasantly formal manner that lent an air of importance to the least important sort of functions.

Had breakfast been served in Mrs. Hudson's small but well-regulated *ménage*, indubitably it would have been announced with an impressive opening of double doors, and served by respectful, liveried attendants. Moreover, there would have been a correctly morning-coated gentleman for each lady of the party, for the express and especial purpose of offering her his arm and escorting her to the card-marked table!

Nor was that all. There were those who called Mrs. Hudson a "bug specialist," and attributed her social success to this interesting form of enthusiasm. Her entomological research was conducted with considerable originality and on lines that differed radically from the method of the late Dr. Gordon Hewitt, similarly called by a large group of affectionate and admiring associates. In Mrs. Hudson's case, "bug specialising" signified an ardent (and inconstant) pursuit of a fad, or a person, or a combination of both. Rarely did a stranger with any claim whatever to renown, escape from Ottawa without enjoying her hospitality, and it must not be forgotten that she frequently dragged absolute obscurities out of their gloom and played most happily with them for a time.

Azalea Deane said that Mrs. Hudson was the most recent development of The Big Game Hunter—game and bug being interchangeable, if not synonymous in her mind. The truth of the matter was, she made a serious study of the state of being termed Society. She attacked the problems and the methods of succeeding in it, with the same energy and concentrated purpose that a man gives to a great commercial enterprise. It was her business and she made it pay. Mob psychology and regimentation of thought were the fountains from which she derived her source of supply, and judicious investment added to her power. People often wondered how Mrs. Hudson had achieved social eminence when women with superior claims had failed. The answer lies just here—her life was spent in a conscious striving for it. Never a move, an invitation, an acceptance, a salutation on the street, was made without forethought. She made Society her tool. Most people are tools, themselves. Usually, Mrs. Hudson was described as a "character", which meant that she was different from ordinary people. Her peculiarities—and she wore them consciously, like a crown—were called odd; her vulgarities, original. She was clever enough to keep the fact that she *was* clever from being realised, and many people were sorry for her! She had married a man several years her junior, and loved to confess that he was an answer to prayer!

"I saw him first at a concert," she was wont to remark, "and the moment my eyes fell upon his dear, unsuspecting head, I said to myself, 'Thank God! I have found the man I intend to marry, and need look no further!' I went home, and prayed for him, and I got him!"

What effect this disclosure may have had upon the spiritual trend of the community, what intensity of supplication or increase of attendance at the churches, there is, unfortunately, no means of estimating. It can scarcely have failed, however, to have exerted some marked influence upon the spinsters of the Capital, and many a married woman, I am told, bent a devout knee because of it, arguing hopefully, that if the Lord could give, He could also take away!

Mrs. Hudson loved her husband with a sort of cantankerous affection that was like the rubbing of a brass bowl to make it shine. She was always prodding him, or polishing him, or smacking at him with her hands or her tongue. Marriage had robbed her of the joy of believing him a genius, but she was fond of him in her peculiar, rasping way.

"Is anyone else here?" she enquired, wiping out the hundreds of people about her with a gesture.

"Mrs. Long," she was told, "and a strange man."

"Ah-h-h!" cried Mrs. Hudson. "Speaking of Mrs. Long, have you heard . . . can't we sit down, my dears? They say," she continued, after the group had recaptured their corner, "that her bridge winnings are simply fabulous; and that if she can't get money, she'll take the very clothes off your back. Of course, you've heard what happened at the Country Club, the other afternoon?"

The group drew in closer, and Mrs. Hudson set forth on the most dangerous of all adventures, the telling of a half-truth.

"She invited Mrs. Knowles, Madam Valleau and little Eva Leeds to lunch, at which, my dears, *they say*, far too much Burgundy was served, (especially for Eva, who is not used to it) and afterwards, of course, they settled themselves at the bridge table. I'm not saying that Eva is free from blame. Indeed, I have spoken to her most frankly on the subject, and she knows that I think her behaviour most culpable. Gambling amongst women who can afford it is bad enough, but that those who can't, should be given an opportunity to imperil their husband's meagre Civil Servant's salary, is a crime that should be punishable by law."

"It might be done, too," murmured Lady Elton, who was an agitative member of the National Council. "If we can prohibit the sale of liquor to a drunken man, I don't see why we can't restrict gambling to persons of a certain income." The sum which occurred to her was, of course, amply covered in her own case and that of her companions. "But, go on—what happened then?"

"Well, Eva lost, and lost, and *lost*! But do you think that Hattie Long would stop playing? Not a bit of it! At last—this really is too awful, my dears, you'll never believe me—"

The ladies had already foreseen this possibility, but like everyone else they liked the colourful romance of Mrs. Hudson's stories, so they urged her to continue.

"Very well," she agreed, "but mind, not a breath of this must go any further! To make a long story short, when they stopped, Eva was so badly in the hole that she couldn't cover her loss by an I.O.U. for Tom Leeds' *monthly cheque*!"

"Horrible!" whispered the group, genuinely shocked.

"What did she do?" asked Lady Elton.

"It seems that a few days before, she had bought from Leila Brant an Empire table. How she buys these things, I've no idea. The point is, that Hattie Long was crazy about that same table, too, and fully expected to have it. When she found Eva had got ahead of her she was simply wild, and offered almost double the price—certainly more than the thing was worth."

"And Eva refused it?"

"I'm obliged to say she did. No one can admire her for doing so. I repeat, I don't think she has behaved properly, but the point is that she had the table Hattie Long wanted, and so, when she had been driven into this quagmire of debt from which she could not possibly extricate herself, Hattie, with devilish finesse, suggested that she should give up the table and call the matter settled."

"She didn't do it?"

"She had to! Her I.O.U.'s for . . ." Mrs. Hudson had the grace to pause ". . . such a sum were utterly valueless! So, bright and early the following morning there was a transfer at her door and now the table decorates Harriet's reception room."

At that instant the crowd parted, and before either faction could avoid an encounter, Mrs. Long and her newspaper man stood beside them. Elaborately amiable greetings were exchanged. Mr. Reginald Harper was introduced. Inured as they were to association with the owners of great names, there was not a member of the group who escaped a sudden palpitation upon meeting this world-famed monarch of newspaperdom. It was not easy to keep gratification out of their manner when acknowledging the introduction, but by tacit agreement they were obligated to flick Mrs. Long over his innocent head.

"Are you living in Ottawa, Mr. Carter?" asked Lady Elton, deliberately mis-calling his name, but with a charming show of interest.

Mr. Harper had only arrived the day previous, for a brief stay.

"The place is full of strangers," volunteered Miss de Latour. "It scarcely seems like home, any more."

"It's the fault of the Government," declared Mrs. Hudson. "New people are always getting in. I don't understand how they work it, but there you are. Are you connected with the Government?" she asked the stranger, coyly.

Mrs. Long flashed a sharp look at the questioner and answered for her guest. "Only to the extent of financing our poor little country," she replied. "Mr. Harper,"—she turned to him, archly—"I suppose I may tell it? . . . Mr. Harper has just concluded a loan for a few paltry millions which a New York syndicate is advancing, so that the salaries of the Civil Service,"—her glance rested for a fraction of a second on the trio—"will be paid as usual."

The elder Miss Angus-McCallum hurriedly changed the subject. "How stunning you look, Hattie," she said. "But then, you've a style of your own and can wear those inexpensive things. *I* saw that costume in Hammerstein's window, and thought it charming."

Hammerstein was an obscure costumer of Semitic origin, who had recently benefited by one of his frequent fire-sales, and the implication that Mrs. Long's exclusive tailor-made had been purchased there was so obvious as to border on crudity. Mrs. Hudson could have done much better!

Mrs. Long ignored the thrust. "There seem to be so few men at these parties, nowadays," she observed, at no one in particular. "But when one looks at the women, one can hardly blame them."

"If we had a little gambling," said Miss de Latour, "no doubt they would find it more attractive."

"But there would be complications." Mrs. Hudson objected.

"In what way?" prompted Miss Mabel Angus-McCallum.

"Well, my dear, they couldn't play for the Vice-Regal furniture, could they? They'd get into immediate trouble with such stakes, for the furniture belongs to the taxpayers of Canada and is not negotiable."

In the sharp silence, Mrs. Long flushed slightly, realising that the incident to which this remark referred had been grossly distorted under Mrs. Hudson's capable and imaginative manipulation. She was about to make a stinging retort when she thought better of it, promising herself a day of reckoning in the future. Just how, did not at the moment occur to her, but time would show her the way.

"There's Captain Teddy beckoning us, Mr. Harper," she said. "We must go," and over her shoulder she explained, "Mr. Harper has never enjoyed the delicious terrors of tobogganing. The Princess is going to take him down. Goodbye!"

"That's that," snapped Miss de Latour. "Now, look out for yourself, Mrs. Hudson!"

The well-known purple velvet and ermine of Lady Denby caught Mrs. Chesley's attention. "She's got Azalea with her this afternoon, and who in Heaven's name is *that*?"

Lady Denby did not leave them long in doubt. "You must all know Mrs. Dilling," she said. "Mrs. Raymond Dilling, from Pinto Plains. Her husband is a Member, you know, and one of the most promising young speakers in the Party."

The ladies bowed frostily, not because they bore any particular grudge against Marjorie, but because they could not afford to miss this golden opportunity for expressing their dislike of Lady Denby, who, though glorified by a title, was not "of their set". They looked upon her as an "uplifter", living well within her husband's income, and exuding an atmosphere, not only of economy, but frugality; one who allied herself with organizations for the benefit of the human race, notably of women and children, and preached the depressing doctrine, that "Life is real, Life is earnest, and the grave is not its goal!"

Marjorie was embarrassed. She had been embarrassed all the afternoon, and something inside of her old fur coat ached intolerably. She noticed that an air of hostility prevailed over the entire throng. She did not realise, however, its fundamental cause; that the acknowledgments of friendships was a delicate matter within the grounds of Government House, for, as a man is known by the company he keeps, so the guests were desirous of being ranked in a higher classification than that in which they ordinarily moved. Which is to say, that although Mrs. Polduggan and Mrs. Crogganthorpe were friendly neighbours, and quite ready to acknowledge one another on their own verandahs, the moment they entered the skating pavilion their vision became blurred, and they saw for the most part, only the Ministers' wives, persons who were especially prominent, or, better than all, chatted with the wife of a Foreign Consul who was too polite, or too ignorant of Western conditions, to take a decided stand with regard to class distinctions.

"Dilling, did she say?" asked Mrs. Chesley, as Lady Denby and her protegées moved away. "What an impossible person!"

"Who is she?" asked Miss Angus-McCallum. "Should we call?"

Pamela de Latour shrugged her shoulders. "I haven't anything to do on Wednesday afternoon."

"Lunch with me," said Lady Elton. "We'll all go together."

"One never knows . . ."

The crowd had thinned perceptibly by the time Lady Denby released Marjorie from the strain of constant introductions, and went away to have a moment's chat with Miss Denison-Page, the statuesque Lady-in-Waiting.

Marjorie indicated a tall, florid gentleman with a shock of silver hair, who loitered at the doorway in a manner that suggested he was waiting for someone to go home.

"Who is that?" she whispered to Azalea.

"Where? Oh, that's Rufus Sullivan, the Member for Morroway," answered the girl. "I meant to have pointed him out to you earlier in the afternoon, only I had no chance. He's Lady Denby's pet aversion. One dares not mention his name in her presence."

"But why?"

"Lots of reasons. He's quite a character, you know. Heavens, how he stares!"

Marjorie turned away with flaming cheeks. She was loath to admit that he had not only been staring, but that he had been at her elbow during the entire afternoon. This distressed her, for, according to the ethics of Pinto Plains, a man impressed his attentions only upon the woman who encouraged him, and Marjorie felt that something in her manner must have been very misleading. She resented his pursuit less than she felt ashamed of herself for inspiring it, and was inexpressibly relieved when he finally left the room.

The terrible disorder of the pavilion sickened her housekeeper's soul, and she turned to Azalea, impetuously.

"Just look at this place! Isn't it disgusting to expect any human being to clean it up?" Then, a little afraid of her own daring, "Wouldn't you just love to open the back door and let a drove of pigs come in?"

"Yes," answered Azalea, shortly, "after you'd opened the front door and let them out!"

CHAPTER 6.

Marjorie was far from happy. The experience at Government House haunted her. Incidents that she had scarcely noted at the time, recurred in the pitiless glare of a good memory to harry her and rob her of her peace of mind. It had all been so different from what she expected!

Sunday dragged wearily on. The children seemed fretful and unusually difficult. The roast was tough and the furnace went out, so that Raymond was obliged to devote most of his precious afternoon to re-lighting it. By the time, therefore, that the children had sung their evening hymn, had each chosen a Bible story to be read aloud, and had been put to bed, Marjorie felt that she could bear no more, and she invaded the disorderly "drawing-room," too troubled to be repulsed by the unwelcoming expression in her husband's eyes.

"Well, what is it, my dear?" Dilling closed the volume upon his long, thin finger, and tapped it with a slender pencil. "Is anything especially the matter?"

"I don't know," sighed Marjorie. "That's just what I want to ask you, dear. Something *must* be wrong, somewhere, only I can't find it! I seem to be so stupid here, Raymond, and people don't like me. I know I oughtn't to bother you, dear," she said, noticing how his eyes strayed back to the book that at the moment she almost hated, with its chrome leather binding, its overwhelming contents, and the voluptuous overpowering odour that reflected the literary richness of its substance, "and I won't stay long, but *can't* you help me, and tell me what to do, so that I'll be more like the Ottawa people?"

Dilling stared down into the mist-blurred eyes, only half seeing them. His thoughts were snared by his own problems and he could not free them immediately. His casual words of encouragement carried no comfort to his wife, who stumbled on,

"You're so clever, dearie! If you aren't sure of a thing, you always know where to learn all about it. . . and that's all I'm asking you, Raymond—to tell me some book that will explain these queer things that I don't seem to understand."

"What kind of things?"

The question was not exactly brusque, but to anyone less troubled it would have suggested a definite desire for a brief interview. Marjorie raised her hands and let them fall to her sides helplessly.

"Hundreds—hundreds!" she began. "All sorts . . ."

"Give me a concrete illustration. Tell me one."

"Well, I never do anything *right*! Yesterday—you *do* shake hands with people when you meet them, don't you?—well, yesterday, Lady Denby took me to the Skating Party at Government House. I thought it was going to be so nice, Raymond. We always thought so at home, you know, but it wasn't just like what we imagined—in fact, it was awfully different."

"Yes, yes. But the point of the story, Marjorie?"

"I'm trying to tell you, dearie. You see, if you haven't been there, it's so difficult to understand the queer customs of the place. I'd been introduced to Captain Dodson—he called out the names, you know, standing just beside Their Royal Highnesses—and when we got into the room where they were receiving, Lady Denby went first, and I came second, and Miss Deane last, and you understand, Raymond, I couldn't see whether Lady Denby spoke to him or not, and so when I came along and he saw me and sort of smiled, I said, 'How do you do, Captain Dodson?' and held out my hand. You *do* shake hands with people, don't you, Raymond?"

"Never mind just now. Go on."

"Well, he didn't shake hands with me! Worse than that, he put his hands behind his back and said, 'Mrs. Raymond Dilling,' in an awful voice, and Miss Deane simply *pushed* me past him! I didn't know what to do when I got there in front of the Duke and the Duchess. I didn't know whether to shake hands or not, and I'm—I'm afraid, darling, that I behaved like a terrible simpleton. It was easy enough to see that Lady Denby was frightfully annoyed. She said that to shake hands with Captain Dodson was *not* the thing, and to shake hands with Their Royal Highnesses, *was* the thing, and altogether, I'm so muddled, I don't know what to do! Raymond, what on earth *is* THE THING?"

Dilling drew his finger definitely from his book, laid the volume on the table, and gave his attention to the question.

"Well, Marjorie," he said, "although I've never formed a considered opinion on this subject, I'll lay the facts before you, and we'll reason it out together."

Reasoning a subject out together between Marjorie and her husband was a merest euphemism for a philosophical lecturette with Dilling on the platform and his wife supplying the atmosphere. With his characteristic gesture when entering upon a discussion of some remote topic that interested him—an upward sweep of the right arm with the sensitive fingers coming to rest on his rapidly-thinning chevelure—he proceeded to instruct her.

"*The Thing*, my dear girl, as I see it, is one of the forms of what the Polynesians call 'Tabu'. In the large, 'tabu' may be said to be negative magic—that is, abstention from certain acts in order that unpleasant or malefic results may not ensue. Do you follow, so far?"

"Yes, dear . . . I think so . . . a kind of rule, you mean, don't you? One can see that, but what puzzles me, is that it works both ways. How does one learn *when* it is right, and when it is wrong? Isn't there some starting point?"

"Most certainly! 'Tabu' originated in religion, and was rooted in fear. Moreover, it was common to all peoples in their tribal beginnings. It is associated with the Totem of the North American Indian and the Fetish of the African races; it oppressed the alert Greek mind for an astonishing period, and prevailed amongst the Romans. Some day, you must read about the Flamen Dialis—a member of the priestly caste, who stood next the King in sacerdotal rank."

"I was thinking especially of shaking hands," murmured Marjorie.

But Dilling ignored her. He slipped easily into his Parliamentary manner, as though addressing Mr. Speaker, and his political associates. Furthermore, he was enjoying this opportunity to open doors that led into little-used rooms in the treasure-house of his mind.

"So rigid were the laws that governed the Flamen's conduct—er—so drastic was the discipline of The Thing—that even a knot in the thread of his clothing was practically a crime against the State! Can you imagine it? He couldn't spend a night outside the City. He was forbidden to ride— even touch—a horse. He . . . well, I could continue at length, but this is sufficient to show you that The Thing, as you term it, is no new, prohibitive measure, designed for your particular embarrassment."

"Oh, I didn't think that . . ."

"I forgot to mention that it was not The Thing for the Flamen to suffer marriage a second time—an historical statement, my dear, which has no personal application, I assure you! You see, the wife of the Flamen became sacrosanct, and passed, also, under the iron rule of the 'Tabu'."

Marjorie nodded hopefully, and urged her husband to explain how women were affected.

"If you are thinking of the Flaminica," returned Dilling, "she was affected very severely. I seem to remember that she was forbidden to comb her hair at certain intervals; also, she became unable to discharge her religious duties unless purified by a sacrifice, after hearing thunder. Upon my word," he broke off suddenly, "I shouldn't wonder if the wide-spread fear of electric storms may have taken its root from this very law! You have provoked a most interesting train of thought, my dear!"

"I'm ever so glad," was Marjorie's quick response. "But do you remember anything about her shaking hands?"

"Not at the moment. However, I venture this opinion ... the Flaminica was the foundress of those social 'Tabus' which have held the minds of women in bondage for so many ages; that she was the dictatrix of moral and social etiquette, to-day. You can readily understand how ladies, supporting this distinguished but irksome office, would seek to mitigate its rigours by using their rank to the discomfiture of less favoured members of their sex." He began to chuckle. "In short, I believe that Mrs. Grundy and Queen Victoria were her lineal descendants."

"Queen Victoria?" echoed Marjorie.

"I mean, my dear, that the Flaminica was the mother of Snobocracy, the divine High Priestess of the Order, whose code is expressed in the cryptic formula, 'It is—or is not—The Thing!'."

The alarum of the kitchen clock startled them both. Marjorie frowned. Althea must have been naughty again. She had been distinctly forbidden to touch it.

"I'm afraid I'll have to leave it at that, my dear," said Raymond, as he opened his book. Its peculiar odour enveloped her like a puff of smoke. "This report is somewhat more tricky than I had anticipated. But you have the main facts of the case—haven't you? To-morrow, I'll bring you a book from the Library."

As Marjorie closed the door, a sharp whirr sounded from the telephone.

"Hello," she said, wondering whether Raymond would mind being called.

"Is Mrs. Dilling at home?" asked a mellow voice at the other end of the wire. It was a voice that vibrated, and struck some unfamiliar chord within her consciousness; a voice that unreasonably disturbed her.

"I am Mrs. Dilling," answered Marjorie, and waited.

"My name is Sullivan," the voice continued. "Rufus Sullivan, the Member for Morroway."

"Oh!" cried Marjorie, startled. Then, "Oh, yes?"

"I am wondering if you will allow me the pleasure of calling on you, Mrs. Dilling. I have been a fervent admirer of your husband ever since I heard his speech in the House, last week, and I'm very eager to meet you. It is scarcely necessary for me to tell you that we have not had Dilling's equal in Parliament for many years."

"You're awfully kind," murmured Dilling's wife, to the accompaniment of a pounding heart. She didn't know why, but she was trembling.

"Well, I'm not sure about being kind," laughed the Hon. Member easily, "but I confess that I am desperately jealous. There's something about a man of Dilling's calibre that accuses us old chaps of unappreciated opportunities and wasted youth. One begins to taste the ashes of discouragement."

"Nobody should be discouraged," returned Marjorie, feeling the words inadequate, but not knowing what else to say.

"No, no! You're right, of course! As Walpole tells us, 'It's not life that matters; it's the courage you put into it.' Just the same, courage is acquired rather less by an effort of will, than by inspiration, don't you think so?"

"Ye-es," returned Marjorie, not very sure after all.

"I was wondering, Mrs. Dilling," the Hon. Member went on in a lighter tone, "if I might be admitted to the list of your acquaintances? If you would permit me to call?"

"I should be very pleased."

"Thank you ... thank you ... I can't say more! Are you busy this evening, or have you other guests? It goes without saying that I should not care to intrude."

Marjorie explained that she was quite free and that a call would not be the slightest intrusion, but that "Mr. Dilling" seemed to be very much engrossed in a book, and she wasn't quite certain—

"Don't think of it!" cried Sullivan. "I understand perfectly, and wouldn't allow you to disturb him for the world. Just let me slip in quietly, and when he has finished, perhaps he will join us. I do want to know your husband better, Mrs. Dilling, but it's quite impossible to form any intimate contacts up there on the Hill, and in the midst of the turmoil of our every-day existence. I won't say any more, however, through the medium of this unsatisfactory instrument. I will be with you in a moment."

He was. Before Marjorie had decided whether or not it was The Thing to entertain a Member of Parliament in the dining-room (where the table was set for breakfast) she was summoned to the door by a discreet tinkle of the bell.

Although his enormous bulk nearly filled the tiny passage, Sullivan's handclasp was very gentle and his voice was low.

"No words, Mrs. Dilling, can convey to you my gratitude for this privilege! I am a lonely man, a shy man for all my huge body, and I do not readily make friends!"

The house seemed to quiver as he followed her to the dining-room, and Marjorie was distressed at her failure to regain her composure and to still the strange quaking within herself. She had never been affected like this, before.

"What a cosy little nest!" exclaimed her guest. "And are there *three* birdlings?"

His fine brown eyes turned from the children's places—where neat oilcloth bibs and porridge bowls stood ready for the morning—back to her face.

"Yes, we have three children—two girls and a boy."

"Wonderful little woman," he breathed, reverently, "and she's only a slip of a girl, herself."

"I'm twenty-seven," declared Marjorie.

"A golden age," he sighed. "But tell me about the children—do! One of the bitterest disappointments of my life is that I haven't half a dozen ... I'm a lonely old bachelor, Mrs. Dilling. Few people realise just *how* lonely."

It flashed through Marjorie's mind that he had lost his sweetheart years ago. Perhaps she had died. Perhaps she had married someone else. In either case, Mr. Sullivan had remained true to her memory. She liked him for his constancy. Her embarrassment faded a little.

"It's dreadful to be lonely," she said, feeling that it would not be polite to ask why he had not married. "I've been a little lonely, myself, since we came to Ottawa."

"Poor child!"

Mr. Sullivan pressed Marjorie's hand with bland sympathy. The gesture reminded her of Uncle Herbert, whose comfort, in the face of any trial, expressed itself by a clicking of the tongue and that same spasmodic crushing of the hand. Indeed, now that she grew more at ease with him,

Marjorie noticed that Mr. Sullivan was quite an old man and she attributed that mysterious something in his manner to the eagerness of a lonely man to make friends. She smiled, brightly.

"Oh, you mustn't pity me," she cried. "I like Ottawa. All my life I have dreamed of coming here, and now the dream has come true. But, it is only natural that I miss some of my dearest friends. I wouldn't be a really nice person if I didn't, now, would I?"

Mr. Sullivan knitted his brows and said that, try as he would, he could not imagine her being anything but a fine friend. There was just the slightest suggestion of a pause before he added—

"You remind me of the noblest woman I ever knew."

"Did—did she—die?"

The great, white head sank slowly. Again, Mr. Sullivan sought her hand. "She was just twenty . . . I was a youngster, too. Life has never been the same . . . But there! I mustn't burden you with my sorrows. You were going to tell me about the children. I don't suppose you would let me peep at them—just a little tiny peep, if I promise not to wake them?"

"Would you really like to see them?" asked Marjorie, now thoroughly at ease with her guest.

"I can't tell you how much."

"Then, of course, you may!"

With an unconsciously coquettish gesture, she laid her finger on her lips and led the way up the creaking stairs. Her thoughts were of the children. Had she been careful to wash all the jam from Baby's rosebud mouth? Althea, she remembered, had pulled the button off her Teddies and she had found it necessary to resort to the ubiquitous safety pin. And Sylvester—well, there was no prophesying what might have happened to Sylvester since she heard his "Now-I-lay-me," and kissed him.

The thoughts of Mr. Sullivan, on the other hand, were concerned with almost everything but the children. He was wondering why that door at the foot of the stairs did not open and a voice ask what the devil he was doing, prowling through the house. He was trying to decide whether Marjorie had advised her husband of his coming and he was being deliberately ignored, or whether Dilling habitually shrouded himself with aloofness, and indifference to the affairs of the home and the personnel of his wife's callers.

At the landing, Marjorie turned to whisper.

"Please don't look at the room. It's so hard to be tidy with babies, you know."

Mr. Sullivan hung yearningly over the cots where Althea and Sylvester were sleeping. He did it very well, and Marjorie was delighted.

"Beautiful," he murmured, and he indicated that he found a strong resemblance to her.

Beside the baby's little crib he was overcome with emotion, and Marjorie's heart went out to him as he groped hastily for his handkerchief and passed it across his eyes. "The cherub," he whispered, "the exquisite little flower. She has her father's cast of features, but—" transferring his expression of adoration to the face nearer his "—but I'll wager she has her mother's eyes!"

When they creaked their way downstairs again they were on the friendliest terms, and Marjorie could scarcely reconcile this kind, elderly gentleman and his interested, avuncular air, with the debonair gallant who had caught and held her attention so unpleasantly at Government House.

"It only shows," she reproved herself, "how you can misjudge a person. And he's old enough to be my father . . ." which state was always synonymous to her with extreme rectitude and respectability.

He would not hear of her disturbing Raymond, nor would he allow her to make cocoa for him, fond of it as he avowed himself to be. But he made her promise that she would let him come soon again, when the children were awake, and that when he was especially lonely, he might telephone her; and moreover, that once in a while she would have tea with him in order that he might prove what an excellent and handy man he would have been . . . under different circumstances!

"This has been for me a wondrous night," he said, holding her hand and looking affectionately down at her, "and one that I shall never forget. There is little I can do to prove my gratitude for a glimpse of real home life, and the joy that has eluded me, but perhaps there may come a time when you feel that I can serve you. Will you put me to the test, then, Mrs. Dilling?" he queried, softly.

Touched, Marjorie nodded. "I am very pleased to have had you come in like this—"

" '*Sans ceremonie*,' as our French friends say," interrupted Sullivan, looking furtively over her head at the closed door behind which he knew that Dilling sat. "The strength of the weak," he murmured, "the courage to endure the emptiness of solitary days and weary evenings. I've been through it. I understand. God bless you, little woman! But there can be no more loneliness for us so long as we are . . . friends!" He pressed her hand and was gone.

As she went upstairs, Marjorie wondered whether or not she had imagined a shade of difference in him as he left her.

PART II
They Saw

CHAPTER 7.

Azalea Deane was a much befamilied young woman, who was leaving "mile 30" behind so rapidly that it was already quite blurred in the distance. Ahead, there stretched a bleak and desolate roadway, leading right into the heart of that repository for the husks of men—Beechwood—and at the best of times, she found her journey wearisome and uninspiriting.

She did not cavil at her fate. No one ever heard Azalea complain—of poverty, obscurity, dullness or villenage. She accepted her destiny with a fine stoicism, which reflected itself in well-feigned indifference and enabled her to proceed along the same monotonous route at the same monotonous speed, with the same monotonous companions month after month, and year after year, without developing gangrene of the soul or breaking into open revolt.

"Oh, God," she prayed each morning, before descending to the agitated atmosphere of the breakfast table, "keep me from being difficult to live with!"

And Heaven heard her prayer.

No one really knew Azalea—least of all, her family. Perhaps, no one ever really knows anyone else, a phase of ignorance which, personally, I am not inclined to deplore. Souls should be clad no less than bodies. They should be gowned with decency, and in so far as possible, loveliness; and if, now and again, the garment slips or wears thin, then should the beholder turn his eyes away, nor seek to pry into anything that may be so terrible or so sublime.

Outwardly, as Lady Denby had said, Azalea was a plain little person. She should have been dainty of form, but through some irreparable miscalculation, the Creator had dowered her with the large features, hands and feet designed for some much more ample person. Therefore, she gave no pleasure to the sensitive, artistic eye, and this was an acute grievance to her who possessed a deep and pagan love for Beauty. She was a toneless girl, with thin, straight, dun-coloured hair which she could not afford to keep marcelled. Her eyes were unarresting, as a rule; too sharp to be appealing and not lustrous enough to sparkle. Her skin had a sandy cast and usually shone. Even when rouge and the ubiquitous lip-stick assumed the respectability of universal usage, Azalea's appearance was scarcely improved, for the former would not blend, and lay like a definite glaze upon her cheeks, while the latter only accentuated the flatness of her too-ample mouth, and made one wish that she had not tampered with it at all.

Her wardrobe was an appalling miscellany of discarded grandeur. Ladies whose clothes were too passé for their own adornment, bestowed them upon Azalea with the remark,

"You can see, my dear, that these are scarcely worn, and anyway, they are not the sort of things one could give the servants!"

She had learned to smother the hot rebellion that flared up in her heart, to thank them prettily, and to convey huge, unwieldy bundles through the streets and hold her tongue when her family commented upon the generosity of Lady This or Mrs. That. But she often wondered that her father never divined that Lady Elton's cloth-of-gold dinner gown remodelled by her impatient and unskilled fingers, caused abrasions upon her spirit deeper than sackcloth could have produced, and blithely would she have consigned every stitch that she owned to the flames, for the joy of buying the most ordinary, commonplace, inexpensive frock at a bargain sale.

The future of the Deanes stretched behind them. The best of the family lay underground. Mr. Grenville Harrison Deane was the sole male survivor of an illustrious line that could be traced (so he declared) with an occasional hiatus, back to Alfred the Great! It was never clear to the upstarts whose genealogical tree took root in England about the time of the Conquest, or thereafter, how he arrived at his conclusion, but if antiquity of ideas was anything of a proof, then they were forced to admit that there was justification in his contention, for his views of life antedated those of Britain's noble King.

Aloofness from fatiguing toil had rewarded him with an erectness that was impressive, and a complexion that a flapper might have envied. A Dundreary of silver gossamer caressed his cheeks, and his clear, lustrous eyes looked out from an unfurrowed setting. His chief characteristics were piety and an Eumenidean temper. The former, which should have been broad, was constricted to the dimensions of a number ten needle, and the latter, which should have been narrow, expanded to encompass impartially every one who held views divergent from his own. Particularly, was it directed against the blistering injustice of the Civil Service.

The Civil Service had served him faithfully for thirty-five years, despite his eternal villification of it. Recently, his incompetence had been recompensed by superannuation and the payment of seven-tenths of his salary—shall it be said, seven times as much as he was worth? But Mr. Deane had always fancied himself in the Premier's place, or at least in a Ministerial capacity. Failing that, a Trade Commissionership, or even a Deputy's post would have appeased him. Therefore, to be superannuated after thirty-five years' inconspicuous hampering of the postal service, appeared to him as a blot upon the integrity of the Nation.

He was forever "taking up his case" with this or that influential person. What his case was, Azalea had but a misty idea, and whether he actually took it up or merely gloated over the notion of doing so, she had no means of ascertaining. Anyway, the matter had long ago ceased to interest her.

Mrs. Deane was the type of woman now happily becoming quite extinct, who was born to be dominated, and ably fulfilled her destiny. The eldest and most unattractive daughter of a rural English divine, she had won her husband by a trick for which he never forgave her, though he realised that she was in no way responsible. He had fallen fatuously in love with Dorothea, her younger sister, and had received the parental sanction to an engagement before setting sail for "Kenneda" and a post that his name might dignify. Six months later, Dorothea, who had quite innocently intrigued the affection of a visiting curate—a nephew of the Dean of Torborough, no less—had been prodded weeping to the altar, while Fanny was trundled on a steamer and shipped to Montreal to console the palpitant bridegroom, who had not even been apprised of the fact that a substitute had been forwarded.

The agony of that trip left its mark on Fanny Deane. A kindly lie would have spared her so much—for a time, at least. But the Rev. Arthur Somerset deemed suffering a salutory need, for others, and stated the case to his first-born with unequivocal lucidity . . . One phase of a woman's duty is to grasp the opportunity for marriage and thus clear the way for her younger sisters, who, also, must have husbands. The prospect of fulfilling this duty in St. Ethelwyn's was slender, and Fanny was no longer young . . . Did she want to be a burden in her old age to her family? . . . Dependent upon them for a home . . . Such inconsideration in a daughter of his was unthinkable . . . And as for young Deane, the Rev. Arthur waived his preference aside with a clerical gesture calculated to display advantageously his well-kept hand . . . Any man might be proud of a wife begotten and bred by Arthur Somerset, D.D.

"You must carry it off well, Fanny," he adjured her, at the close of the interview, "for otherwise, you will be stranded in a strange country where . . ." the alternative was painted in no mean and unromantic terms.

Fanny "carried it off" successfully enough, though by no fault or virtue of her own. Too ill, almost, to stand, she crept down the gangway, and cowered before the eager-eyed young man who did not even recognise her when she addressed him.

Ah, if she had only been told that kindly little lie, and could have raised a radiant face to his, whispering,

"Here I am, dear! It was too wonderful that you should have sent for me!"

Instead, with ashen lips and shame-filled eyes, she muttered, "Mr. Deane, they married Dorothea to a curate—she couldn't help it—she wanted you to know! Here is your ring . . . and . . . and . . . they made me come . . . For God's sake, don't send me back! I'll work for you till I drop dead . . . I'll be your servant—anything—only, for God's sake, don't send me home!"

He stared at her while the devastating truth burst over him like an engulfing flood. He shook with rage, with the anguish of blighted hopes and his own impotence in escaping the net that had been spread for him, while Fanny cringed beside him praying that God would strike her dead . . .

And Heaven did not hear her prayer.

Speechless, they faced one another. After a bit, he took her roughly by the arm.

"Come, girl," he said, "we'll get this rotten business over, quickly. The license reads 'Dorothea'—I suppose I'll have to get another one. There now, for God's sake, don't sniffle! People are looking at us."

To give him credit, Grenville Harrison Deane never charged her with the deception of her parents. He never referred to it in so many words. But for two and forty years, Fanny lived in connubial torment, under the shadow of this smothering humiliation, and the fear that he might some day be led to speak of it. Often, there was that in his manner, that threatened to burst into violent and comminatory reproach.

She tried to efface herself, to reduce herself to nothingness, and to spare him the reminder of her substitution. She had a way of watching him, endeavouring to divine his whims and moods, that was loathesome in its humility. Her entire life was an apology for having failed to be her sister.

Unfortunately, Fanny never suspected that the greatest need of her overlord was association with a strong-minded tyrant, who, in the guise of the clinging-vine—or any other—would have thrust upon him the unexperienced pleasure of putting his shoulder to the wheel and hearing it creak as he moved it. He would have been happy doing things, being wheedled into service; but, as matters stood, Fanny Deane would have breathed for him, had such been possible. She relieved him of every burden and responsibility, and became a substitute not only for her silly, simpering sister, but for a shabby armchair and a pair of carpet slippers. Azalea, who was the youngest of five daughters, went so far as to say that the tomb to which his mortal envelope must one day be committed, would never equal in comfort the padded sepulchre her mother provided him while living.

Azalea's earliest remembrance centred round a very common occurrence—her mother kneeling in the midst of broken toys and howling children, pleading,

"Don't cry, my darlings! We will mend them! Sh-sh-sh—*Please* be quiet! *Don't* irritate your father."

She lived in constant dread of irritating a man who would have kept his temper had he really been vouchsafed anything to be irritated about; and her life was one which no self-respecting dog would have endured.

No one was more surprised than Fanny Deane when her four elder girls found husbands. Naturally, perhaps, she regarded marriage as a difficult and sordid undertaking—for parents, that is to say. Many a night, as she sat beside a moaning baby, the thought that one day she might have to engineer her children into the State of Holy Wedlock was like a deadly stricture about her heart. However, Hannah, Flossie, Tottie and May all married without any fuss or flurry, in a satisfactory, chronological fashion, the Civil Service yielding up its living dead to provide their sustenance. They became the Mrs. Polduggans and Mrs. Crogganthorpes of Ottawa; that large, uneasy, imitigable body—scrabbling, straining, jostling, niggling, fighting for the power to give rather than receive—snubs!—and living largely in the hope of supplanting their superiors and lifting themselves out of the ruck composed of other women, whose husbands, like their own, were merely "something in the Government".

But Azalea was different. Marriage, in her opinion, was neither the subliminal pinnacle of feminine felicity, as her father claimed to conceive it, nor the Open Door to Independence, as her sisters averred. Shrewd observation led her to the conclusion that of independence there was little, and feminine felicity there was none. Always interested in the dark side of life, e.g., the married side, Azalea divided the women of her acquaintance into two classes—the parasites, who slyly or seductively tapped their husbands and appropriated their material and spiritual substance without suffering the smallest compensatory impulse, and the antithetical order, who resigned themselves to a stronger will and found matrimony a state of reluctant vassalage.

Azalea dreamed sometimes of an ideal companionship, or perhaps, a companionable ideal, but the paradigmatic young men whom her sisters (with the patronage of the successful angler who has already gaffed his fish and offers to instruct the novice how to bait a hook, and cast) enticed for her selection, inflamed her disgust rather than her romanticism.

Her greatest hunger was for economic independence, and this was summarily denied her.

Mr. Deane, drenched in archaic theories, confused idleness with refinement, and work with degradation. Moreover, he would have felt a sense of incompetence, mute reproach, even contempt, had he permitted his daughters to join the restless ranks of the employed. By such a measure, would he have confessed his inability to support them as befitted women of gentle breeding, and to provide them with all the amenities that their natures craved. That one of them should possess a bank account of her own and feel at liberty to spend money without the humiliating necessity of applying to him, was a condition that smacked of positive shamelessness. It was characteristic of him that although he never wished to perform any useful task unaided by the members of his household, he never allowed them to perform the task alone.

He had a genuine horror of the modern business woman who could look him unflinching in the eye, without that sweet deference which testified to his superiority. All business women were, in his opinion, coarse; besides, economic independence resulted in their getting "out of hand", and a woman who got out of hand, was, in Mr. Deane's judgment, a very dangerous proposition. Therefore, he refused Azalea the freedom she craved. He immolated her self-respect (and that of the community for her, in a measure) on the altar of his vanity, and condemned her to a life of servitude far more degrading than anything she would have chosen. She was depressed under the burden of obligations that gave her little benefit and no pleasure, and she secretly despised herself for being forced to accept them.

"Do let me go away and work," she used to entreat, "I could teach. That's a lady's profession."

But her mother made vague gestures of distress that said,

"Don't bring up this dreadful subject again! Please, my dear, be careful or you will irritate your father!"

And father, giving every promise of fulfilling this prophecy, would reply,

"So long as I live, I hope that no daughter of mine will be forced from the shelter of her home, and out amongst the ravening wolves of commerce. When I am gone . . ." he left an eloquent pause ". . . But in the meantime . . ."

The words, not to mention the gesture that accompanied them, implied somehow that caravans of voluptuous commodities assembled by his protean labours, should continue to arrive at their very door.

He was unctuously proud of her friends, and actually toadied to her in deference to her association with the aristocracy of the Capital. So did her sisters, and their husbands, and the "char", and the tradespeople, all of whom knew that she enjoyed sufficient intimacy with Lady Elton to assist at a luncheon or dinner-party—assist, that is to say, in the kitchen. And the splendid thing about this kind of assistance was that she received no honorarium for her services. That was where she took conspicuous precedence over Mrs. Wiggin, the char, and Ellen Petrie, who "waited on all the exclusive affairs of the city". To work without salary was Mr. Deane's conception of a lady's highest calling, and a means whereby she might be kept from getting out of hand.

He was supported in this attitude by one of the foremost ladies in the land, who argued that "no woman engaged in earning her own living should be presented at the Drawing Room!"

The Dillings struck a new note in the monotone of Azalea's existence. She had never seen their like, and was profoundly touched by their genuineness, their simplicity. For the first time in her life she felt that she had come into contact with people to whom friendship is dearer than the advantageous acquaintanceship that travesties it; for the first time in her life she could show an honest affection without being suspected of having an ulterior motive. At that time, Azalea had nothing to gain from the Dillings. On the contrary, she had something to give—an ineffably joyous experience—and she delighted in the sensation of being for once the comet instead of the tail; instead of the trailer, the cart.

Towards Raymond Dilling, she was conscious of an intense maternalism. Mentally, she acknowledged him her master, but in every other respect, he was an utter child—hard, undemonstrative, cold, but, despite that, a very appealing child. And she saw with her native shrewdness that mere mentality would never gain for him the success which he deserved. Ottawa, she knew, was thronged with brilliant people whose gifts were lost to the City—to the Dominion—because they lacked the empty artifices and consequent social standing which enabled them to get a hearing. No strolling mummer in the Middle Ages needed ducal patron more sorely than does a mere genius in the Capital of Canada.

And Dilling liked Azalea. She was a new and interesting type to him who had never considered feminine psychology a topic that was worth pursuing. His wife's friends in Pinto Plains were, he realised, estimable creatures running to fat and porcelain teeth at middle age. They were conscientious mothers, faithful to their husbands and earnest seekers after a broader knowledge than that provided by their homely tasks. But they wearied him. Whenever he encountered a group of them, his dominant wish was to escape, and he rarely failed to gratify this desire by excusing himself with some such remark as,

"I'll just slip off and leave you ladies free to discuss the three D's", by which he implied (with some degree of justification, doubtless) that the conversation of women is restricted to the topics of Dress, Domestics and Disease. He hated women's chatter.

Azalea Deane was the only woman he had ever known who possessed what he later termed a bi-sexual mind. He was never irritably conscious, as was the case with Marjorie's other friends, of the fact that she was a woman. Even when she discussed the three D's, there was a broad impersonality, a pleasing and quizzical tang to her remarks that he chose to arrogate to the mind of man. Before he had known her any length of time, he discovered that, unlike Marjorie she not only understood what he said, but that in some startling and inexplicable manner she divined thoughts which he had expressly refrained from putting into words.

For him, she was a novel experience, whose flavour he enjoyed rather more intensely than he was aware. Not that his emotions were even remotely touched by the personality of the girl. No! She was a mental adventure which he followed with frank curiosity and a diminishing display of patronage. Her mind was full of exhilarating surprises, and he was astounded to discover how easily she ornamented arid facts with garlands plucked from her rich imagination. She had a neat twist in the handling of them which Dilling was not slow to see and imitate. She guided him into many a pungent domain of thought, where he lost himself completely in an exciting pursuit after some winking little light, that led to the very middle of an icy stream into which he fell, spluttering, only to find Azalea calm and dry, on the opposite shore, laughing at him. He contracted the habit of reading extracts from his speeches to her, and presently, he tried the effect of an entire discourse. Now and again, he sounded her as to what he considered saying, and discovered that her enthusiastic understanding was like an extra filter to his already well-clarified intention.

He stored up particularly smart bits of political repartee to tell her, while his own triumphs of wit were laid at her feet rather than those of his bewildered wife. And all this time, the prevailing fancy that overlaid his subconscious mind, was,

"Quite a good sort, that girl! Pity she isn't a man!"

He voiced this latter sentiment to Azalea one evening shortly before prorogation and his return for the summer to Pinto Plains. In their sharp and peppery fashion, they had been discussing the Budget, inflated, Azalea contended, beyond all reason by the conscienceless demands of those picaresque buccaneers, Eastlake and Donahue, whose issue of private enterprise was begotten in the womb of the public treasury, when Dilling turned to her and cried,

"You've made out a good case, Miss Deane! You should have been a man!"

The girl's cheeks burned a painful brick tint. But she laughed and retorted,

"By which you tactfully imply my unsuitability for the state to which it has pleased God to call me, and regret that physical limitations prevent my choosing a more adequate sphere. I confess to you in strict confidence, that frequently, I have deplored this condition, myself."

"Come along into politics," invited Dilling, a touch of seriousness behind his banter.

"Right-o! Just so soon as you amend the B.N.A. and offer me a refuge in the Senate," she answered, and changed the subject.

Later that night, Marjorie hinted that he had hurt Azalea.

"Eh?" cried Dilling. "What are you talking about? Hurt her—how?"

"By what you said."

"What did I say?"

"That she should have been a man."

Dilling carefully twisted his collar free from the button. A violent physical action of any kind was foreign to him. Running the curved band between his fingers, he gave an abstracted thought to the possibility of wearing it again on the morrow, even while he turned to contradict his wife. "Nonsense, Marjorie, she liked it! All women like it; it's a tribute to their mentality, my dear. One often has to say some such thing to a perfect ninny, but in this case I happen to be sincere and I think Miss Deane knew it."

Marjorie did not contest the point. She never argued with Raymond, but once in a while she felt, as now, that his non-combatible correctness covered an error in judgment. Of course, he was sincere in paying a tribute to Azalea's cleverness, and, of course, she knew he meant what he said. But that was the very trouble—the very barb that pierced her spirit!

In a strange and mysterious way (of which she was somewhat ashamed) Marjorie often reached perfectly amazing conclusions that were directly opposed to Raymond's incontrovertible logic. And Azalea's hurt was a case in point. Just why the words had stung, it was beyond Marjorie Dilling to explain. Orderly thinking and systematic juxtaposition of facts found their substitute in flashes of intuition which, throughout the ages, have stood for women in the place of reason. But she knew, without knowing how she knew, that Azalea would rather have impressed Raymond with her incomparable womanhood, than the fact that she was the possessor of a brain that should have functioned in the body of a man.

As for Azalea, she was not conscious that Marjorie had heard the echo of that discordant note, and she would have been inexpressibly surprised had she suspected it. Years of rigid discipline had taught her to conceal all the emotions she thought she had not strangled, and she was accustomed to being treated as a man when not as a nonentity. Times without number she had paid for an evening's entertainment by escorting timourous and penurious ladies safely home in the silent watches of the night . . . a delicate assumption that she, herself, lacked sufficient fascination to stimulate brute design. On other occasions, hostesses frankly asked her to slip away quietly, "so that my husband won't feel obliged to take you home, dear." And once, a particularly considerate host glimpsing the blizzard that raged beyond his portal, had placed her in the care of a diminutive messenger boy, of some nine years, who struggled through the snowdrifts and sniffled that he had come from Hewitt's Service, and please where was the parcel?

So Dilling's words cut without producing an unendurable pain. The spot was well cocained and would ache long after the incision had been made. Azalea listened to his defence of his leader, his Party, and Messrs. Eastlake and Donahue, sensitive to a breath of discouragement beneath his words.

"I came to Ottawa expecting to find co-operation, and in its place fierce competition confronts me—competition," he said, "within the very ranks of the Party! It may strike you as being particularly naive, but I confess that I had not expected to find this sort of friction. It puts a different complexion on politics."

This was a tremendous admission for him to make, and in one of those flashing visions that supplemented her more leisured mental processes, Azalea saw that just as Marjorie groped along her level, so Dilling stumbled into pitfalls in his particular sphere, that a cumulus vapour of disenchantment threatened the horizon of his career, and that even as his wife bade fair to be a victim of the Social Juggernaut, so he would be crushed beneath the wheels of the political machine.

And they thought that this was The Land of Afternoon!

CHAPTER 8.

*T*he Dillings returned to Ottawa refreshed in body and spirit. Their summer in Pinto Plains had been a prolonged triumph and its effect, beneficial. Not only had they been welcomed with affectionate deference, entertained sedulously, and permitted to depart with honest regret and a dash of frank envy, but they had been reclaimed by that splendid illusion from which six months in the Capital had freed them.

By the time they turned their faces eastward, they were quite prepared to attribute their disheartening experiences of the previous winter to hyper-sensitiveness—the difficulty generally felt in accommodating oneself to a new environment.

It was during the last stages of the journey that uneasiness returned, and expressed itself in remarks such as,

"Just think . . . this time last year we were strangers, and now, it seems almost like coming home!" or

"It's nice to know that we have friends here, isn't it? We won't be so lonely, this year, will we?"

Each in a characteristic way tried to capture a sense of confidence, a glow of happiness, and to feel that being no longer aliens, Ottawa would be different—that is, as each would like to find it.

Marjorie succeeded better than her husband.

"It's awfully exciting, isn't it?" she cried, as the train panted along beside the canal, and familiar landmarks unfolded before her.

Across the muddy water where barges and the Rideau Royal Pair were tied up for the winter, she could see the Driveway, spotted with children and women casually attendant upon perambulators. The Pavilion at Somerset Street, where she used to sit with her little brood, looked bleak and uninviting, but she was glad to see it, just the same. Two lovers occupied a bench in front of the Collegiate, and kissed shamelessly as the train moved past. Marjorie's heart warmed to them, not that she approved of kissing in public places, but because there was something human about them; they added weight to her theory that Ottawa was not so forbidding and formidable, after all.

Dilling stared out of the window, too, but he did not see the lovers, the Armouries, the Laurier Avenue Bridge, the Arena, nor the warehouses flanked by the Russell Hotel. He saw a straggling little lumber village, gay with the costumes of Red Men, voyageurs, and the uniforms of sappers and miners, who were at work on the Canal. What a mammoth undertaking and how freighted with significance! By the building of a hundred and twenty-six miles of waterway that linked Kingston with the infant Bytown, English statesmen provided an expedient for adding to the impregnability of the British Empire!

"War," he mused. "How it has stimulated the ingenuity of man! With sacrifice, with blood and tears, we carve a niche for ourselves out of the resistant rock, in the hope that there we will find peace, but immediately the task is finished, we set ourselves to fortify it against the hour of war."

He pictured the Cave Dweller, bent over his crude instruments of destruction, clubs of bone and stone, which, in all probability, the modern man could scarcely lift. He considered the inventor of primitive projectiles. That was a long step toward the mechanism of modern homicide. One could lie, ambushed, behind a mound and use a sling, a boomerang, a blow-pipe or a javelin, and arrows . . . he gave a mental shudder and thanked God that he had not lived a hundred years ago. There was something about an Indian that made his flesh creep; a traditional antagonism that he did not try to overcome. The romance of the Red Man never gripped him. Like all unimaginative people, his prejudices were sharp and immutable.

He picked the word "blunderbuss" from a confusion of pictures that combined Gibraltar and Queenston Heights, and cumbrous cannon that were dangerous alike to friend and foe, and repeated,

"War! Always fashioning some new tool to strengthen the hand of Death. They spent a million pounds on a 'military measure' to safeguard the Colony from invasion on the South . . . and behold, the Rideau Canal!"

He started when Marjorie thrust parcels into his arms, and observed that at last they had arrived.

Azalea met them at the station. She had opened their tiny house, and with the assistance of Mrs. Plum had put it in order.

Hers had been an exceptionally uneventful summer, and she had looked forward to the Dillings' return with an impatience that astonished her.

From the last of June until the first of September, Ottawa is like a City of the Dead. Despite the fact that these are the pleasantest weeks of the year, the town is deserted by every one who can get away, even though the exodus extends no farther than Chelsea, on the other side of the river. But Azalea hadn't even got so far, this summer. Her time had been pretty fully occupied carrying out commissions for more fortunate friends. Lady Denby who had gone to the sea, asked her to superintend the installation of the winter's coal. Mrs. Long preferring the irresponsibility of Banff to the responsibility of presiding over her country home and a succession of unappreciated house-parties, decided that this was an excellent opportunity for papering some of the obscurer portions of her town residence, and 'knew that Azalea wouldn't mind overseeing the work'. She interviewed a cook for Mrs. Blaine, hunted up a photograph of Sir Mortimer Fanshawe taken on the golf links (before he had acquired the game) and excellent as a pictorial feature for a sporting supplement. She shopped, exchanged articles, paid bills that had been forgotten, and found herself generally confronted with the *res angusta domi* of a woman without an income. She did not grumble. At the same time, she could imagine a hundred happier ways of spending a summer.

Mr. and Mrs. Deane left the shelter of their comfortable home to suffer in turn the hospitality of each of their married daughters, who holidayed according to their means (i.e., spent a good deal more money than they could afford, and returned home soured by the necessity for retrenchment). Azalea could have gone, too, but there were limits even to her endurance.

The Dillings fell upon her joyously, not only Marjorie and the children, but Raymond.

"You must come home with us," he cried, "and tell us all the news. Is it true that Pratt is running for the Federal House? I heard a rumour to that effect on the train."

Azalea nodded.

"You can't be surprised. This has been his wife's ambition for years. She'll achieve it, too, if there's anything in persistent campaigning. But I've something else to say—I wrote you about it a few days ago, before your wire came. The house that Lady Denby has been so keen for you to take, is empty. I have an option on it in your name."

Marjorie could not suppress an exclamation. The house in question was large, and in her opinion, unduly pretentious. Their living expenses would be more than doubled. It seemed strange to her that people of their modest means should be encouraged—urged, indeed—to make such extravagant outlay. Display of any sort was, in the eyes of Pinto Plains, vulgar, and a cardinal sin upon which her friends felt themselves qualified to sit in judgment, was that of trying to appear above one's station.

To Marjorie, one of the most amazing features about life in the Capital was the discovery that women who dressed with most conspicuous elegance, lived in impressive style and drove in motor cars, commanded only a Civil Servant's meagre salary. Later, she learned that over their heads a cloud of debt continually hung, but it caused them no more distress than did the dome of the sky. The infamous credit system in the city was responsible for these moral callouses which she simply could not understand. Debt, to her, was synonymous with dishonesty, and that anyone could become accustomed to living in its shadow, was beyond the limits of her comprehension. It was a shock for her to learn that respected families had unpaid accounts at the large stores extending over a period of twenty years!

Virtually, any tradesman would supply merchandise on account to a Civil Servant, because although the salary could no longer be garnisheed, they hoped that a small payment would be snipped with regularity from the infallible Governmental cheque.

"Why don't you buy a set of sectional bookcases for your husband's books?" asked Azalea's sister, Flossie, during the progress of a call.

Marjorie's reply was ingenuous, naively truthful. "We've been under so much expense lately," she said, "I felt that I couldn't afford them."

Mrs. Howard, whose husband was an anaemic little man, occupying a humble post in the Department of Labor, opened her eyes in genuine astonishment.

"You don't have to *pay* for them," she cried. "Hapgood is most considerate in the matter of his accounts. I generally have to beg for mine!"

This latter remark was not strictly in line with the truth—not in Mrs. Howard's case. She had heard it, however, dropped from the lips of one of Ottawa's twenty-three millionaires, and appropriated it, she felt, with some effect.

But Marjorie couldn't see any future happiness at all, knowing that she would be faced with financial problems, and she was absolutely unable to understand the attitude of Lady Denby, who, throughout the previous winter, had stressed the necessity for making a better appearance "for the sake of the Party".

"When people are wealthy and have an assured position," she counselled, "they can enjoy a freedom of action that is denied those less fortunately conditioned. Mrs. Hudson is an example. She could, if one of her extraordinary whims dictated, dine at Government House in her great-grandmother's faded bombazine, without injuring her position in the slightest degree. On the other hand, should *you* attempt the smallest unconventionality, I assure you the result would be socially disastrous. The same principle applies in the matter of entertaining. You are no less a part of public life than is your husband, and you can render him no greater assistance than by displaying a judicious and well-regulated hospitality. Cultivate *nice* people—er—the Minister's wives, and so on ... Entertain them and entertain them well, but—" she broke off, abruptly, "—you can't do it *here!*"

It quite took Marjorie's breath away to learn that Lady Denby considered women important in politics, and that they might sway their husbands for or against a fellow member was an idea that had never entered her mind. Neither could she understand how her own popularity could be a factor in Raymond's success, and that it was dependent upon maintaining a position she would not afford, instead of living according to her means and simplicity of requirement—was an attitude of mind that she never completely grasped. But the necessity for it all was made evident even to Raymond, and by no less a person than Sir Eric himself, who ably coached by his wife, remarked that "to save, one must first learn to spend!"

"Establish yourself, my dear fellow," were his words, "establish yourself in the life of the Capital, and when the roots are firmly implanted in this loamy soil, draw in your horns—if one may be permitted to mix a metaphor. I am not advocating a reckless expenditure of more than you have to spend," emphasised the advocate of all the verbotens, "but rather the point that it is not advisable for a young politician to appear to hoard his salary. Education, you say? The children's education will, I trust, be well provided for by a generous and appreciative country."

So the Dillings moved, and Marjorie memorialised the occasion by issuing invitations to a large tea.

"I suppose you didn't keep a visiting list?"

"No!"

Azalea had expected a negative answer, so she was not disappointed. But Marjorie added,

"I'm sure I shan't forget any of my friends."

"Doubtless! The difficulty will lie in remembering all your active enemies!"

"Oh, Miss Deane—I mean Azalea—what shocking things you say! Surely, I don't have to ask people who have—that is, who haven't—who aren't exactly what you might call friendly with me?"

"Positively!"

"Oh, but that doesn't seem right!" protested Marjorie, in dismay. "It's deceitful! There's no use liking people if you treat the ones you don't like just as well!"

"Sound logic, my dear, but impractical from a social standpoint. You see, it's something like this—" Azalea slipped a thin gold bracelet from her arm, pouring within and about it, a quantity of pen nibs. "Society is like this bangle, and these nibs are the people who compose it. I'll jostle the desk and then see what happens to those who are not safe within its golden boundary. They fall off and go down to oblivion. The others, though disturbed, are in a sense secure, so you can see, my dear, that the paramount business of life in the Capital is to get *inside*. Of course, there are circles within circles, and you must learn about them, later. But for the moment, concentrate upon getting within the shining rim. Once there, you can stick, and prick, and jab, and stab to your heart's content, and you need not treat your friends and enemies alike. But until you *do* get there—well, you really won't matter, one way or the other. Your friendship will be prized scarcely more than your enmity will be deplored."

"But," objected Marjorie. "I never heard of dividing people into lots, unless—" a sudden thought occurred to her "—unless you mean that all the nice people are inside and the other kind are not. Is that it?"

"Indubitably," laughed Azalea. "And you must affirm your belief that this is so, on each and every occasion."

"I don't know what you mean."

"Why, you must find all the people within the circle charming and brilliant and desirable, and all those outside commonplace and dull, and not worth while. You must like the former and despise the latter. Oh, it's quite simple, really!"

Marjorie smiled the smile she reserved for her husband's excursions in wit. She thought, of course, that Azalea was joking.

"Now, there's sometimes a little difficulty in classifying people who teeter on the edge," she poised a nib on the golden circle to illustrate her point. "A little push one way or the other will decide which way they will go, and until they get pushed, I admit they are something of a problem. However, we'll begin with the certainties, and then I'll borrow a list from Lady Denby, so as to be sure not to overlook anybody ... The Ministers' wives—Mrs. Blaine, Mrs. Carewe, Mrs. Haldane, Mrs. Carmichael, Lady Denby ..."

Azalea wrote rapidly for a few moments, carefully spelling the French names as she recalled them.

"Then the wife of the Black Rod: she goes everywhere—"

"And I like her," interrupted Marjorie. "She's not a bit stiff, is she?"

Azalea laughed and shook her head. Marjorie's dread of women who were "stiff" and men who were "sarcastic", amused her.

Between consultations with Lady Denby, the Parliamentary Guide and the Telephone Book, the invitations were issued, and Azalea sat back, sighing after her labours.

"Now you will have paid off all your tea obligations," she said, "but you really must keep a list. Separate ones for luncheons, dinners and suppers. Probably, a dinner will be the next thing."

"And who must I ask for dinner, when I give one?" enquired Marjorie, ignoring in her distress the rules of grammar.

"Why, the people who have had you, of course! Not luncheon people, not tea people, mind!" Azalea was quite stern. "But the people who have had you for *dinner*! It will be simple until you have been entertained frequently, and then you will have to sort out members of different sets."

"I don't like it," said Raymond Dilling's wife. "I don't want to entertain that way. I tell you, it's deceitful!"

"Entertaining," said Azalea, with a suspicion of hardness in her voice, "is an admirable illustration of the 'eye for an eye' transaction mentioned in Holy Writ. Only, in the Capital, an astute woman schemes to obtain two eyes for one optic, and a whole set, upper and lower, for the molar she has sacrificed. When she accomplishes this, my dear, then she has achieved real social success. Bismillah!"

CHAPTER 9.

Several circumstances combined to make possible the large and representative crowd that attended Mrs. Raymond Dilling's first big crush. The day was fine, the season was only beginning so that there were few counter-attractions, and the Parliamentary set, who were hearing with increasing frequency of the fervid young prophet of the prairies, went out of curiosity to see, as Mrs. Lorimer tactfully put it, "*What* he had married."

Dilling had already made a strong impression—partly favourable, and partly the reverse. But it was definite in either case.

Lastly, the Hollingsworth house, into which the Dillings had moved, was a landmark which still bequeathed a flavour of by-gone grandeur to its successive tenants, although no member of the illustrious family had lived beneath its roof for close upon half a century. But no matter who lived there, it was a mansion into which one could pass with dignity and a certain satisfaction, secure in the knowledge that even should it be converted into a boarding-house, there would remain the manifest though indefinable air that differentiates the messuages of patricians from the tenements of the proletariat.

That the Hollingsworths' should be transformed into anything so needful as a private hostelry, however, was almost inconceivable, for Ottawa's last concern was her housing problem.

Accommodation was so scarce at the seat of Government that many Members began to fear, after a discouraging search, that they would have to stand. Over-furnished rooms, and under-furnished houses were offered at opulent rentals, but of comfortable pensions, there were none. There are but two or three to-day. What solution has been reached, may be attributed to the number of picturesque old residences that have been remodelled and split into half a dozen inconvenient mouse-traps.

Inside, the Hollingsworths' was a riot of fantastic ugliness. A gaunt reception hall engulfed the visitor and cast him, from beneath a series of grilled oak arches, into a sombre drawing room. One end was bounded by folding doors that resisted all efforts at movement, and beyond, there yawned a portentous bay window that invited invasion by the house next door and reduced the cubic contents of the dining-room. Strange abutments, niches that looked as though they had been designed for cupboards and abandoned before completion, appeared in unsuspected places. Angles were everywhere. The ceilings were lumpy, like the frosting of a birthday cake, and there wasn't a gracious line to be seen.

Marjorie's hangings, chosen with the idea of giving a cheerful touch, looked somewhat as a collar of baby ribbon might have looked upon the neck of an elephant. Her Brussels rugs were suggestive of a postage stamp on a very large envelope, while the Mission furniture and mahogany What-not, added to the general air of discord. With several violent examples of the lithographers' skill on the walls, there was completed a terrorising picture that might aptly have been labelled "The Carnage of Art".

Marjorie stood in front of the cherry-wood fireplace and tried not to be nervous, but she couldn't forget that immense issues depended upon the success of this tea—Raymond's entire future, perhaps! It was a thought that almost petrified her.

Pamela de Latour was one of the first guests to arrive. She was early because she was assisting, and she was assisting because Lady Denby had made the matter a personal favour to herself. It was customary, in Ottawa, for unmarried ladies to "assist" in the dining-room, no matter what their age, while matrons, either old or young, officiated at the tea table. It therefore frequently developed that youthful matrons—brides, indeed—were comfortably seated behind the tea-urn, or that they cut interminable ices, while spinsters thrice their age, percolated kittenishly among the guests on high-heeled slippers, deprived by man's short-sightedness, of the rest which their years were craving.

Miss Lily Tyrrell, aristocrat by inclination and democrat by necessity—a charming woman whose family had been both wealthy and conspicuous in an older generation—also assisted, as did the wholesome Misses McDermott. These latter were so much in demand that their "assistance" had become almost a profession, as had tea-pouring for Mrs. Chalmers, wife of the Black Rod, and presiding at meetings for Mrs. B. E. Tillson.

"I'm so pleased to see you," said Marjorie to Miss de Latour, a little too precipitously, and spoiling the effect of Hawkin's announcement.

Hawkins "announced" at every function of any importance, and infallibly employed the precise nuance of impressiveness with which to garnish each name.

"Miss de Latour," he called, and in a tone which plainly said, "Here's Somebody!"

"Missus 'Anover," he droned, a moment later, looking over that lady's shoulder, and taking a deep breath before booming,

"*Lydy Denby!*"

That was his way.

"It was so good of you to come," Marjorie continued. "I didn't know but that you would have forgotten me."

"Not at all," murmured Miss de Latour, gazing with a sort of outraged intensity about the room. "Had you a pleasant summer?"

"Oh, wonderful, perfectly wonderful! It was so good to get home and feel . . ."

"Missus Moss," observed Hawkins, listlessly.

"Pleased to meet you," said Marjorie, nervously cordial. (She recalled later, with considerable puzzlement, that most of her guests said briefly, "How d'y do?" If they reciprocated her friendly sentiments, they displayed admirable restraint in suppressing the fact.) "Isn't it a lovely day?"

"Glorious," agreed Mrs. Moss, estimating Miss de Latour's dress at an even hundred. "I suppose you're glad to be back in Ottawa? Those little prairie towns must be so dull!"

Before Marjorie could spring to the defence of Pinto Plains, Mrs. Hotchkiss was announced. The smile with which she was prepared to meet her guest changed to a look of surprise. The rather plain little person advancing towards her was not the dashing Mrs. Hotchkiss she so greatly admired.

"You were expecting my namesake, I see," laughed the newcomer, easily. "Yes, there are two of us—no relation. She's the good-looking Mrs. Hotchkiss. I'm the other one!"

"Pleased to meet you," said Marjorie, magenta-colour with embarrassment. "Have you had—I mean, won't you have your tea?"

"Mrs. Plantagenet Promyss," blared Hawkins, as though impatient to get Mrs. Hotchkiss out of the way.

A small, untidy woman plunged into the room.

"How d'y do?" she said, not only to Marjorie, but all who were within hearing distance. "I hope I'm not too late for a nice hot cup of tea! There's nothing so depressing to me as a third lukewarm steeping . . . and that's what a good many sessional hostesses give one, my dear!" Then catching sight of Mrs. Long, "I've just come from a meeting of the Little Learning League, where Lady Elton read a perfectly delightful paper called 'Good Buys in Old By-town'. You know, she's so clever at bargaining and that sort of thing . . . eh? The Little Learning League, my dear Mrs. Dilling, is the only organization of its kind in the Capital. It concentrates once a fortnight, the essence—absolutely the essence—of feminine culture and intelligence.

Mrs. Lauderdale Terrace is our president. You probably haven't met her . . . yet," she added, kindly.

As a rule, Mrs. Promyss found the literary afternoons very wearisome. She possessed a pretty gift for modelling in soap, and was eager to instruct her fellow-members in the use of this charming and ductile medium. So skillful was she that her copy of the famous Rogers' group, "You Dirty Boy" was once mistaken for the original. Indeed, she was so intrigued by its artistic quality, that she was disposed to argue that soap should be used for no other purpose, whatsoever!

Lady Elton's personal title, however, combined with the smart caption of her paper, had quite enchanted the sculptor, and she was in high good humour. "You must come to see me in my studio," she called, as one of the Misses McDermott led her away to the dining-room and a hot cup of tea.

Marjorie smiled and shook hands until faces, like great expressionless balloons, wavered in the air. She lost all power to distinguish what was being said to her, and had no idea what she replied. Now and again phrases tumbled against her ear out of the general uproar but they seemed to have very little sense.

". . . very proud of his children," shouted a richly-dressed person on her right.

". . . me, too," came from a group on her left, "only we fry ours in butter."

From the direction of her leatherette divan drifted a remarkable statement—". . . and she learned to swim . . ." "with a floating kidney . . ." ". . . and came ashore at Quebec in a Mandarin's coat!"

Mechanically, she took the tea Azalea brought her, and approached a group of Cabinet ladies.

"Appalling," one of them was saying. "Like something in a nightmare!"

"Do you think she'll ever learn?" murmured another. "He's really clever."

They turned suddenly.

"We were just admiring your house," exclaimed Mrs. Carewe. "This room . . ."

"Oh, I'm so glad you like it!" Marjorie's voice trembled with happiness. "I feel very small in such grandeur, but we're not using the top floor at all, and that helps a little. It was fortunate that our furniture was dark, wasn't it?

I used to think there was nothing more gorgeous than a gold drawing-room suite, but even if I could have it, it wouldn't do at all in here, would it?"

"Positively not!" agreed the ladies, heartily.

At the other end of the room, a group of Ottawa's youthful Smart Set sought to extract a modicum of enjoyment from what they termed a dee-dee party.

"They're getting damnder and duller," sighed one.

"I thought nothing could beat Lady Denby's, but this has it skinned to a finish!"

"Can't any one think of a funny stunt?" asked another. "I'm so bored, I could lie down on the floor and sing hymns."

"Do it," dared Mona Carmichael, obviously the leader of the group. "Go on, Zoe . . . I'll bet my new pink knickers, you haven't the nerve!"

"Nerve's my middle name," declared Zoe, with a toss of her head. "But the trouble with me is Mother. She's prowling about somewhere in the festal chamber, and she never appreciates my originality."

"Let's eat," suggested Elsa Carmichael, the Minister's second daughter. "That always fills up time."

"My time's stuffed full," observed Mona. "Had an awfully late lunch."

Their shrieks of laughter sounded above the din.

"Sh—sh—sh—!" warned Zoe. "Little Nell from Pinto Plains is looking at us."

"Well, let's do *something*," insisted the first speaker. "Couldn't we go upstairs and hide things?"

Mona objected that this form of recreation was stale.

"We might smear their tooth brushes with cold cream," suggested Elsa.

"Perhaps they don't use them," Zoe returned.

"I say," cried Mona, suddenly alive to a new thought, "how many olives can you hold in your mouth at once?"

Nobody had ever tried.

"Let's do it now," they agreed with one accord.

"Me first," said Mona. "It was my idea."

They seized a plate from the table, surrounded the experimentator, and watched half a dozen large, green olives disappear.

"My word," breathed Elsa, "she's swallowing them whole!"

"Eight," counted Dolly Wentworth, her cousin. "Nine, ten—my Sunday hat, doesn't she look like a chipmunk?"

This was too much for Mona. She gulped, grabbed the plate now almost empty, and shot explosively, ten whole olives into it.

Screams of delight rewarded her.

"Look," panted Zoe, "she hasn't even bitten them!"

"You beast," said Elsa, "now we can't tell t'other from which."

"Sorry," replied her sister, "but you know I can't eat them. They make me disgustingly sick."

"You've got to eat them," cried Dolly. "If you don't, they'll be served up at the next party."

The thought threw them into agonising spasms of mirth. Oh, this was wonderful ... priceless ... *mervellus* ... the very best ever! They really expected to expire ...

"Slip them back on the table," commanded Mona, as she saw Marjorie approaching.

"Not a minute too soon," whispered Dolly. "Now then, girls, your best Augusta Evans smile ..."

"Have you had tea?" asked Marjorie, finding something about their hilarity that was as incomprehensible as the sombreness of the other groups who appeared to be too bored for words. She had little time for reflection, but there flashed through her mind a comparison between this and a tea in Pinto Plains, where a friendly atmosphere was inter-penetrating and a hostess wasn't ignored by her guests.

They turned to her with the insolence of people who felt they had graced her home by their presence. Mona Carmichael answering for her friends, replied, "Quarts ... thanks."

As that seemed to be productive of no further conversation, Marjorie moved away, suddenly conscious that there was a slight commotion at the door. A late guest was arriving. To her amazement, she recognised Mrs. Augustus Pratt, coarctated in a sapphire velvet, whose fashionable slit skirt revealed a length of limb that fascinated, while it unutterably shocked her.

"Mrs. Pratt," confided the lady to Hawkins.

"Parding?"

"Mrs. Pratt," she repeated, bending a shade nearer.

"Missus Spratt!" he relayed, resentfully.

Hawkins knew Mrs. Pratt. He knew that she was marching round the golden circle seeking a weak spot through which she might force an entrance, and he felt it an insult to his position that he should have to deal with any one outside the charmed enclosure. He hated Mrs. Pratt.

Mrs. Pratt bore down upon Marjorie, and in her wake followed a girl who was obviously a relative.

"I came because I knew you must be expecting me. I said to Mod '... something has happened to that invitation, and your father would never forgive me if I didn't make a particular effort to get down to Mrs. Dilling's this afternoon'. This is Mod, Mrs. Dilling. I suppose she's a little older than your children?"

Marjorie was unequal to the occasion. She was surprised that Azalea had asked Mrs. Pratt. Azalea was surprised, herself, although she took in the situation at a glance, knowing that it was not unusual for persons of Mrs. Pratt's calibre to attend functions at Government House—and elsewhere—with a sublime disregard for the necessity of an invitation.

Maude was impaled upon the group of smart young ladies who stared disapprovingly at her, while her mother wandered about for half an hour with the intention of having everyone in the room know that she was there. Later, that night, she took the precaution to telephone Miss Ludlow, society reporter of THE DIAL, and, with cunning innocence, offered the item about Mrs. Dilling's tea as a means of helping the girl to fill up her column—or colyum, in Mrs. Pratt's phraseology. She believed in helping women, and she realised how difficult a task confronted the reporters. At any time, she would always be willing to confide information, and advised Miss Ludlow (who listened with her tongue in her cheek) not to hesitate to call upon her.

As the crowd thinned, a chic little motor drove up to the Dilling's door, and, after a tired glance in the direction of the bright chintz curtains, the driver settled back to await the pleasure of his lady.

He was discovered almost immediately by the group standing in the dining-room.

"What slavery," murmured Mrs. Long. "I wonder if it's worth it."

"Perhaps he doesn't mind," suggested Mrs. Blaine.

"Oh, I should say it's part of the day's routine," said Miss de Latour. "He calls somewhere for her every afternoon. One can grow accustomed to anything."

"They say she's writing a novel," confided Mrs. Long, "an acrimonious tale about all of us in the Capital."

"How delicious," cried Miss de Latour. "Dante will be jealous, I fear!"

"But it isn't a novel," Mrs. Blaine informed the group. "At least, that's not what she calls it."

"What is it, then?"

"Well," said Mrs. Blaine, "I've never seen it—nor any of the other literary productions of which she is guilty, but she told me that it was a sort of allegory, a child's story, called "The Fable of the Fairy Ferry-boat" ... and she's having it multigraphed for free distribution among the children of the English peerage."

"Be careful," cautioned Pamela de Latour, "here she is!"

Mrs. Hudson fluttered to the window in response to the summons of Azalea Deane. She waved a sprightly hand in the direction of the waiting car, and mouthed,

"Coming, directly, darling!" as though speaking to a young and inexperienced lip-reader.

"Isn't it absurd?" she cooed coquettishly to the others. "But he *will* come! One would think we were bride and groom," and she made an ineffectual effort to blush.

"Some men are lovers always," sighed Mrs. Blaine.

"That's Bob to the life," cried Mrs. Hudson. "No wonder I'm so spoiled."

"You certainly look exceptionally well," remarked Mrs. Long. "Such a becoming hat ..." the fibs trickled fluently from her lips "... such an artistic blending of gay colours ... I like bright colours on any one who can wear them. And your hair has grown so beautifully white ... not a dark strand to be seen anywhere ..." Her eyes wandered to the patient car "... And Mr. Hudson looks like a perfect boy ..."

CHAPTER 10.

Mrs. Pratt was racked by indecision. She was faced by a stupendous problem. She could not determine whether to invite the young girls who had so frankly snubbed "Mod" to drive home in her limousine, or whether to honour herself by cringing before a group of elderly notables. She had not possessed a motor long enough to understand that people to whom driving would be a boon, do not expect to be invited, and that only those who own cars, themselves, or are perfectly able to hire taxis, should be asked to enjoy the convenience of a motor.

So she made the mistake of offering to drop Miss Lily Tyrrell at her remote apartment, and prodded Maude into urging the Carmichael sisters to be driven home.

"We could easily take a couple more," she announced from the doorway, rather as a barker tries to fill up his sight-seeing car. "No trouble at all!" But as couples were slow in stepping forward, she strode off with the persons already captured.

There was silence for a space after Mrs. Pratt had telephoned directions to her chauffeur. A sensitive stranger would have suspected that each member of the party was waiting for the other to throw the first stone. But such was not precisely the case. The unpleasant *timbre* in the atmosphere was due to the fact that between each individual there existed a definite sense of animosity which was clothed with the filmiest cloak. Each seemed to be waiting an opportunity to step into the open and club the others into sensibility of her own importance.

Mrs. Pratt looked at the ears of her chauffeur. Miss Tyrrell turned her head towards the window and thanked Heaven she would soon be able to take off her shoes. The Carmichaels maintained a series of signals by kicking one another beneath the lap robes, and Maude stared into her folded hands, wondering vaguely why people were born at all. Chickens and dogs and cats seemed so much more worth while.

"Where do *you* live?" asked Miss Tyrrell, with just the proper shade of patronage. She wished to make very clear to the Carmichael sisters that there existed no intimacy between Mrs. Pratt and herself.

The former plunged into a minute description of the improvements she had effected in the Tillington place, and warned Miss Tyrrell that she would scarcely recognise it, now.

"I suppose in its day, it was considered all right," she said, "but it was quite impossible when I took it over. You must see it . . . Of course, you *will*! With a husband in Parliament, I shall have to do a lot of entertaining. Do you like to dance?" she asked Mona, suddenly.

"I adore it," returned the girl, with elaborate indifference. "You don't, do you?" she demanded of Maude.

"Oh, yes, I love dancing."

"Really? I never see you, anywhere."

"Mod is just home from school," said Mrs. Pratt. "I don't believe in a girl carrying all her brains in her feet. She went out rather more than was good for her in Montreal . . . not being vurry strong. That's why I can't let her go to the University, as she wants."

"What a pity," murmured the sisters, in a tone that made Miss Tyrrell bite her lips to keep from laughing.

The moment they were alone, Mrs. Pratt wheeled upon her daughter. "Whatever will I do with you, Mod?" she scolded. "Aren't you ever going to learn to say anything for yourself?"

"I don't like those girls," muttered Mod.

"I should hope not! But is that any reason why you shouldn't make friends with them?"

"I don't want to have friends that I don't like."

Mrs. Pratt was struck speechless by such philosophy. It had never occurred to her that anyone could hold views at variance with her own, least of all, her daughter. She found herself at a loss for an argument, a retort, indeed. The girl might just as well have said she didn't like having two hands.

"But everybody has!" exclaimed Mrs. Pratt. "There's no getting around it! Look at your father . . . look at me!"

Maude looked.

"You don't suppose I went to that Dilling imbecile's tea because I *liked* her—or any of the people there, for the matter of that—do you?"

"Then why did you go?" asked Maude, sullenly.

"Why—why—how absurd you are! I went, and you will have to go because other people do—because it's the way of Society, because, whether you like it or not, it's THE THING!"

They found Mr. Rufus Sullivan enjoying the fruits of the cellar when they reached home.

"Blame Gus, not me!" he cried. "Heaven knows I've tried to take myself off half a dozen times. Is this your girl?"

"Yep," answered Pratt, his harsh voice softening. "This is our baby."

"Too big for me to kiss, I suppose," said Sullivan, secretly congratulating himself that this was so. Maude bore a striking resemblance to her mother.

Mrs. Pratt acknowledged this witticism with a dry cackle, and invited the Hon. Member to stay and take *pot-pourri* with them. She slurred over the words cautiously, never quite certain as to the correct application of the phrase. Some people, she knew, said pot luck, but this had, to her way of thinking, a vulgar sound.

"That's the stuff," cried Gus. "We can go back to the House together after a bite of supper."

"Dinner," corrected his wife, coldly. "You're quite all right as you are, Mr. Sullivan. None of us will dress."

"I should hope not," breathed the irrepressible Pratt, and drained his glass with a smack. "Sullivan's no party."

As it had been this gentleman's intention to stay and talk with Mrs. Pratt, he demurred politely, calling himself an inconsiderate nuisance and other equally applicable terms. But in the end he allowed himself to be persuaded, and settled down to accomplish the object of his coming.

"It's a great pleasure to meet a woman with so keen a sense for politics," he remarked, speaking to Pratt but indicating his wife. Mr. Sullivan was one of the few men who could eat and talk at the same time, without seeming to give undue preference to either operation. "Our Canadian women take shockingly little interest in the life of the country."

"Don't blame 'em," mumbled Pratt, struggling with a very hot potato.

"Augustus!" Between telegraphing reproach to her husband, and directing the maid in what she conceived to be the correct serving of a meal, Mrs. Pratt's heavy eyebrows attained a bewildering flexibility. "He pretends not to take his position seriously, but leave him to me, Mr. Sullivan, leave him to me!"

"With confidence, Madam," returned the Hon. Member, gallantly. "Would that I had half so much in the other women of the Party. Is it not curious," he went on, "that a politician's wife rarely appreciates the extent of her influence in shaping her husband's career? The parson's lady identifies herself with his interests; the doctor's wife realises that she can attract or repel patients; and only the other day, the wife of a small-town banker confided to me that she never misses an opportunity for doing a stroke of business on her husband's behalf. As a matter of fact, I understand that she was largely responsible for the rival institution closing its doors, and leaving the field. Yet, a politician's wife as a rule, seems to take pride in holding herself aloof from politics."

"Dirty business for a woman," commented Pratt, stroking Maude's hand underneath the table.

"Not a whit dirtier than Society, my dear fellow, and there she likes to wallow. Am I not right, Mrs. Pratt? As a woman of the world, I feel sure you will agree with me."

Mrs. Pratt, who desired above all else to be a woman of the world, agreed with him, darkly. In this coalition, they seemed to form a vague but tacit compact from which the recently-elected Member for Ottawa was excluded.

"What, in your opinion, is the vurry best way for a woman to help her husband, politically?" she enquired, as they rose from the table.

Sullivan managed to assume an arch expression as he pressed her arm, and answered,

"How can you ask such a question of a mere man?"

"I can ask anything of anybody when there's something I want to find out," was the blunt retort. "Gus—Augustus—has *got* to make good."

"He will! We have the utmost faith in him . . . and may I add, in you. You'll be a tower of strength to Gus, Mrs. Pratt, with your keen sense for politics. Only the other evening, I was making this statement to my little friend, Mrs. Dilling."

"Mrs. Dilling?"

"Yes. Wife of the Member for Pinto Plains. You should know her, Mrs. Pratt. A creature of rare beauty and charm."

Mrs. Pratt confessed to a slight acquaintance in a tone calculated to chill her guest's enthusiasm. "She gave a big tea, this afternoon. Mod and I were there."

"Really? I am glad to hear it. You two ought to be great friends—with interests that are so nearly identical." As Mrs. Pratt said nothing, the Hon. Member continued—somewhat more easily, noting that his host and

Maude had left the room—"I'm so fond of her . . . almost *too* fond, I'm afraid! She's a wonderful little woman, Mrs. Pratt—and I've known a good many in my day. Do you realise that Marjorie could simply *make* her husband, if she had a tithe of your political sense . . . if she only knew how!"

"You surprise me," said Mrs. Pratt, and in her tone the Hon. Member was gratified to detect the ring of truth.

"Well, it's a fact. Dilling's a marvel, my dear lady. Even the Opposition concede him the respect due a powerful antagonist."

"He's not a bad speaker," admitted Mrs. Pratt.

"There isn't a man in the House who can touch him! Now, is there?"

Mrs. Pratt hedged by suggesting that the country looked for something more than forensic eloquence.

"A profound remark!" Mr. Sullivan could not restrain his admiration. He beamed and stroked his knees, deriving from the performance, apparently, much satisfaction. "Trust you to dig right down to the root of the matter! Not that he hasn't principles, dear lady, and also the courage necessary to express them. We mustn't overlook that. Moreover, it's almost impossible to defeat him in argument . . . Such disconcerting agility of mind, you know. He lets the other fellow expend himself in an offensive, and then, without apparent effort, stabs and thrusts until his opponents fall in regular—er—regular—"

"Windrows," suggested Mrs. Pratt, whose unacknowledged relatives were honest farming people.

"Windrows, a capital comparison! They fall in regular windrows before him. Why, he can prove that black is white any day in the week."

"Men are fools!" was the lady's oracular remark.

"Unfortunately for them . . . us, I really ought to say. I, myself, have felt the force of that young man's power, and I've been absolutely putty in his hands."

Mrs. Pratt drew her lips into a thin, straight line, and forbore to comment on this weakness.

"The trouble is—as, of course, you are aware—he has been trained in a bad school, and it may take some time to undo the effect of early education. Then, naturally, he's only human and the wine of success is a heady beverage. He's somewhat determined—"

"Mule-ish," amended Mrs. Pratt.

"No, no, I protest," cried the Hon. Member, playfully. "You must not be too hard on the fellow. All he needs is a little guidance—perhaps even a shade more definite opposition. For example, this elevator and freight idea of his . . ."

"G'aranteed to plunge the whole country into roon," interrupted Mrs. Pratt, whose investments were centred strictly to the East.

"I anticipated you would take the view of the better minds," returned Mr. Sullivan, perceiving that the time had come for him to discard the subtler implements of finesse, and employ the rough, but honest trowel. "But when all's said and done, it may be better to support a man with whose policies we are not in accord than to split into groups, and eventually be forced from our seats into the benches on the opposite side of the house."

Mrs. Pratt watched her guest with unmistakable bewilderment in her hard blue eyes.

"I see that you agree with me," he went on, "and you are probably wondering, just as I am, how soon the need will come for us to prove our Party loyalty. It can't be far away, dear lady. I have ten dollars in my pocket that says there'll be a Cabinet vacancy before the spring."

"And Dilling will get the portfolio!" barked Mrs. Pratt, thrown completely off her guard.

"What a head you have!" cried Sullivan. "I'll wager there aren't a dozen men who have suspected it! But he needs support . . . he must have it. We must stand solidly behind him, for no matter how divergent may be our views upon this question of western freight, we've got to train up a man—a good strong fellow—who will sweep the country and be able to step into the shoes of the Prime Minister, some day!"

"Prime Minister!" gasped Mrs. Pratt, and fell to preening herself in order that she might hide the trembling of her hands.

She hated the Dillings—Raymond for his reputed genius, the clear, cold brilliance that would not be eclipsed, and Marjorie for her childish friendliness and ingratiating ways. The meek might inherit the Kingdom of Heaven without provoking her envy, but that they should also inherit the earth was a contingency that aroused her cold fury.

She saw them sought after, deferred to, taking precedence over everyone save the representative of the King! Her thoughts fell into narrower channels and she pictured Marjorie opening bazaars, lending her patronage to this or that gathering of Society's choicest blossoms, arriving at the state where she would be unstirred by invitations to Government House!

Under the turquoise velvet, her bosom rose and fell, heavily. At the moment she hated her husband no less fiercely than she hated the man whom she chose to consider his rival. What could Augustus carve in the way of a career? How could he ever hope to triumph over this aggressive man from the West? Where would she be when Marjorie Dilling had become the wife of Canada's young Prime Minister?

The suave voice of Rufus Sullivan fashioned itself into words. The first ones she failed to catch, but the last pierced her like the point of a white-hot rapier.

". . . and then, naturally, a title. And how graciously she will wear it, eh?"

A title . . . Mrs. Pratt felt suffocated. A portfolio was bad enough; the Premiership was a possibility that she could not consider without a cataclysm of emotion, but a title . . . the pinnacle of human desire, the social and political apogee . . .

Sir Raymond and Lady Dilling . . . Lady Dilling . . .

She rose abruptly and strode to the door. Pratt avoided a collision with difficulty. He was just coming in.

"No more time for philandering," he cried, with vulgar geniality. "On to Pretoria! Nelson expects every man to do his duty!"

Mrs. Pratt watched their departure with contradictory sensations. The Hon. Member for Morroway was not the man to spoil a good impression by an inartistic exit. He made a graceful adieu, managing to convey the idea that, although now and again he might be the bearer of news that was disturbing, on the whole he was a man who could be mulct by a woman of astuteness, of the most intimate and useful information.

Augustus Pratt, M.P., arrived home on the stroke of midnight to find his wife and daughter in the midst of a litter of stationery, calling lists, telephone and Blue Books.

"What's up now?" he demanded, picking his way across the floor as one hops over a brook by means of stepping stones.

"Look at that," cried his wife, and pointed to the evening paper.

Pratt gave his attention to the item indicated. It headed the Personal column, and read,

"The following ladies and gentlemen had the honour of dining at Government House last evening . . . and Mr. and Mrs. Raymond Dilling."

"Well," he yawned, "there's nothing very startling about that! I don't see the answer."

"No! Naturally you wouldn't!" Mrs. Pratt pounded a stamp on an envelope.

The M.P. turned to his daughter. "Tell her old dad what it means, little Maudie."

"Mother's giving a big dinner party, on the seventeenth."

"Oh, my God!" sighed Augustus. Then, "I've got to go to Montreal on that date, Minnie—honest, I have!"

"You dare! And listen, Gus, while I think of it; if I ever hear that you've given one atom of support to that Dilling, I'll have my trunks packed and the house closed, before you can get home! Now, don't forget!"

"Dear, dear!" Pratt assumed an air of panic. "What's the poor beggar been up to now?"

"He's up to getting himself into the Cabinet, if men like you don't want the job, yourselves—that's what he's up to. And once in the Cabinet, you know where he'll land next."

"Where?"

"In the Prime Minister's seat," returned Mrs. Pratt, sourly.

"In the Senate, you mean," laughed Augustus, and pinched Maude's ear.

"Your idea of jokes is sickening," Mrs. Pratt declared. "Sometimes I wonder why I bother with you. Now, Mod, read out the names on those envelopes down there!"

Dutifully, Maude complied . . . "Mr. and Mrs. Chesley . . ."

"Like enough they won't come," interrupted her mother. "We've never called."

". . . Mr. and Mrs. Long! Mr. and Mrs. Robert Hudson . . ."

"There's another hateful snob. This afternoon I could have strangled her!"

"Mr. and Mrs. Herbert Truman . . ."

"They say she only goes to Government House," mused Mrs. Pratt. "However, I took a chance. It only cost two cents—and you never know."

"You bet you'll never know," said the Member. "Minnie, you're plain crazy asking all these swells that you don't even know when you see 'em! Why don't we have any *real* friends, nowadays?"

Mrs. Pratt answered with a baleful glance that was more eloquent than words. Then, assured that there would be no further interference from her husband, directed Maude to finish her work.

". . . Sir Eric and Lady Denby . . ."

"They ought to come, anyhow," she groaned, hopefully, "seeing it's the Party. The Fanshawes, the Howarths, Sullivan and Azalea Deane . . . she's sure to come . . . that makes twenty-nine. There's one more envelope, Mod!"

"Mr. and Mrs. Raymond Dilling," read the girl.

"Dilling?" echoed her father.

"Of course, Augustus. Don't gape at me in that way!"

"But you just told me—I thought you had your knife into the Dillings."

"So I have, you fool!"

"Then why the hell do you ask them to your party?"

Mrs. Pratt so forgot herself as to stamp her foot. "Can't you see," she cried, "that they're getting on?"

CHAPTER 11.

*F*or a time, Dilling was entertained by the visits he received from ladies of varying ages and mixed intentions. He found their vapoury subterfuges or engaging candour equally amusing. But presently, this type of diversion, so eagerly welcomed by many of his confrères, began to pall, and he developed amazing ingenuity in the avoidance of such callers.

He had grown suspicious of "deserving cases," and "ancient grievances"; he found himself totally unsympathetic towards the erection of monuments commemorating the questionable valour of somebody's obscure progenitors; he could sit absolutely unmoved and listen to schemes which were being projected "at considerable personal inconvenience," in order that he might attain immortality. The measures he was asked to father in the House ranged from the segregation of the feeble-minded to prohibition of philandering.

"He's a cold fish," complained more than one lady, after failing to elicit the smallest response, either to her project or her personal charms.

It was true that Dilling's emotional reactions were slight, but it was equally true that had they been vehement, he would have forced himself to a course of conduct commensurate with what he conceived to be the demands of national welfare. He never could accept the idea that the Government Service was an institution in which hundreds of persons—like Mr. Deane—might find a comfortable escape from the storm and stress of a fruitful life, and render in return but a tithe of the work that even their small abilities could fairly perform. He never could sympathise with the attitude of those who looked upon the public funds as private means, and he opposed, in so far as he was able, every effort to tap the Dominion Treasury for individual gain.

There were times when he thought with discouragement about these things; times when he was oppressed with the basic insincerity of public life. It was so vastly different from what he had imagined! He felt himself eternally struggling against the malefic urge of partisanship—and partisanship was not always, he found, an expression of high principle.

And he saw also that, as his success gathered head, petty jealousies—and great—sprang up on every hand. The very persons who assisted in his rise would be the first, he knew, to herald his downfall. He used to think that because a man was prominent, he possessed universal good-will, but now he knew that the exact reverse obtains.

"I am the most unpopular man in the House," he said to Azalea, one evening. "On the floor, they cheer and applaud me, but in private or social life, I am shunned."

Another woman would have contradicted him. Such a course did not occur to Azalea.

"Do you mind?" she asked.

He considered a moment.

"I'm not sure. It seems to me that the popular Members don't *do* anything. They're too busy being popular . . . too busy being agreeable to a herd of tireless parasites."

"Which is quite out of your line, is it not?"

"Well, why *should* I snivel and crawl?" he defended. "One respects a man or one doesn't. Popularity is, after all, only an expression of mob psychology; as you know, it is unstable—having either the vaguest of excuses, or palpable insincerity behind it."

"You mean the insincerity of the person who is popular?"

"Of course! What man feels genuine friendliness towards enough people to make him 'popular'?"

Azalea shook her head in the characteristic way that implied her resentment against accepting the inevitable.

"But don't you feel that a certain amount of studied affability is—let us say—necessary to the attainment of success in public affairs?"

"No! I believe with Lincoln that the conduct of a statesman—and that is my high ambition, if it be God's will that I attain to it—should be moulded upon three principles; 'malice towards none, charity for all, firmness on the right'. These principles are not compatible with the flatteries and lightly-regarded mendacities of a popular idol. A statesman ought to be less of a man and more of an ethical inspiration. It's not an easy ideal to live up to," he concluded, "but at least it's a clean one, and I think the only one that history justifies."

"Yes," repeated Azalea, as though careful that her voice should not betray her true opinion, "it's a very clean one."

Recalling that conversation, Dilling found himself musing rather pleasantly about Azalea. What a curious little creature she was! What a stimulating companion! He could not, for the life of him, visualise her features, but he could bring to mind many an illuminating twist of her thoughts. Times without number, he realised, he had invoked her extraordinary intuitive powers and transmuted them in the crucible of his logic, into what Sullivan was pleased to designate as invincibility in debate.

"She's more than half responsible," he told himself. "I couldn't have achieved my present position by any process of reasoning alone."

He looked over his crowded desk with a sensation of helplessness. How could any man, single-handed, clear that accumulation away? He wondered if other Members allowed their business to get into such a distressing tangle, and if they had better luck than he when a stenographer came in for a few hours, to reduce the congestion?

"It's this eternal speech-making," he reflected. "That's what takes so much of my time. I wish . . ."

He left his chair and began to pace about the room, surrendering to an access of restlessness that was quite foreign to him. Azalea Deane . . . there was the solution! Why not? Why should she not come to him as a permanent assistant . . . a sort of private secretary?

"She could relieve me of a myriad minor duties," he thought. "Foreign press . . . correspondence . . . research work . . . She's amazingly accurate . . ." He smiled as he caught himself suppressing the familiar corollary, "for a woman!"

Yes, that was the solution! He would ask Azalea Deane to work with him. "We'll get on famously together," he thought. "She's so quick to catch the drift of my intention. She really understands me."

He sat down again, amused at the recollection of an original view expressed by Azalea in answer to Marjorie, who complained of Ottawa's persistent misunderstanding.

"There's no cause for distress in being misunderstood," she had said. "It's the opposite condition that we should dread! Imagine one's stupidity, covetousness and smallness of spirit being laid bare! Unthinkable, isn't it? You mustn't forget, my dear Marjorie, that being misunderstood works both ways, and through imperfect understanding we are frequently credited with motives and qualities that are quite as flattering as we could wish. Heaven forfend that I should ever be thoroughly understood!"

Dilling applauded her and reminded his wife that if men were compelled to write their thoughts and wear them as phylacteries on their foreheads, few, indeed, would carry themselves bravely in public.

"And why should they do that, dear?" Marjorie enquired, her pansy eyes clouded with perplexity.

"He is only trying to be clever," explained Azalea. "He is subtly suggesting that if the very best of us proclaimed our thoughts upon our foreheads, there would be jolly few who didn't pull their hats low above their brows."

Azalea did not wear her thoughts upon her forehead, Dilling reflected, and he smiled at his conceit in thinking that if she did, they would probably be written in a language that was difficult to read! It suddenly occurred to him that he knew very little of what was passing in Azalea's mind. His endeavour had been directed to an opposite course—assisting her to understand what was in his thoughts.

"She's a curious creature," he repeated, "a problem. But she has rare intelligence and imagination. I need her ... She is necessary for the advancement of my work. I can't concentrate in this hopeless muddle ..."

The idea excited him more than he realised. In planning a schedule for their day's routine, he did not recognise his keen desire for a closer intimacy with the girl's mind, the assurance of her esteem, the stimulus of knowing that she expected him to conquer unconquerable things. He began to wear down her arguments, to win her from possible disinclination. She must agree! She must come!

He pictured a scene with her tiresome old father, when he should ask not for her hand but for her brain. How insensately stubborn the old antiquarian would be! How damnably unreasonable!

He consulted his book of appointments ... not a minute Wednesday ... nor Thursday ... Ah! Mrs. Pratt's dinner party ... Good! He would ask her then ...

A thin smile touched his features as he said to himself,

"If I can move the Opposition in the House, surely I can override the objections of Grenville Deane!"

Mr. Deane would have swelled with pride had he known that his daughter was engaging the attention of more than one Parliamentary Member that day. In a room above that occupied by Raymond Dilling, the thoughts of three other gentlemen bent themselves fleetingly upon her.

"The fellow's not only clever," grumbled Turner, "but he's too damned careful. We'll have some trouble in pinning anything on him."

Sullivan sipped his whisky reflectively. "The trouble is that he never meets the right sort of people."

"God knows they go out enough," protested Howarth. "According to the Personals which I've read conscientiously for several weeks past, they go pretty much everywhere."

"Because he's become the vogue, in a manner of speaking," said Sullivan. "But that won't do us any good. It won't last long enough. Socially, they are failures and always will be ... Mark my words, the time will come when they will be asked only because their political position requires recognition, not for their personal charm. Church-workers and unambitious obscurities will be their particular friends ... her particular friends, perhaps I should say. He won't have any."

"Still, he'll meet some interesting women," objected Turner.

"I grant it, but not deliberately interesting," returned Sullivan, with a wink. "In other words, he won't stumble into a trap. He'll have to be led into it."

"Why won't he stumble?" Howarth asked. "Other men do."

"His temperament is a safeguard, for one thing. He is not sufficiently attracted by women to go exploring, and only those who wander into unfamiliar places get caught in traps."

Howarth remarked that his wife had reported a warm friendship between the Dillings and the Deane girl.

"Yes," said Sullivan, "I've been watching that. Mrs. D. tells me that he admires the girl intensely."

"Humph!" commented Turner.

"I've never met the lady," said Howarth, "but judging from her looks I should think that a man's intensity of feeling for her could not be much more than a mild passion of the imagination."

Sullivan laughed. "That's not bad for you, Billy. I'll go even further and opine that Dilling's intensity of feeling for anyone will be like the passion of a fried sole! However, the Deane girl won't do."

"What about de Latour's daughter?" suggested Howarth. "She looks clever, and might help, 'for the sake of the Party,' as our estimable Lady Denby says."

"Good God, Billy," groaned Sullivan. "We don't want anyone who *looks* clever! Don't you know me better than that?"

"Well, the sweet young thing should be easy to find," said Turner.

"No good, either. In the first place, it's hard to find one with any sense, and in the second, he gets that type as a daily diet."

"Those Carmichael girls seem to be consistent winners," suggested Turner, once more. "Some brains, and good looks . . ."

"Too young," said the old campaigner. "Undependable! Kids are apt to lose their heads and weaken, when it comes to using the scalping knife. First thing we know, they'd give the whole show away. No," he went on, reflectively, "what we want is a regular stunner, who'll stick right at the game until she has his scalp at her belt . . . a woman of the world, you know, chock full of horse sense and able to handle men with as little difficulty as an expert trainer handles cats."

There was a short silence.

"I can't think of anybody," Turner's tone was sodden with discouragement.

"Nor I," said Howarth. "Haven't you got anybody up your sleeve, Sullivan?"

The Hon. Member for Morroway modestly admitted that there was a lady of his acquaintance who combined all these alluring vices.

"Either of you ever heard of Mrs. Barrington?" he enquired.

Turner thumped his approval. Howarth took his satisfaction more cautiously.

"I've seen the dame. Kind of flashy, eh?"

"Tastes differ," replied his friend.

"Just moved here lately, hasn't she?"

Sullivan nodded.

"Hangs round the House a good deal, trying to put something over for her husband, I've heard."

"You're remarkably well informed, Billy," mocked the older man.

"Did you ever know her before?" asked the unabashed Howarth.

Sullivan confessed to a previous acquaintance. "Her mother's first husband was my sister's brother-in-law. So, you see, she's a sort of relation."

"Not too close to be interesting," observed Turner, who had his private opinion about Sullivan's relations. "Has she been sounded? Do you think she'll take on the job?"

The Member for Morroway was hopeful, "provided," he said, "she is not absorbed in any other emotional adventure. They are chronic."

"Is that the only provision?" Howarth wanted to know.

"Well—er—as you, yourself, remarked, she seems to be determined to get Barrington a nice, cushioned berth in which he will be well protected against the rigours of enervating toil. I understand that she fancies the Chairmanship of the Improvement Commission."

William Howarth, M.P., expressed relief, and the opinion that this was "pie".

"We'll just put little Augustus Pratt on the job," he said. "How soon could we see the lady?"

Sullivan didn't doubt that she was somewhere in the House at the moment.

"You trot along and find her, then," urged the other. "Bring her up here and let's hold a friendly little conference. The sooner we get her started on this escapade, the sooner our young friend will lose his head!"

CHAPTER 12.

A light but insistent tapping put an end to Dilling's reflections.

"Come in!" he called, impatiently, and turned towards the window as if intent upon the landscape.

There was a slight pause, and then, like a well-timed bit of stage business, a woman stood framed in the open door.

Dilling appreciated the dramatic note even while he resented it. On general principles he despised the theatrical.

"Oh, I *am* lucky!" cried his visitor, in a well-disciplined contralto. "I scarcely dared hope to find you alone. Every atom of courage I possessed oozed out of my finger-tips at the thought of interrupting a secret caucus, or some other of the dark conspiracies that are supposed to occupy our Members' time!"

She advanced and extended an ungloved hand. Dilling touched her fingers without speaking.

"My name is Hebe Barrington," she went on, "Mrs. Arthur, on my calling cards, you know . . . and I'm here on a desperately serious mission. Its success means everything to me, and you, yourself, Mr. Dilling, have buoyed me up with the hope that I shall not fail."

She shifted her position slightly, contriving to draw her skirt close about her long, slender limbs like a sheath.

But Dilling was not looking. He had taken a penknife from his pocket, and was giving First Aid to an untutored finger-nail.

"How shall I begin?" she went on, watching him from beneath her lashes. It was one of her prettiest gestures.

"Perhaps, if you made some notes and sent them to me—"

"Oh, please!" she protested. "That's heartless of you. And *do* sit down! I can't think while you wear that 'Time's up' expression. It drives every idea from my head. I tell you frankly, Mr. Dilling, I expected you would be much more kind."

She flung him a smile that had dazzled many another man. Dilling received it with indifference, in a wholly unprecedented manner. Mrs. Barrington found the experience somewhat disconcerting.

In his expression there was no appreciation of her loveliness. Neither was there the disapproval that betokens a recognition of it, or a sign of that wariness by which man betrays his knowledge of its danger. There was nothing.

In the abstract, Dilling saw men as trees, walking, but women he saw scarcely at all. Emotionally, he was vestigial. Artistically, he was numb. Beauty in any form registered only through his outward eye. He missed the inner vision that should have quickened his soul.

Mrs. Barrington was not an unfamiliar figure to him, although he had never been sufficiently interested to ask her name. Frequently, of late, he had seen her in the restaurant, or in the corridors, sometimes surrounded by a group of Parliamentary gallants, and sometimes in earnest tete-a-tete with just one man. If he thought of her at all, it was to conclude that like other women who haunt the House, she was engaged in the popular occupation known as lobbying, and he felt an instinctive opposition to whatever request she might be about to make.

On her part, Mrs. Barrington felt the disappointment of one who has been unexpectedly repulsed at the first line of attack, and sees the necessity for finer strategy. She laid aside the ineffectual weapon of physical charm, and took up the subtler blade of flattery.

"I have come to you," she said, "because you are not only essentially, but so patently, sincere. Not your speeches alone, but your whole manner, proclaim it. I suppose that is a good deal to say of a politician, is it not?"

"By no means!"

"There is little evidence to the contrary! Most of them rant about a loftier patriotism, service for the public weal that knows no respite and the realisation of a higher idealism for Twentieth Century Canada, but their actual performances are not marked with the large disinterestedness they profess. You are different. Perhaps you won't like my saying so, Mr. Dilling, but as you sit in the House, surrounded by your colleagues, yours is a noticeably solitary figure. I felt it the instant I saw you, and the impression has grown steadily stronger . . . with reason. You have brought a different element into politics, Mr. Dilling. Like Disraeli, you are on the side of the angels! You have brought what I call practical spirituality, a force that can and will defeat materialism, if—if—you do not get discouraged, and tired of struggling on, alone."

"Aren't you rather disheartening?"

The question was asked with such utter unconcern that Mrs. Barrington could not deceive herself into thinking she had made an impression. Had Dilling taken her seriously, or accorded her half the sincerity she professed to impute to him, he would have been unconscionably embarrassed. As matters stood, her words, like her beauty, failed to touch him. He heard them as he heard agreeable music, without annoyance, but without pleasure. It was said of him, that once, in Pinto Plains, when asked if he enjoyed piano playing he had answered, "Oh, I don't mind it!" and he could aptly have applied the same phrase to this woman's conversation.

He didn't mind it! He was listening without giving particular heed to what she said. He knew that she had come to ask a favour, and he was not sufficiently amenable to feminine wiles to lose sight of the methods of a shrewd campaigner.

"I may be disheartening," he heard her say, "but I am sincere. Would you have me pretend—tell you how popular you are, and how certain to become the idol of the people? Do you not remember that the Cæsars and Lincolns of history have been slandered and slain by their friends and compatriots, and can you hope to escape a similar fate at the hands of our people—even though despotism is not tempered with assassination here, as it was a hundred years ago in Russia?"

Dilling was conscious of a flicker of interest. It was curious, he reflected, that this woman should have come to him and given expression to the very thoughts that had been uppermost in his mind. He wondered whether she had been talking to Azalea.

"And what has all this to do with your mission?" he asked, closing his penknife with a snap.

"Everything!" she cried, vehemently. "Everything depends upon the honesty behind your protestations, upon the fact that you are not merely content to talk about idealism, but will work to see it blossom throughout the country. Moreover, I have counted on your vision, your ability to see the benefit of what, to others, may look like an impractical measure. Any other type of man would laugh at me," she added.

She stopped and waited for him to speak. But he made no comment.

He was not insensible to the cleverness with which she assembled her points. There was about her address a climacteric quality that compelled his admiration. But her speech fell flat because he failed to pick up his cues. The obvious retort that she must have anticipated, was never spoken; so each pause was pregnant with the suggestion of finality, of failure.

"I felt as though I were being driven, blindfold, along a crooked passage," she said, later, in describing the interview to Sullivan. "Each time

I turned a corner, some one rose and struck me in the face, so that I reeled and lost my bearings and had to wait a bit in order to recover myself and my sense of direction."

Dilling half suspected this. He did not, however, assume a difficult and disinterested manner, deliberately, nor did he act with conscious rudeness. He simply felt no curiosity in Mrs. Barrington nor in the object of her visit, and no obligation to pretend that he did.

"I have come to you," she said, again, "because you are the embodiment of all the qualities I have mentioned. Your sympathy, I take for granted, for the reason that the cause I plead is a spiritual cause, Mr. Dilling. I am asking for the development of a nation's soul."

"Oh!"

This response, though almost imperceptible, affected the woman as applause breaking suddenly over an unfriendly house, stimulates an actor to greater achievement. She left her chair and stood before him, a vision of aggressive beauty. She nearly lost herself in the part she was playing, and allowed impulse rather than design to dominate the moment.

"We admit that in the fierce struggle for existence, a young country must concern itself primarily with material problems, and that the song of the spirit is often stifled by the cry of hungry children. But has not the day arrived for us when our thought, and at least a small part of our resources, should be devoted to providing nourishment for the Canadian soul? I know that this sounds like the spell-binder's affluence of speech, but, believe me, Mr. Dilling, I have a practical proposition behind it."

"Well?" said Dilling, without enthusiasm.

She pointed to the Little Theatre movement, to various literary and dramatic organisations that have sprung up throughout the Dominion, as a proof that we are seeking a means of artistic expression, for spiritual development, that we are feeling a reaction from the wave of materialism which, in these times, holds the land in thrall. "In a word," she said, "we are looking for happiness, only just realising that we have striven without it all these years. We are not a happy nation, Mr. Dilling."

"Show me a more prosperous one," he cried.

"Ah! But there's our trouble. Prosperity and happiness may lie at opposite poles. The one is of the earth and its fulness, the other of the spirit, and in our pursuit of the former, we too frequently forget the needs of the latter. Happiness depends upon the emotions, Mr. Dilling, and Canadians have almost suffocated theirs."

Obviously, the spark of interest she had ignited had turned to ashes. He was silent, so she hurried on.

"We need Art—the medium through which spirituality flows into the life of man. We want to hear the symphonies of our composers, the songs of our poets, as well as the throb and thunder of motor factories and power plants. I would ask the Government to recognise the organisations that are endeavouring to promote artistic creation, and to give financial assistance to the conspicuously talented artists throughout the Dominion!"

"Hold on!" cried Dilling, stung into repelling this premeditated attack upon the National Treasury. "We maintain a big Gallery out at the Museum. We subsidise Art."

"Yes," she countered, quickly, "but not the artist. What you do only goes to swell the pay-roll of the Civil Service . . . You don't go far enough! Hasn't the Government helped to build up the industries of this country? Has it not pap-fed factories and commercial enterprises of various kinds? You know it has! If I should want a water-power for some silly little saw-mill, shall I not have it from my Province, for the asking? There's not a doubt of it! Yet, no one thinks of providing a greater power and one whereby this growing unrest can be composed. We are making a great point of conserving our natural resources, but who thinks of conserving our *spiritual* resources, Mr. Dilling? We need the one no less than the other. Men are reaching out towards Art!"

"Government is organised to legislate for peace and order in the community."

"Aristotle said that Government was organised to make people happy. I scarcely think we have made good along his principles, do you?"

"You can't legislate people into happiness."

"No! But you can provide the things that will create that state of mind. I should like to see a National Theatre, Mr. Dilling, in which the struggles and triumphs of Canada might be told by her own sons and daughters. Love of our common country can be fostered in no happier way. Let us have annual prizes for excelling talent in the Arts, and Science, and Literature!"

"Have we any poets worth recognising?" interrupted Dilling.

"Ah, I knew you would make that objection!" cried Hebe Barrington. "I knew that your thoughts would fly at once to Milton, and Keats, and Shelley . . . and the greatest of them all, Shakespeare. You immediately compare us with the immortals, and feel that we lose by the comparison. I don't profess to offer you a Homer or a Sappho. But there were lesser poets in Athens whom Pericles favoured at the expense of the people's purse. It's harder for poetry and the Arts to flourish to-day, than two thousand years ago—Oh, don't you see, *we* need a National Theatre?"

"It's an idea," conceded Dilling, with caution.

Hebe Barrington was clever. She did not press her slight advantage but prepared to beat a strategic retreat.

"I knew that you would see it," she cried. "How else can we make idealism real save by expressing it first through Art and then weaving it into our practical experiences? How else can we keep alive the traditions that have given us our Empire? How teach them to the young? I am full of schemes for working this thing out. May I come to see you again—or better still," she amended, watching him intently with her great, soft eyes, "will you come to me, say this day week?"

"If you like," he said, opening the door.

Presently, he opened the window, too. The room was close with a heavy, sweetish odour that offended him.

He looked down the river, past the Mint and the Archives. Catching sight of the smoke-clouded roof of Earnscliffe—once the stately residence of Sir John Macdonald—he fell to wondering what the Grand Old Man would have said to such a proposition . . .

A National Theatre!

The Greeks, he remembered, spared neither time nor money on their dramatic temple, which was free! On the other hand, the Canadian theatre was almost prohibitive in point of admission fee, and far from being the object of Governmental support, it was controlled by a group of Semitic gentlemen whose habitat was Broadway and whose taste reflected anything but a Canadian National spirit. In Rome, Mommens had taught him, there were fewer occupations more lucrative than those of actor and dancer— Roscius, one of the former, receiving the equivalent of $30,000 as his annual income, and Dionysia, a fairy-footed maid, $10,000 yearly—more than twice the amount of his Parliamentary indemnity!

Why should Canada not have her theatre?

He had dreamed of leisure to write—a drama of the West. Often he had pictured its theme unfolding in a mighty spectacle that would rival those of Ancient Rome, when six hundred mules passed in review across the stage of a military pageant, and whole armies were in requisition to give verisimilitude to a production.

He saw vast herds of buffalo and cattle; he heard the thunder of their flying hoofs and the yells of the pursuing Red Men. From the south and east, troops of devil-may-care cowboys burst upon the scene. The whirr of arrows, the snap of rifles, beat across his consciousness. And as the play progressed, over the flaming prairie there crawled a slow, white streak, coming to a halt at last in what looked like the heart of infinity. And presently, there appeared a tiny farm.

Deep in moonlit gorges, Dilling saw fur traders, whiskey smugglers, Indians, and cattle thieves, threading a cautious way. Then came the flash of scarlet coats and diminishing disorder.

And along the trails made by the thirsty buffalo, followed by wary Red Men, rediscovered by ambitious young surveyors who found that wisdom was born in brute, and even in primeval man, before it made its way to books, the railway flung its slender arms across an infant nation; and settlers came hard upon the heels of construction crews, a strange assortment who spoke their parts in the music of unfamiliar, polyglot tongues.

And on the site of some forgotten Indian encampment, where patient squaws pounded out their corn, there grew a field of wheat which gave way to a small settlement, and then a town where gigantic storehouses now husbanded the grain!

Ah, God, the glamour of the West—his West! Suddenly, it sang in his blood, it shone in his eyes, it dazzled him and provoked emotions that no woman had ever stirred.

A National Theatre? Well, it certainly was an idea, but he must not be intrigued by it; there was no hurry. The proposition needed thinking . . . Dilling crossed the room, took the receiver from its hook and called up Azalea. He was unaccountably disappointed to learn that she was out.

He realised with a sense of shock that she was the only friend he had made since coming to the Capital. At the moment, he felt that she was more than a friend . . . that she was a necessity. But he resisted this weakness as he would have resisted dependence upon a stimulant or sedative. Dilling liked to believe in his self-sufficiency, his detachment from all human ties. He could not deny, however, that Azalea fed him intellectually—food convenient for him.

"She feeds my mind," he repeated, surprised that this should be so. "Isn't it curious that she should possess this power . . ." It was all he asked of God.

His feeling was one that did honour to Platonism and now, as he sat reflecting upon it, Raymond Dilling wondered just what Azalea thought of him. Did she think his standards worthy of his calling? Had she faith in his singleness of purpose, and did she commend his policy for its wisdom? Or could she have misunderstood him, read into his unashamed confessions, the easy cant of him who makes a profession of sincerity?

He had taken for granted that she was in accord with his political creed, that she appreciated his native worth; but never before had he asked himself the question . . . did she like him? He had no assurance that she did. Admitting her acceptance of him upon his own terms, so to speak, might she not feel for him as we so often feel towards estimable persons whose blameless characters inspire us with nothing but respectful tolerance? On the other hand, suppose she did not regard him as a worthy figure, would she dislike him? Are there not natures to whom an impostor presents a personality unreasonably appealing? Has not the world had its Casanovas and Cagliostros?

What manner of man did Azalea like? What type stirred her rich imagination?

These unanswerable questions provoked him to an unwonted consideration of the girl, but he failed to recollect an occasion when she had revealed her inner thoughts and aspirations to him. What heart throbs, he asked himself, pulsed beneath that strange, drab exterior? What spirit wounds were covered with the cuirass of her whimsical satire? What was her philosophy of life, and what did she really think of him?

He had no idea, but he did know that he wished to be her friend.

Dilling couldn't recall ever formulating a definite opinion on the subject of friendship, and he was not at all sure what Azalea might require of him. Sympathy, he mused, might be helpful in times of strain, but he was not prepared to admit that friendships were vital. A man could—perhaps should—be independent of their fetters, unseeking and unsought. Friendship had its rise in the emotions according to philosophers, and was therefore a weakness. Yet, was it? History showed that great men transmuted it into strength.

Which would it be for him, a weakness or a source of strength? And if the latter, how best could he convert its power into fuel for his energy?

He looked at his watch. Almost time for lunch. Azalea should be at home now, he thought. Again, he turned to the telephone.

In the room above, Mrs. Barrington was eagerly accepting a whisky and soda from the hospitable Member for Morroway.

"You look as though a little stimulant would do you no harm," observed Howarth, busily attentive with the cigarettes.

"Without it, I shan't last till sundown," returned the woman. "Never have I spent such a half hour . . . and never again!"

"Difficult, eh?" asked Sullivan.

"Impossible! Why, Uncle Rufus, that man's not human! Heaven knows, I'm not a vain woman," she declared, "but for all the notice he took of me, he might have been a graven image, or I might have been one of the shrieking sisterhood! There wasn't a smile . . . there wasn't a flicker of response! I kept thinking all the time of Congreve, and his *Lady Wishfort* trying to captivate that stupid ass, old *Mirabell!*" Her full voice trembled with excitement and anger. Into her cheeks flooded a wave of natural colour, beneath their expertly applied rouge. "I'm through . . . I'm through," she cried. "He made me think of a eunuch contemplating a statue of Venus!"

CHAPTER 13.

Mrs. Pratt stood in the hard glitter of too many electric lights, in a hard, encrusted green gown, and greeted her guests with a hard, set smile that froze any budding sense of enjoyment they may have brought with them. Maude was silent and sullen. She had caught the backwash of her mother's ill-temper throughout two trying weeks, and the party had become a nightmare to her. Augustus, miserable in his evening clothes, and perspiring under the weight of admonitions that warred with his sense of hospitality, watched her in a passion of sympathy. After a succession of violent scenes, he was dolorously conscious that he and Maude together, were no match for the determined woman whom he had meekly followed to the altar.

"She's got too damned much gulp," he thought to himself, wondering how to reduce this hampering characteristic in his daughter.

A vigorous jab in the side reminded him that something was amiss. "Eh, my dear?" he whispered. "What's wrong?"

"Take your hands out of your pockets, Augustus," hissed Mrs. Pratt, "and don't you dare to call Dr. Prendergast, 'Doc'!"

"Doctor and Missus Bzen-an-Bza-a!" announced Cr'ymer, from the door.

Cr'ymer was a very recent acquisition to the Pratt ménage. Mrs. Pratt would have preferred a Japanese but for once she was overruled by her husband, who harboured the malicious belief that every man of foreign birth, especially negroes and Orientals, look upon the women of our race with lascivious eyes. So when Cr'ymer applied, and upheld his cleverly-forged reference with a plausible story, Mrs. Pratt engaged him—bibulous mien and Cockney accent, notwithstanding.

Having been but a few weeks in the city, and most of that time comfortably soothed by vinous refreshment, Cr'ymer was not conversant with the names of social Ottawa, and even had he been, it is doubtful that those of Mrs. Pratt's guests would have been familiar to him.

"How d'ye do?" asked Mrs. Prendergast, annoyed to find that no one else had arrived. There was a suggestion of over-eagerness in being early.

"How do yuh do?" returned Mrs. Pratt, wishing that she was Lady Elton or someone worth while. "Sit down, won't you? I think you'll find any of my chairs comfortable, and there's no need for you to stand because we have to . . . The others can't be long, now."

"They can if they choose," remarked Dr. Prendergast, who liked his dinner in the middle of the day and a substantial supper at six o'clock. "Never saw anything to beat the people, to-day. They don't start out till it's time for decent folks to be in bed. Things get later and later. Shouldn't be surprised to see the hour for dinner set at eleven o'clock . . . Outrageous!"

"Well, with so many engagements to crowd in of an afternoon, and with the House sitting till six o'clock, it's vurry difficult to dine much earlier than seven o'clock," argued Mrs. Pratt. "Oh, here are the Leeds. How do yuh do? Augustus, meet Mrs. Leeds!"

"How do?" mumbled Augustus, and prayed for the coming of the cocktails, which, as an antidote for the concoctions of an atrocious cook, he had made extra strong.

Mrs. Pratt aspired to a good cook, by which she meant a person who could disguise the most familiar comestibles so that recognition was impossible. Personally, she liked plain and wholesome cooking. Most people do. But she laboured under the misapprehension that members of the aristocracy ate strange and undistinguishable dishes; moreover, that the degree of exaltation which one had attained, was evident by the kind of food one ate. For example, she could not conceive of His Majesty enjoying a rasher of liver and bacon, nor a Duke sitting down to the staple pork and beans so familiar to the humble farming class. Long hours she pondered the question of food, rising gradually through the ragouts and rissoles, ramakins and casseroles, to ravioli, caviare, canapes and the bewildering *aux* and *a la's* that make a wholesome menu so picturesque and indigestible.

The cook that Mrs. Pratt had in mind, was one who had served at least an Earl, and had titillated the palates of his class. But at that time—now half a decade past—social distinctions were drawn quite as finely in the kitchen as the drawing-room, and the woman who would exchange her culinary gifts and aristocratic associations for the wages of a mistress not even an Honourable in her own right, had not been found.

The hour set for dinner had past. In the drawing-room, a noticeable chill tempered the atmosphere. Mrs. Pratt was not an easy hostess. The word "entertaining" was, for her, the most perfect euphemism, and in ordinary circumstances, she would have taken satisfaction rather than pleasure by gathering people at her home. On this occasion, she was denied satisfaction, and a rising resentment gave her far from gracious manner an added acerbity. Conversation lost all semblance to spontaneity, and every eye seemed to be fixed upon Mrs. Pratt, who sat stiffly on a Louis Quinze chair and hoped that Rufus Sullivan was sensible of her displeasure.

She blamed him for this contretemps. It was he who had asked her to invite the Barringtons, laying delicate emphasis upon their social importance no less than upon their importance to the Party.

"Strangers," he said, "but excellently connected and frightfully smart—rather too smart for parochial Ottawa, I fear, dear lady! However, they're well worth cultivating, and a clever woman could make no little use of Hebe Barrington."

Certainly, she was not difficult to know. Her acceptance of Mrs. Pratt's laboured and formal invitation—delivered for lack of time by telephone—was so casual as to startle that good lady. This was not her conception of the manners of the elect.

And now they were quite fifteen minutes late. Mrs. Pratt's anger rose.

She had just decided to proceed to the dining-room without them, when there was a furious ring at the bell, a hurried step on the stair, and Cr'ymer signalled her that they had arrived.

"My dear Mrs. Pratt," cried Hebe, sweeping forward, "*is* there an apology profound enough to touch the hearts of your guests—not to mention your husband and yourself? How do you do, Mr. Pratt? And your daughter . . . why, you dear child, kiss me! Fortune has indeed smiled upon this family . . . Mr. Dilling? What a delightful surprise . . . Mrs. Pratt," she went on, bowing and smiling impartially, drawing everyone about her, if not actually, at least by suggestion, "*do* tell me that I am to sit next to Mr. Dilling, and—" with an arch glance at her host, "not too far from Mr. Pratt!"

"Mr. Dilling is to take you in to dinner," replied the hostess, tartly.

The cocktails, supplementing Mrs. Barrington's entrance, infused new life into the party. Most of those present walked from the drawing-room in a pleasant frame of mind.

"They say that society is divided into two classes," said Hebe, as they took their places at the table, "those who have more dinners than appetite, and those who have more appetite than dinners. I don't know that I should confess it, but I belong to the latter class. I'm always ready for a meal . . . Ah, what a charming room this is!"

With one or two exceptions, the guests were unpleasantly impressed by this expression of frank admiration. According to their canons of etiquette, personal remarks were not The Thing. But if the impulse to make one proved utterly irresistible, then it should be prefaced by some such phrase as,

"If I may be pardoned for saying so, that is a beautiful . . ." or, "I hope you won't be offended if I pass a remark on your . . ."

Even Mrs. Pratt was only slightly mollified. The personnel of her dinner party differed radically from what she had designed. Indeed, of the eleven guests who took their places at the table, there were but three whose names had figured on her original list of invitations. Besides, she was not conscious of the instinctive liking for Mrs. Barrington that Sullivan had predicted. Quite the contrary! In the first place, she disapproved of her gown—a shimmering sheath of opalescent sequins infinitely more striking than that which Mrs. Pratt herself was wearing. In the second place, she did not like a(nother) woman to monopolise the conversation. In the third place, she objected to the manner in which Augustus was being captivated right under her very eyes, and these were but a few of the items that she set down upon her mental score. But that Mrs. Barrington was smart could not be denied; and as illustrious names slipped artfully into the recital of her experiences and associations, most of the assembled company found themselves giving her a grudging respect. There were four exceptions—the Dillings, Sullivan and Azalea.

"I'm sure I've heard of you, Dr. Prendergast," she glowed at that gentleman. "But where, or from whom, I simply can't remember. I have the most dreadful habit of forgetting names . . . if it weren't for Toddles, there, I'd forget my own. He's just as good at remembering as I am at forgetting, so we manage famously, eh, my fond love?"

Barrington hid a smile and mumbled something that passed for an answer. He was a delightful little man who had become accustomed to his wife's brilliant impertinences, and rather enjoyed them when they were not carried too far.

He had not been taken into her confidence, of late, but suspected that she had some telling reason for imposing these curious people and this abominable dinner upon him. It was his nature to be amiable under trying circumstances, so he made himself agreeable to the ladies on either side, and tried to look upon the occasion as a bit of a lark. Mrs. Leeds was not lacking in charm—a pale little creature whose mouth had a discontented droop and who was ashamed or afraid to meet her husband's eyes. She talked bridge throughout the evening, bewailing the sums she had lost because someone at the table had failed to bid or to play according to the rules of the game. It was quite distressing to hear her re-play hands that should have added to her score below the line, but which built the tower for her opponents.

"For example," she said, under cover of Dr. Prendergast's monologue, "only last night, the most unheard-of thing happened! I declared no trump.

Though weak in spades I had every suit protected, and was perfectly justified in my declaration. The man on my left bid two spades. My partner passed, telling me he had no protection in that suit, but I felt safe in raising to two no trump, because, supposing that the bidder held ace, king to five, *at least*, I knew that my queen was sufficiently guarded by two little ones. Do you follow me?" she asked, anxiously.

"Perfectly," lied Barrington. "And then what happened?"

"Well, the bidder led the seven of spades. My partner laid down his hand which only held the ten. Picture my horror when this woman—" she indicated an imaginary third player "—took the trick with the ace, and then *led the Jack through my Queen*! Of course, my hand was shot absolutely to bits. They took five straight spade tricks and two in diamonds before I had a look in. Time after time, I am penalised just that way by playing with imbeciles who don't know how to bid."

"Rotten luck," sympathised Barrington. "What the devil is this we are eating?"

Mrs. Prendergast was the simplest person to entertain. When not giving undivided attention to her husband, she was entrusting to her sympathetic partner a list of his outstanding virtues as a citizen, husband and father.

What "the Dawkter" thought and said provided her with an inexhaustible topic for conversation. Apparently she had no opinions of her own, but, as her husband was quite willing to listen to the echo of his oracles, they were an exceedingly happy couple.

The Doctor was a generous-waisted gentleman whose talents exercised themselves in the field of proprietary medicine. PRENDERGAST'S ANTI-AGONY ALIMENT was just beginning to fraternise with Best Wear Tires, Breakfast Foods and Theatrical Attractions on the bill boards. Presently, however, as a result of sapient advertising and the deplorable ignorance of English by the people who speak it, "aliment" merged into "ailment" and PRENDERGAST'S ANTI-AGONY AILMENT became the popular specific for those to whom all advertising makes direct appeal.

And so carefully generalised was the nature of the disorder it was supposed to correct that the decoction was consumed indiscriminately by sufferers from rheumatism, chilblains, dyspepsy, sciatica, high blood pressure and sclerosis. According to the testimonials that made their way into the press it did many people . . . good.

The Doctor's mind was full of human ills, and the value of advertising. To the latter he was a recent convert, and inevitably fanatical. Requiring several thousand dollars to carry on his campaign, he was doing his best to bring the others to his point of view.

With the exception of Mrs. Barrington, no one gave him any encouragement. Throughout three entire courses, she murmured, "Incredible! Amazing! It sounds like a fairy tale!" at moments when he might have given some one else an opportunity to speak, and started him off again with renewed zest and vigour. Under cover of his eloquence, she talked to Raymond Dilling.

Dilling was suffering acute mental and physical distress. Fastidious always about his food, he could not eat the dishes put before him, and the little bit he did manage to swallow was flavoured with the scent which Hebe Barrington perpetually exuded. Positively, he would have preferred the odour of moth balls.

He had never seen a woman so naked ... not even his wife. Marjorie emphasised a characteristic which she called modesty and, having no curiosity whatever about the human form, Dilling respected her reserve.

He sat at the corner of the table, next to Mrs. Pratt, and found that he could not escape contact with the warm mundanity of Mrs. Barrington. Although the table was not crowded, she seemed to give him no room. Once or twice, he shuddered, and she mistaking his movement, smiled provocatively into his eyes.

"You haven't forgotten about Monday afternoon?" she whispered. "I've been thinking of it all week."

Dilling had forgotten.

"There's really nothing to be gained by discussing the proposition yet," he said. "We've been so busy in the House, I haven't had time to think about it."

"No matter. We can become friends," she murmured, significantly. "Can't we?"

A sudden silence relieved him of the necessity to answer. Dr. Prendergast had run down, and was looking at Mrs. Barrington.

"Positively the most interesting thing I ever heard," she cried. "Toddles, I wish *you* could invent something other than tarradiddles. *Do* send me an autographed bottle, Doctor! I haven't a thing the matter with me, and don't promise to use it. I'm so disgustingly healthy. But I'd love to have it to put on the shelf with my signed books and other treasures. Won't it be nice, Toddles?"

Azalea bent her head above her plate and scarcely knew whether to be angry or amused. Sitting on the same side of the table as Mrs. Barrington, Dilling and the Doctor, neither she nor her partner, Leeds, could see exactly what was going on. But what she did not divine, was reflected in the varying expressions of Turner, who sat on Mrs. Pratt's left, Eva Leeds and Marjorie. Even Pratt, who had fallen an instant and unresisting victim to Hebe Barrington's charms, gave her more than inkling of the by-play at the other end of the table.

She was very much alive to the presence of Sullivan, who sat directly opposite and assumed towards Marjorie an air of offensive proprietorship. Prejudiced against him perhaps by the opinion of her friends, she had never felt for the man active dislike until this moment when every slanderous tale she had heard leaped into her mind. Although he had become a frequent visitor at the Dilling home, she had met him for the first time this evening, and had not the slightest desire to continue the acquaintance. Furthermore, she wondered if Marjorie could be persuaded to put an end to such a friendship.

"Are you having a good time, little woman?" she heard him whisper.

"Yes, thank you," replied Marjorie, hoping that telling a polite lie would not be a sin.

"Not so good as though we were having dinner alone—without all these dull people?"

"No," admitted Marjorie.

"When shall we have another party . . . of our own?"

"I don't know just now. Perhaps next week."

By the furious colour that surged into Marjorie's cheeks, Azalea knew that Sullivan had caressed her under cover of the table.

"It's always at this point that the liveliest dinner begins to grow dull," cried Hebe Barrington. "Have you ever noticed it, Mrs. Pratt? No? Dear me, *what* partners you must have had! I believe there *are* super-women with whom men are never tiresome. How do you account for that, Doctor?" Then, without waiting for an answer, she went on, "I have a theory of my own regarding this slump in brilliancy and wit. It is simply a matter of being too well fed. The animal wants to stretch and sleep. What do you think?" she smiled at Augustus, who was so disturbed by this sudden attention that he interfered with Cr'ymer's unsteady serving of the wine and between them they managed to upset the decanter.

"Oh, Mrs. Pratt!" Hebe turned in mock terror to her hostess. "I throw myself upon your protection. He is going to blame me! I'm sorry, but I'm innocent. Uneasy looks the face that wears a frown, Mr. Pratt! If you will only forgive me, I'll promise not to speak to you again all evening."

"Wish you'd get the missus to go that far," retorted Augustus, avoiding his wife's eye.

There was a laugh in which Mrs. Pratt did not join. Conversation dropped to a murmur between couples. Hebe repeated her question to Dilling and received from him a grudging affirmative. A ponderous hummock of doughy consistency was tasted and thrust aside, and the hostess rose from the table.

"Poor Augustus!" whispered Hebe, as she sank down beside Azalea in the drawing-room. "Won't hell-fire be his when we've gone?"

"Perhaps if we're especially nice to her, she will have forgotten by then."

"Not a chance, my dear! I don't know the individual, but I know the type. Death will be his only escape . . . But, tell me, just who are you?"

"Nobody in particular," answered Azalea. "That's why I'm here," she added, with an unusual touch of malice.

Mrs. Barrington was startled at this thrust. Into her eyes there shone a budding respect for the girl.

"Yes, but who *are* you? What's your name?"

Azalea told her.

"Deane? Oh! You're a great friend of the Dillings, then?"

"You seem surprised."

"I am," confessed the other woman. "I've heard of you, but—er—" she ran an appraising look over the reconstructed gown that had adorned the person of Lady Elton for three years—"I thought you would be different."

"A doubtful compliment," suggested Azalea.

"As you like," returned Hebe, and seated herself at the piano.

Somewhat to Azalea's surprise, Mrs. Barrington made no effort to capture Dilling when the men re-joined them. She turned the battery of her fascinations upon Pratt with an occasional shot at the Doctor. Dilling made his way directly to Azalea and dropped on the chair beside her.

"How long do these things last?" he enquired, under his breath. "Can't we go home?"

"In a few minutes. Wait until Mrs. Barrington stops singing. The bridge players will probably stay on."

Dilling made a frank signal to his wife, then turned back to the girl. "Do you mind coming to the house with us?" he asked. "I will see you home. There is something particular I want to say."

The song ended abruptly, and Azalea raised her eyes to meet those of Hebe Barrington. There was something in their expression that made her flush. And there was the same suggestiveness, the same mockery in her words at parting.

"If Miss Deane will wait until I have redeemed my promise to Mr. Pratt and sung him one more song, we will drop her at the door and save Mr. Dilling the trouble."

"Cut him out of that pleasure," amended Barrington, quickly.

"Even pleasures are troublesome, Toddles, dear," said his wife, "look at me, for an illustration. However, there may be another time . . . You must all come and see me. They say my parties are rather fun. I'm usually at home on Friday evenings, and nearly every Sunday afternoon."

Azalea did not speak for a moment after Dilling had made his proposition. She dared not trust her voice.

"You can't be offended?" he asked, bluntly.

She shook her head.

"On the contrary, it gives me the most extraordinary sense of pleasure that you want me . . . that you think I can be of some real service to you."

"Well?"

"Well . . . that's all! It's simply out of the question! I know my father will never hear of such a thing."

"He must! I'll see him to-morrow. I'll show him that he's wrong. I'll say . . ."

"You'll say," interrupted Azalea, forcing a laugh, " 'Sir, I have come to make a formal request for your daughter's . . . shorthand!' And then, "I'm glad, for your sake, Mr. Dilling, we don't own a dog!'"

"You can't discourage me," cried Dilling. "I've made up my mind that we will work together, and if you consent I feel that the thing is as good as settled."

It was. The following morning, when Azalea carried in her father's breakfast tray, she found that he had passed out of life as he had passed through it, easily, and without toil or struggle.

CHAPTER 14.

*T*wo months had passed since Azalea had undertaken her secretarial duties. She felt that she had entered into a new life, that a wonderful renascence was hers. Never in all her imaginings, had she dreamed of days so replete with happiness.

A sense of deference to the dead prompted Mrs. Deane to protest against her daughter's accepting the appointment. They talked at one another across an abyss that widened daily and separated them.

"You shouldn't do it, Azalea," she cried. "It doesn't seem right. You're disobeying your father when he's scarcely cold in the grave . . . It isn't as though you didn't know that . . . I mean, I suppose it wouldn't be so bad if he had been dead a long time . . ."

"Disobedience is a matter of principle, not time, mother!" returned the girl. "Don't you see that I have no choice? We can't live without the equivalent of father's superannuation allowance!"

"Well, I'm sure I don't know what to do," Mrs. Deane whimpered, "Business is so difficult for a woman to grasp . . . Oh, Azalea, if he knows it, he will be so dreadfully annoyed! Isn't there some other way? If you had only been married . . ."

"Please, mother, let's not go into that! I'm sorry to have disappointed you, but for myself, I haven't a single regret. I don't look upon marriage as the only solution of a woman's financial problems, you know."

"It's a convenient one," argued Mrs. Deane, rather more pertinently than usual. "There are the girls . . . they don't have to work."

"If they don't, then they are cheating their husbands," cried Azalea, purposely misunderstanding. "And too many married women who don't cheat their husbands are being cheated—like you," she nearly ended.

"Oh, my child!"

"I can't look upon marriage as a refuge from the dangers that beset a female traveller on the Sea of Life. To me it is a tricky craft that may play you false as it operates between the two inescapable ports of Birth and Death."

"And you are our baby, too," sighed Mrs. Deane, as irrelevantly as Mrs. Nickleby.

"A baby who has grown up at last, and thanks God for the opportunity that has come disguised as a necessity; a baby, dear mother, who does not look upon congenial work as a test of courage, but as a divine privilege."

Curiously enough, once she was established in her new position, unreserved approval was expressed among her friends. Many of them attributed the move to some suggestion of their own. Lady Denby and Mrs. Hudson both remembered having advised Azalea to take some such step years ago. Lady Elton thought she had shown her good sense at last, but hoped that Mr. Dilling would not be too exacting. Entertaining was a bore under the best of conditions. She simply could not imagine getting along without Azalea's assistance. Mrs. Long saw an opportunity for picking up odd bits of political gossip that eluded the ordinary reporter, and making a neat little income on the side.

"You're clever enough to do it, my dear," she said. "Now, don't be thin-skinned. Spice is what the people want—any of them who bother to read the papers."

As for Dilling, he felt himself infused with new zest and enthusiasm. He was conscious of a greater capacity for work, an accession of power. His brain seemed to function tirelessly and with amazing clearness. He developed a veritable rapacity for what appeared to be ineluctable problems, and he who had been a model of industry became a miracle of inexhaustible energy.

It was about this time that men began to look to him as the most able exponent of their political creeds; it was upon him that they called to master such questions as Newfoundland's entrance into the Dominion, trade with the West Indies, reciprocity with the United States, and upon his slender shoulders fell the burden of carrying on the most contentious debate of latter times—Canada's Naval Policy. In short, it was to him that his Party turned, as the only man capable of grasping those knotty issues of international importance and presenting Canada's case in a masterly way before the Council of the Nations.

"I've been invited to join the Golf Club," he announced one morning, as Azalea came into the office.

"I'm glad! You're not hesitating about it, are you?"

"Oh, I don't know. What do you think?"

"I think you are becoming no end of a social lion," she replied, smiling, "and that soon you will be roaring as lustily in drawing-rooms as on the floor of the House. Seriously, I think you should accept. It will be good for Marjorie."

"I'm not so sure. She hasn't many friends among that crowd. However, I think I see what you mean."

Azalea hoped he did. She was desperately anxious for him to realise that in the Capital success is regarded from only one angle, the Social. Professional, literary, political, all these are but feeders to the main issue.

"I spent the afternoon with your exceptionally brilliant Dr. Aldrich," said Sir Paul Pollock, the eminent British anthropologist, during the course of a dinner the Chesleys had given in his honour.

"Aldrich?" echoed the company. "Who's he?"

Sir Paul did not take the question seriously. "I don't blame you," he laughed. "Two scientists at the same party would be excessively heavy wheeling."

"But who *is* he?" insisted Miss Mabel Angus-McCallum. "I never heard of him."

"Nor I . . ."

"Nor I . . ."

"Well—ah—ha—if you are not pulling my leg," answered the amazed guest, "perhaps you will be interested in knowing that he is one of the most famous biologists living. But—ah—ha—! I expect you are just stringing me."

It was gradually borne in upon him that they were not, that they had no desire to cultivate the men and women whose lives are devoted to the advancement of their race, that even the names of such people were unfamiliar to them and that prominence in their especial sphere was clouded by a total eclipse of the social solar system.

It was this latter point that Azalea ardently wished to make Dilling recognise. He was so immersed in his public life that there was little time for the consideration of any other question, and Marjorie had not sufficient astuteness to make the most of her advantage or profit by experiences.

She seemed incapable of keeping step with her husband, of acquiring a broader vision than that which was hers in Pinto Plains. In her eyes, a thousand dollars was always a staggering sum, five hundred an immense concourse of people.

"But, dearest Marjorie," cried Azalea, in affectionate exasperation one day, "you *must* learn to see beyond a home-made dress and a parish tea-party!"

"If my clothes and my food mean more to people than I do, myself," argued Marjorie, "then I don't want to have anything more to do with them. We're just plain Canadians, and I don't want to pretend otherwise!"

"Yes, but—but—" Azalea often found herself at a loss for illustrations that would co-ordinate with her friend's code of ethics, "conforming to certain conventions isn't exactly pretence. You might look upon it as a ceremony, ritual, something that is an adjunct to a position."

"A lady is a lady anywhere," murmured Marjorie conscious, herself, that she was not precisely strengthening her argument.

"So is a clergyman," replied Azalea, "but you would not like to see him conduct a Service in a pair of tennis flannels or a bathing suit."

"Oh!" The point had gone home. "What have I done that's wrong?"

"Nothing so very wrong, you dear lamb," said the older girl, kissing Marjorie's troubled mouth, "but try not to be so humble. Humility is a splendid virtue, sometimes—but not when we're heading for the Cabinet!"

"It frightens me to think of it."

"But you must overcome that, and feel perfectly at ease with Mrs. Blaine, Mrs. Carmichael, Lady Denby and the others. You must make them your friends."

"I can't be friends with people if they don't want me!"

Azalea tried to explain that in public life friendship and association are more or less interchangeable terms. "You were not friends with all your classmates at school," she said, "but you associated with them, especially on formal occasions. It was then that your status was fixed by your class. It is exactly the same with your position as Mr. Dilling's wife. You must feel yourself worthy of belonging to the highest class—the class which has been reached by a very prominent man, who will be known in history as one of the greatest statesmen of his country."

"What must I do?" asked Marjorie, as Mrs. Deane might have said it.

"Learn and observe social distinctions. Everyone else does. Show that you respect your husband's achievements and others will follow your lead. Why, the Society Columns are read to better advantage by the tradespeople, the gas inspector, the telephone operators, the very cab drivers, than you."

"I don't know what you mean," said Marjorie, very close to tears.

"I mean that those people almost unerringly place the rest of us in our proper class. They observe the rules of precedence, which you don't. If there happened to be but one cab at a stand, and both you and Mrs. Blaine wanted it, which one of you would get the thing?"

Marjorie did not answer.

"Mrs. Blaine! You know it! Why? Because she goes to Church regularly on Sundays, pays her bills promptly, refuses to gossip and slander her neighbours? Not a bit of it! Because she puts a value on herself that is compatible with her husband's position . . . at least, that's near enough the mark to serve my purpose in scolding you!"

"All right," sighed Marjorie, "I'll try to be stiff with people, if that's the way to help Raymond. I don't believe it, you know, Azalea, but I think I see what you mean."

Azalea, however, was not so sanguine.

"Do you play golf?" she asked Dilling.

"Oh, I've handled the clubs once or twice. But I won't have any time to devote to the game."

"You must make time. It will do you a world of good. All play and no work will make you an ideal politician," she teased.

"You will come out with us to dinner, the first night we go?"

"Oh, no!" she cried. "You must take someone infinitely more distinguished. You must shine and let your light be seen before men. If I might make a suggestion, give a very exclusive dinner party and invite the Chief."

"But you must come, too!"

"We'll see. In the meantime, hadn't we better tackle this formidable mail? It seems to grow larger every morning."

Towards the middle of the afternoon, a spare, thin-lipped little man came into the room.

"Howdy, Raymond?" he greeted. "Been tryin' to run you down to your hole this last half hour. Got kinder twisted in this big buildin'."

"How are you, Sam?" said Dilling, shaking hands. "It's good to see someone from home. Just get in?"

"Just about. How's the Missus and the kids?"

Dilling assured his visitor that their health was good.

"We've had an awful lot of sickness this winter. First, the baby was taken with swollen glands, and we'd no sooner got her up an' about when Sammy came down with grippe, and on top o' that, the wife had to be operated on for appendicitis. Makes me creep to think what the doctor's bill is goin' to be."

"Don't worry about that, Sam. Halsey is the soul of consideration and patience."

"Still, he's got to be paid. Swell office, you've got, Raymond."

Dilling smiled.

"An improvement on my old one, but modest as offices go."

"This all there is of it?" queried the stranger.

"This is all. We don't have suites, you know, until we get to be Deputies or Commissioners, perhaps. It's plenty large enough."

"Sure. I was only wonderin' where we could have a little talk—a kinduv private confab, as you might say," returned the other, nodding at Azalea's industrious back.

"We can have it right here," said Dilling, promptly. "This is my confidential secretary, Miss Deane. Mr. Sam Dunlop, of Pinto Plains. Miss Deane. He's an old friend and worked hard at the time of my election. Go ahead, Sam. What is it?"

"Well—er—" began Mr. Dunlop, in some embarrassment, "it's about that block of ours out home. You mind when we four bought it from them Winnipeg fellows, the idea was that they would start in putting improvements all around us?"

"In the centre of the town," supplemented Dilling. "I remember very well. There was some talk of street cars. What of it?"

"They're a bunch of shysters, that's what! They haven't spent a dollar on First or Second Streets, they only pulled down a couple of buildings on the Avenue, and they're investin' every dollar they can raise to develop Pond Park and turn it into a summer resort. And business is trailin' 'em right out that way."

Dilling looked grave.

"Has anyone actually moved off First Street?"

"Bowers is moving in the spring. Jennings got an option on the corner of Cedar and the Avenue which takes the two biggest merchants away. After that, all the little fellows will go."

"And the hotel they talked about?"

"If they build, it'll be out the other way. Oh, there ain't a bit of use in you settin' there thinkin' that we've got a chance," cried Mr. Dunlop. "We've studied this thing till it's a wonder we didn't get brain fever. Says Lewis, 'We four went into this here deal as friends and we'll stick together. You go down to Ottawa and see Raymond. He'll look after us, same as we've been tryin' to look after his interests.' Mumford's the hardest hit— next to me, that is! But none of us, outside of yourself, can afford to hold that property an' pay taxes while the town grows in the other direction."

"And what do you think I can do?" asked Dilling, in a hard voice.

"You can recommend the sale of our block to the Government, boy, that's where you come in!" Mr. Dunlop dragged his chair closer and poured forth his proposition in a rapid whisper.

"But Pinto Plains doesn't need another Post Office," argued Raymond Dilling. "The Liberals spent fifty thousand dollars for the one we have only a few years ago, and you were the first to denounce it, Sam. Everyone agreed that the town wouldn't grow up to it in a hundred years."

"But, damn it all, Raymond, can't you see that this is different? Can't you get it through your head that we'll be ruined unless we can sell that property and sell it quick? All of us—of course, exceptin' you—all of us have got to raise interest on the money we borrowed to put into it, and Lord knows where mine is coming from. What's a dinky little Post Office to the Government? Lewis says it ought to be a cinch to put it through, for he can condemn the other one, easy! How long do you figger it'll take to get the matter settled, son?"

"It's settled right now, so far as I'm concerned."

"How do you mean?"

"I can't undertake such a job."

"You . . . what?"

"You're asking me to betray the confidence of the country, Sam; to rob the Treasury. That's the proposition in plain English, isn't it?"

Mr. Dunlop denied this accusation eloquently, if irrationally. He cajoled, he stormed, he pleaded, he threatened. He reminded Dilling that during his election campaign, support had been based on friendship, not a strict adherence to truthfulness, and that the boys had not stopped to consider every lie that was told on his behalf.

"Runnin' the country ain't the same as runnin' a Sunday School," he added, in justification.

"The governing principles should be the same," answered Dilling. "No, Sam, I can't do it. Argument is useless. When you and the boys think it over, you will agree that the man who would have carried out your proposition is not the type that you would have to mould the policy of the Nation. I hope that Pinto Plains will never send a chap like that to Parliament! You'll come down to the house, of course, won't you?"

But Mr. Dunlop did not hear the invitation. He was so absorbed in expressing his opinion of the man he had sent to Parliament, that he failed to recognise Sir Robert Borden whom he passed in the corridor, and ran violently into Sir Eric and Lady Denby without uttering a word of apology.

"We'll fix him," he muttered under his breath. "We'll fix him!"

In the office there was silence save for the sibilent fluttering of papers on Azalea's desk. Presently, Dilling spoke.

"I'm too indignant at the moment to be sorry for them!" he said. "And it's something of a shock to find that they held me in no higher esteem than to think I would be a party to such jobbery."

"I doubt that they looked at the matter in just that way. Isn't it merely another example of the common practice of bringing your white elephant to feed at the Dominion crib?"

"It's another example of perverted ethics," growled Dilling, and he went angrily off to lunch.

Azalea sat on, thinking. What, she asked herself, would be the outcome of Raymond Dilling's uncompromising attitude with men of Dunlop's calibre? Would he, like Marjorie, persistently close his eyes to the advantage of temporising in matters that affected his political career? Would he never learn that a gentle lie turneth away enquiry and that as Dunlop had so truly said, the country was not run like a Sunday School? She had heard him reject more than one proposition made by men of his own Party who never could be brought to see the criminous side of misappropriation of public funds. She had known him to ignore the Patronage system by refusing positions to incompetents, as bluntly as he had discarded Dunlop's scheme. And a little compromising, or even temporising, would have accomplished his object without loss of good will.

"Custom," he once said in answer to her remonstrance, "can never in my opinion sanctify piracy or brigandage. I don't believe in Patronage and never shall. Incompetency should be treated and overcome if possible, but not rewarded."

Rejoicing, as she did, in this fine adherence both to the letter and spirit of his political creed, yet she could not but feel apprehensive for his political future. As a lamp unto his feet were the rules of the Independence of Parliament, but he was rapidly making enemies when by the employment of a little diplomacy he might have had hosts of friends. Scarcely a week passed without bringing forth some public attack upon him, and the mere fact that he championed a cause was sufficient to win for it a mob of fanatical obstructionists.

Yet Azalea realised that anything less than this unswerving rectitude would have been for Dilling ignominious surrender, and she prayed that he might uphold his ideals at all costs, that he might achieve a spiritual triumph even at the price of material defeat. She wondered how it would all end.

CHAPTER 15.

"You had better go up to the House, to-night," called Long, as he passed his wife's door on his way to dress for dinner.

"What's going on? I'm booked for bridge at the Blaine's."

"Dilling's going to speak. I think you'll be repaid for calling off your game."

"All right. I'll telephone," said Mrs. Long, carefully adjusting a hair net. "Perhaps the others would like to go. Only two tables, I understand . . ."

The House was crowded by the time Mrs. Blaine and her party arrived. The "Ladies of the Cabinet" were shown, of course, into the front row of the Speaker's Gallery, and those of lesser rank were distributed wherever space permitted.

Marjorie had been directed to a seat in the second row, immediately behind Mrs. Carmichael and next to Mrs. Long, beyond whom sat Eva Leeds, Pamela de Latour and Mrs. Chesley. Strictly speaking, none of them deserved a place in the Member's Gallery, but in deference to Mrs. Blaine, whose guests they were, and also to their social status, they were thus happily privileged. The vacancy next Marjorie was presently filled by Mrs. Pratt, although Deputy Minister O'Neill's wife sat several rows behind.

"Well, upon my word," whispered Mrs. Carmichael to Mme. Valleau, wife of the Postmaster-General, "The Virginia Creeper will be clinging to us, next. How does she do it?"

There was no mystery. Mrs. Pratt's superb lack of what her husband termed "gulp" was partially responsible; and, in addition, she knew how to wring one hundred per cent returns out of a five dollar bill. The doorkeeper, who was the object of her investment, was more affected by the frigidity of her reception than she was, herself.

"Good evening, Lady Denby . . . How d'yuh do, Mrs. Blaine? Mrs. Carmichael . . . Good evening, Madame Valleau . . ." She bowed right and left, murmuring names—prominent names—and creating the impression among those who didn't know, that she was on pleasantly intimate terms with every one worth while. "Oh, Mrs. Dilling . . . I didn't notice you!"

"Good evening," returned Marjorie, with strained politeness.

She was determined to be just as stiff as Azalea could have wished. Not that she was converted to the belief that this attitude on her part would be in the least helpful to Raymond, but because she was, by nature, docile and amenable to discipline. Always for Marjorie the word "must" held an ineluctable obligation.

Therefore, when Azalea insisted that she must adopt a greater formality of manner, the time came when Marjorie surrendered.

"Who is that woman in the other Gallery?" asked Mrs. Long, from behind a jewelled lorgnette.

"Which one?" queried Pamela de Latour.

"There—in the front row. She seems to have forgotten her clothes, so far as her torso is concerned."

"Oh," cut in Mrs. Pratt, "that's Mrs. Barrington. They've recently come to Ottawa. Her husband's something or other on the Driveway Commission. I can't akkerately say just what, although Mr. Pratt was largely instrumental in getting him appointed."

"Barrington?" echoed Mrs. Chesley, "why, that's the woman who's rushing Raymond Dilling, isn't it?"

"Sh—sh—sh—" warned Pamela, nodding in Marjorie's direction.

"Well, isn't it?" insisted the other.

"Hush! She'll hear you."

"I suppose that means it is. Does she know?"

"I don't think so," whispered Pamela. "Doesn't see much beyond the kitchen cabinet and the drawing-room curtains, I fancy."

"Lucky woman," murmured Helena Chesley, thinking of her impressionable husband.

"Who's speaking?" Mrs. Long was moved to ask. Until that moment, no one had given a glance at the House.

Mr. Sullivan, it seemed, had the floor. A few Members watched him languidly. Nobody listened.

Pamela de Latour turned attentive eyes upon him for a moment or two. Then,

"There's really something intriguing about that man," she murmured. "If only he would apply a little veneer to cover the knots once in a while, he would be accepted everywhere. No one minds what he does when you come to analyse things; only they mind what he does so openly. Does anyone happen to know the reigning favourite?"

"I hear she is a taffy-haired manicurist," whispered Eva Leeds, wishing they had stayed at home and played Bridge. Her losses had been shocking of late, and she felt that the tide of bad luck would certainly have turned this evening. That was always the way, she never really had a chance! "But there's no telling . . . That may be ancient history. I haven't heard much about him, lately."

"About whom?" demanded Madame Valleau, bending back her handsome head in order to see the speaker. She was supposed to be the best informed lady in the Cabinet—informed, that is to say, regarding the shadowy side of the Members' private lives.

They told her.

"Oh, Sullivan," she cried, in her fascinating broken English. "A delightful dog, hein? I wish there were more men like him in this dull town!"

Mrs. Carmichael, having two young daughters to whom she enjoyed applying the inappropriate word "innocent", protested.

"Why, no woman is safe with him," she said.

"A few," argued Madame, allowing her eyes to travel slowly over the immediate group. "Besides, who wants to feel safe with any man? Not I, for one! If women had been safe with men, there would have been no need for cavaliers, for gallantry. Sullivan is charming."

"I think he's a conscienceless old reprobate," declared Mrs. Carmichael, "and the National Council should make an example of him."

Marjorie leaned forward. It required a good deal of courage on her part to push into this argument, but she felt that loyalty to an absent friend demanded it.

"You misjudge him, Mrs. Carmichael," she defended. "I know him very well and I am certain the things people say about him are not true. He's too kind to everybody, that's his trouble! He is as kind to a—a—manicurist as he is to . . . well, to me! He's always so ready to help people and to give them good advice!"

Mme. Valleau gave vent to a musical little scream that was heard by the Sergeant-at-Arms, and impelled him to shake a playful warning for silence at her.

"Don't kill my enthusiasm for that man by telling me he is giving good advice!" she said. "He won't be doing that for a long while, I'll be bound."

"Why not?" demanded Marjorie.

"Because it's only when Sullivan is too old to give the bad example he will begin to give the good advice," returned the Frenchwoman. *"Mon Dieu,* I hope that won't be for many a long day."

"I don't think you are fair to him," championed Marjorie.

"My child," interrupted Lady Denby, "I should be greatly disturbed if I thought you were trying, seriously, to defend that man! Mme. Valleau has original ideas on every subject, including honour, but for you to express yourself favourably on Sullivan's behalf, or admit friendship with him, would be little short of compromising. I know you too well to misunderstand, but these others might get a sadly erroneous impression."

"But . . ." began Marjorie.

"Stop chattering," cautioned Mrs. Long, who had only just stopped, herself. "Mr. Dilling is going to speak."

The House filled rapidly. Members slipped into their seats and turned towards the slender young man who stood, hand on hip, in the very last row of back benches. In the Press Gallery there wasn't a vacant chair. Representatives of the leading dailies jostled and crowded one another at the desk, and those men who could not obtain so convenient a position, drew sheaves of copy paper from their pockets and recorded Dilling's speech on the surface offered by their neighbour's backs. Pages flung themselves on the steps of the Speaker's dais, and relaxed into an attitude that was almost inattentive. They had learned that while the Member for Pinto Plains was speaking, the House rested from its customary finger-snapping, and, like otiose diversions.

A cheer crashed through the silence. On the right of the Speaker, desks were thumped and feet beat upon the floor. A babel arose from the Opposition, and in the Galleries, visitors forgot that they were "strangers in the House," and that, like the children of a bye-gone generation, they were supposed to be unheard.

"Or-r-der," drawled the Speaker. And the clamour died.

"Bon!" chuckled Madame Valleau. "He has the courage to speak, that Dilling—and behind his words, there is the mind to think!"

"Very good," pronounced the ladies surrounding Marjorie. "Most interesting! Quite excellent, indeed!"

"Thank you," returned Marjorie, so stiffly that they looked at her in amazement, wondering if success had suddenly turned her head.

They wondered still more when a messenger approached her, delivered a note and said there would be an answer. Eyebrows were raised, and incredulity was telegraphed from one to the other of the group.

"What's this?" asked Lady Denby, in what she conceived to be a playful tone. "Have we an admirer in the House?"

A furious blush and confused stammering was Marjorie's reply. With one of those rare flashes of insight for which she could never account, she knew that in view of the recent discussion about Sullivan and her defence of him, he was suspected of being the writer of that letter. She didn't blame the women in the least, for she suspected him, herself.

But she was mistaken. The scrawling signature of Hebe Barrington met her eye as she hastily turned the last page, and the body of the communication was an invitation to supper.

"I have persuaded Mr. Dilling to join us," the letter announced, "and he asked me to say that we would meet in his room, at once. Please come!"

"Mrs. Barrington has invited me to supper," Marjorie explained, with a noticeable moderation of stiffness. "I think I will say good night and hurry on."

"What's got into her?" asked the ladies. "Her naiveté was bad enough, but her snobbishness is insufferable!"

Marjorie had never seen a home just like the Barrington's. It reminded her of the Ancient Chattellarium, and struck her as being a curious place in which to live. There weren't two chairs that matched in the whole house, and the black rugs and hangings she found very depressing. Moreover, the rooms bore names as strange as their furnishings, and she had no idea what her hostess meant by the Cuddlery or the Tiffinaria.

Mrs. Barrington entertained easily. She did not stand in the centre of the drawing-room, beneath the chandelier, and greet her guests with flattering though repetitive phrases. In the first place, there wasn't, properly speaking, a drawing-room. In the second, there was no chandelier. What light there was, came from half a dozen shaded sconces, and a pair of Roman lamps. There were no pictures on the wall. At least, Marjorie did not call them pictures. They were scratchy drawings representing Chinamen engaged in such profitless occupations as contemplating the tonsils of a large-mouthed dragon, or leaning thoughtfully upon a naked blade—naked, that is, save for the head that clothed the point of it. She had never seen their like, before, and thoroughly disapproved of them.

Mrs. Barrington did not stand in the drawing-room at all, but wandered about with a cigarette in one hand and a glass of Scotch in the other, and seemed intensely surprised to see the people she was entertaining.

"Well," she greeted more than one guest, "fancy your trotting away out here. Are you with anyone or did you come alone?"

With the exception of Mr. Sullivan and the Carmichael girls, they were strangers to Marjorie, as, indeed, many of them were to their hostess.

"Who is the young blood so effectively burgling the cellarette?" she would ask her husband. Or, "Toddles, tell me quickly, is that girl in blue some one I ought to know?"

Supper was spread in the Tiffinaria and eaten all over the house. Marjorie was inexpressibly shocked to hear a nice looking young man call to his partner,

"You wait upstairs, old dear, and I'll bring up the victuals. We can mangle them on Hebe's dressing table."

"Peacherina!" answered the girl, throwing her slipper at him. "What's on the menu, this evening?"

A recital of the contents of the table and buffet resulted in guarded approbation.

"Get a dab of everything," called the girl, "and we'll manage to find something we can digest."

A Sheffield tray was dismantled and heaped with food sufficient to have served four persons. Added to this, the young man used as a centrepiece his partner's slipper, into which he had poured a mould of chicken jelly.

The Hon. Member for Morroway was, as always, tenderly solicitous of Marjorie. He made several attempts to find a place in which they could sit to have their supper tete-a-tete, before he was successful.

"Somebody's in the Cuddlery," he announced, backing out of the door and guiding her hastily away. "Oh, excuse me," he cried, to an unseen couple who were occupying a nook under the stairs. "Looks as though we'd have to try the pantry or the kitchen. Let's see if we can find a corner on the floor above."

"Oh, no!" protested Marjorie, "I shouldn't care to do that. Why, can't we go there—into the front room? I don't mind others being about."

"Dear little woman," Sullivan whispered, and drew her close against him under the guise of protecting her from collision with a youth who carried an empty glass, "of course we don't mind, but the ridiculous fact is that *they do!*" He sighed in his most elderly manner. "I do wish that Hebe would infuse some dignity into her parties. Perfectly innocent, you understand; not a hint of harm, but just naturally silly and boisterous. Look at young Creel, there, daring Mona Carmichael to stand on her head! By Jove," he slapped his leg and burst into a laugh that seemed to be a spontaneous expression of hilarious amusement, "he's got her by the ankles and she's going to try!"

But, after being trundled about the room like a wheelbarrow, Mona decided that she didn't want to stand on her head. "I tell you what," she cried, "let's dress up in Toddles' clothes!"

With a whoop they raced for the stairs, half a dozen of them, leaving Marjorie and Sullivan in possession of the room. Shrieks and confused scamperings followed. Evidently, they were much at home, there.

"Who are all these people?" Marjorie wanted to know.

The girls, it seemed, were a dashing and exclusive group whose number, and conduct, had earned for them the sobriquet of "The Naughty Nine". They were the envy of all those who stood without the golden circle drawn round them, and subsequently, by dint of heroic pressure that was brought to bear, their number was increased by three and they became "The Dirty Dozen". The youths were the scions of Ottawa's aristocracy.

"You don't care for them?" asked Sullivan. "You wouldn't like Althea to behave in that way?"

The bare suggestion produced physical pain. "But, she wouldn't," cried Marjorie. "She *couldn't*, Mr. Sullivan! Not that they aren't very—er—bright," she added, seeking to say the kindly thing.

When they returned to the room, the girls were dressed in Mr. Barrington's clothing—business suits, riding breeks, pyjamas and underwear, while the boys had costumed themselves in their hostess's attire.

Marjorie kept telling herself that she was dreaming.

She longed to go home. She could neither enter into the revelry nor did she wish to separate herself from the crowd and stay alone with Sullivan. She had been very uncomfortable with him, lately. Sometimes, almost afraid. She refused to acknowledge this fear, even to herself, but she knew that it existed.

The conversation in the Gallery recurred to her with disturbing vividness—not that slander ever influenced her judgment—ever! The person who was swayed by unkind criticism was, in her opinion, no better than the person who uttered it. At the same time, there was something about the Hon. Member for Morroway from which she instinctively shrank, without suspecting that she was making, by her attitude, a confession of her secret impression of the man.

No amount of reasoning could correct this state of affairs. In vain did she tell herself that he was old enough to be her father, and that his frank affection for them all was merely the enthusiastic expression of a lonely man's dependence upon a kindly household. In vain did she try to overcome a sensation of shame and personal impurity after she had been alone with him.

"My own mind must be evil," she scourged herself, time and again. "He never has done or said a thing that Raymond couldn't know. What *does* make me feel so wicked when I'm alone with him?"

It may have been a sense of impotence that frightened her. She could never see the wheels of Mr. Sullivan's mind in operation, she could never tell what he was going to do. He seemed to arrive at a goal magically, without progressing step by step, and he had such an uncanny way of divining what she was thinking.

She was not conscious of his footfall, nor of the opening of the doors that admitted him to a closer intimacy, but suddenly, he would stand before her, very near to the Inner Shrine of her Temple, catching her, as it were, unclad, or in the act of prayer, and she couldn't put him out.

He was very quiet and respectful and walked as though aware that he was in a Holy place, but that didn't alter the fact that he had passed through those obstructing doors without a sound of warning, and without her permission.

And he took such shocking liberties. For example, Marjorie couldn't possibly have told how he had been allowed to contract the habit of kissing her. To be sure, it had begun in fun, one evening, when they were playing with the children. But she couldn't explain why she found it impossible to deny him the privilege thereafter. It was very curious and disturbing.

Perhaps her difficulty lay in the artful naturalness with which he performed his acts of pretty gallantry, taking so much for granted and trading on her clean simplicity.

"I don't want to behave so that he will think I have nasty notions," she said to herself, and Sullivan knew it.

"You're tired, dear," he said to her, not wholly inattentive to the Vaudeville on the other side of the room. "Lean back against me. Raymond won't be long, now!"

She felt his arm slip round her and moved away in sudden panic.

"Oh, Mr. Sullivan, not here, please!" she cried.

It wasn't in the least what she should have said; but there was no opportunity for explanations or corrections then.

"You're right, little woman," he whispered, "this is *not* the place. I understand."

It was only too obvious that he didn't; that he misconstrued her gentle repulse of all familiarity into a prudish discouragement of this particular expression of it, and his manner suggested satisfaction that she should prefer to receive his caresses when they were alone. It was a case of another door being opened and one which resisted her efforts to close it.

"I'd like to go home," she said. "Do you think you could find Raymond?"

The Hon. Member for Morroway knew his hostess too well to commit himself to a definite promise. But he murmured something hopeful and made his way with a good deal of bluster to the top of the house.

The door of the Eyrie was closed.

CHAPTER 16.

*M*eanwhile, Dilling had been an unwilling victim to Hebe Barrington's charms.

"Your wife is coming home with me for a bite of supper," she had written him, "and I want you, too. The bald truth is—I don't trust Toddles with a pretty woman, so you must be on hand to see her home."

But although he had signified his readiness to perform this happy task several times, she had made it impossible for him to break away.

"Don't you love my little nest?" asked Hebe, closing the door and leading him by the arm to a deep couch, standing well beyond the faint light thrown by a winking oriental lantern.

"It's very unusual," said Dilling.

"Everything here has a history," she told him, "but I won't tell you about any of my treasures just now. You need only know that this room is called the Eyrie, and I want you to feel that it is your own. Any time, day or night, that you want to run away from the abominations of politics, this place is ready for you. You need not even share it with me—if you don't wish."

"Thank you," muttered Dilling, seeing that she expected him to speak.

"And now, let's talk about your speech. It was tremendous! How easy it seems to be for you to avoid the feeble word and choose those that thrill one with a sense of power. Every fibre of my being was alive with response to you, to-night. But why didn't you look at me, Raymond?"

"I? Er—why—I didn't know that you were there," stammered the man who was supposed to avoid the trite and obvious.

"But why didn't you look and *see*?" insisted Hebe. "Is the admiration of mankind in general, and of woman in particular so unimportant? Does it give you no stimulation?"

"Oh, it isn't that," said Dilling.

He was very ill at ease. Admitting her intellectual attainments, yet he never enjoyed talking with Hebe Barrington as he enjoyed talking with Azalea. He was too conscious of her, too acutely aware of the fact that she sought to attach his scalp to her belt, his frail person to her chariot wheels. Instinctively, he was on his guard against a temptation to which he could not imagine himself surrendering.

"What is it, then?" she asked, passing her fingers through his thin hair.

As Marjorie recoiled from Sullivan, so Dilling tried to withdraw from the caresses of Mrs. Barrington. He had never received advances from women—decent women—and he was shocked, revolted. Even her use of his Christian name jarred unpleasantly upon him whose social standards decreed that although a man and woman might address one another familiarly before the marriage of either party, the instant they turned from the altar, rigid formality should be observed. To be called "Raymond" by a married woman whom he had known but a few weeks, smacked strongly of indecency.

"Is it possible that beneath your discomfiting iciness of manner," Hebe continued, "you want to attract men, hold them and make them your friends? Do you feel the need of friends, Raymond Dilling?"

"I am only human," he returned.

Suddenly he felt an overpowering urge to talk, an imperious need for candour. He wanted to open his heart, deplore his failures and the unfulfilment of his desires. He saw his inability to draw men to him, and surround them with a vivid atmosphere of comradeship in political endeavour and a common patriotic inspiration. He felt that men did not like him, that he would never be an adornment to their clubs, one upon whom the success of a social event depended. And, unaccountably, he realised that he cared—cared for himself, and for Marjorie, and for Azalea Deane. As though reading his thoughts, Hebe went on,

"You'll never do it as you are, Raymond. You are suffering the result of the habit contracted, I have learned, in your college days, when you withdrew yourself from all but the few who recognised your talents and thrust themselves upon you for your worldly, and other-worldly behoof. A native shyness of strangers and an inherited reluctance to spend money on the amenities of life, moved you to live in cloistered exclusiveness, when you should have been expanding your soul in joyous contact with your fellow men. Am I not right?"

"I don't think it was so bad as that," said Dilling, fighting against the stupefying effect of the perfume he had learned to associate with her.

"But it was! You avoided human contact, and only by such means is life rid of its tendency to become set and small. Don't you remember the French axiom, '*L'esprit de l'homme n'est malleable que dans sa jeunesse*'? You are still young, Raymond, but it is high time that you began remoulding. If you had only allowed yourself the Paganism of Youth, you would have spared yourself the Philistinism of Maturity."

"It's all very well to preach conviviality and *bon camaraderie*," Dilling returned, stung into making what he afterwards felt to be an undignified defence, "but you must remember that I couldn't afford to hold my own with the roisterers at college." He moved, with a gesture of impatience, beyond the reach of her marauding fingers. "It was not so much inherited caution as immediate limitations that made my 'exclusive cloistering' necessary. I put myself through college, you know," he added, with a touch of unconscious pride, "and I couldn't afford to enjoy it."

"But that's the very point—the very point I'm driving at," she triumphed. "If only you *had* spent beyond your means—if only once you had overstepped your limitations! We all do, all of us who have souls. One way or another, the artist is always spending. The lover never counts the cost. You can't—you shouldn't want to—reduce emotions to blue prints and specifications, and that's what you have done! Listen, Raymond, and forgive me if I offend you. There is a corner of your personality that lies fallow because its dull atmosphere refuses nourishment to artistic taste and sensuous beauty. In other words, you are afraid to spend, even now, lest the ultimate cost may prove to be something you think you can't afford. You are afraid to let yourself go, for emotions lead one even farther than the tangible medium of exchange." Her tone changed. "How you ever came to marry a pretty woman is something of a mystery to me—a frump would have answered just as well. Indeed, I ask myself, why did you ever marry at all. Will you tell me?"

"I don't think there's any mystery about it," parried Dilling.

He was not prepared to confess that love had played a very small part in his relations with Marjorie, nor that his need of her was more that of an amiable associate than wife. With the simplicity that marked so many of his social adventurings, he believed that when he could support a wife and family he should marry; and he chose the least objectionable—and most desirable externally—woman of his acquaintanceship. There was the explanation in a nutshell.

"Have you ever felt the appeal of sensuous beauty?" Hebe Barrington persisted. "No! I am answered. The very phrase revolts you as I speak it. It is an evocation of the Seventh Commandment and a ruined household. Queer fellow! Your insensibility to beauty in line and colour, not only in Art but in life, proclaims you a Philistine."

"You've called me that before."

"And I call you so again. You had no ear for the cry from Paxos, 'When you are come to Pallodes announce that the Great Pan is dead'," she cried theatrically. "Little you understand how it was that Pan's trumpet terrified and dispersed the Titans in their fight with the Olympian gods."

"You have a harsh opinion of me," said Dilling, a little nettled. "I thought I knew my classics."

"You read them—you bathed in their sensuous beauty, but you never felt it, Raymond, even while imagining that you were mewing a mighty youth of the intellect. Deluded boy," she murmured. "Blind boy!" Her hand fluttered over his face and rested upon his eyes. For the life of him he could not respond to this woman, but at the same time he made no definite resistance, judging that by so doing he would lay himself open to the charge of priggishness. Dilling had little dread of ridicule when he trod upon familiar ground, but of late he had realised how virginal he was in the social struggle. Quite still he sat, while Hebe Barrington's hands moved softly about him. He did not know that to her his unresponsiveness was incredible; the web she was weaving was as apparent to him as his power to break it. "It is not too late," she whispered, "to save yourself, to save your soul alive."

"Am I to take that as encouragement?" he enquired, with intentional rudeness.

"As the body in its vigour renews itself every seven years, so it is possible for the spirit to open its doors periodically upon new realms of percipience and creative power. Set about your own rebirth, Raymond! Don't imagine that you can achieve re-genesis by pondering the sources that gave the pagan Greek his apprehension, shall I say, of the joy of life. The Greek lived in a narrow time and in a narrow world, in spite of which he made living glorious. You, on the other hand, live in a big world where there is room for the coming of the superman. Oh, Raymond, lay hold of the sensuous beauty that lies within your very grasp. Come out of your barren cloister and inhale the warmth of the sun and perfume of the blossoming flowers! Mere intellect has never achieved perfect happiness for any man. He must develop his emotional nature in order to get the most life has to offer and in order that he may give her of his best," she added, quickly. "He must learn to understand men and women, and to understand them he must—live!"

"You seem to be very certain that I am one of the unburied dead!"

"Exactly! Every man who doesn't love is dead. Oh, don't point to your wife and children as contradictory evidence. You love neither, Raymond, I mean, with the love that is like a great, engulfing tide, the love that haunts and tortures, and racks and exalts. I mean the love that is like a deep, ecstatic pain, that simultaneously is a feast and a cruel hunger."

Her words poured over him like a warm scented flood. He was conscious of a curious desire to plunge his body into their deeps, to feel their heat and moisture. But the impression eluded him. He could not abandon himself to the enchantment Hebe Barrington was trying to cast over him. No glamorous mist blurred his vision. He saw with penetrating clarity, and his only sensation was one of distaste.

"I am of opinion that life can be useful without these exaggerated, emotional outbursts," said Dilling, "that where so much energy is expended in one direction the drain is felt in other lines of endeavour."

"But will you never open your eyes to the radiant truth that a great love is not a drain but a reservoir, a source of supply? It enlarges one's power and stimulates creation. Did not every conspicuous figure in history have his feminine complement, and is not at least a part of his achievement credited to the stimulation of an overmastering love?"

Dilling was not so sure. Average and sub-average persons, wholly unable to apprehend the subtle forces of will and intellect behind a great achievement, accept it with dull simplicity and dismiss it with a word of praise. But average and sub-average persons experiencing the driving power of emotion in varied degrees think themselves capable of understanding a sublime passion and therefore place it—perhaps unconsciously—ahead of intellectual accomplishment. In fine, we bring others down to our own level, a fact that explains why "human interest" and "heart interest" make a wider appeal than things that live and move and have their being on the higher plane of mind and spirit.

"I doubt it," he said, answering Hebe's question. "I doubt, for example, that Parnell's skill in leadership depended upon the dashing Kitty O'Shea, or that Nelson would have failed at Trafalgar save for Lady Hamilton."

"Do you mean that no *particular* woman is necessary to a man, or that emotional relationship between two persons of opposite sexes is over-estimated?"

"Either, and both," laughed Dilling, and rose. "But I really must find my wife. She will think I have deserted her, and, anyway, late hours are forbidden in our house. Shall we go down?"

But Hebe held him.

"Just a moment," she begged. "I can't allow you to leave me with a wrong impression. Oh, I know quite well how my conduct to-night must appear in your eyes—your blind eyes, Raymond, and it is not a sense of prudishness that impels me to explain that I do not throw myself at you for a narrow, personal satisfaction. It is true that I love you, but I love the big

You, the public man, the orator, the statesman, and I have a supreme longing to see you attain greater honours and bring greater glory to Canada. To achieve this, I am firmly convinced that a closed door in your nature must be opened. You are like a man working in artificial light. He can see, yes—but he attains results through greater strain than is immediately apparent and, therefore, his season of usefulness is lessened. There is sunshine, Raymond, and in its radiance, much of what was work becomes play. Love is my sunshine and is a miraculous creative force. With your frail body, you must draw power from an outside source, Raymond, and what other reservoir is there but Love? Listen, dear, just a moment more," she cried, tightening her arms about him. "I would rather see you love some other woman than not love at all, for I know that the awakening of your soul would be Canada's great gain. And now," she concluded, rising, "will you kiss me before you go?"

Dilling hesitated, and in that instant's delay a step sounded on the stair and a gentle tattoo beat upon the door.

"Come in," cried Hebe, crossly. "Oh, Uncle Rufus, we were just going down!"

CHAPTER 17.

*R*epresenting the constituency of Morroway by no means exhausted the dynamic energy of the Hon. Rufus Sullivan, and he had ample time for engaging in pursuits of a tenderer and more congenial nature. But occasions did arise when concentration upon Parliamentary problems became a necessary part of the day's routine, for they affected not only the political standing of the Hon. Member, but the size and stability of his income.

He sat alone in his office, oblivious for the moment, of the heavy gilt mirror that hung opposite his desk, and to the contents of the drawer marked "Unfinished Business". He glared unwinkingly into space, forgetful of the existence of a fluffy-haired little manicurist who sat waiting for him in an over-decorated, under-lighted apartment of his choosing. Sullivan was carefully reviewing each step taken at the caucus he had just attended, and satisfying himself that his own part in the proceedings would react in an advantageous manner.

The anticipated vacancy in the Cabinet had occurred, and the inevitable complications had developed. Howarth stepped modestly into the spotlight, and put forth claims that were not without justification. Gilbert, the Radical, stood out as an advocate for Reciprocity and felt the power of the Middle West behind him. Dilling, more or less thrust into the contest, was supported by the phalanxes of Eastlake and Donahue, and opposed any such trafficking with the United States.

Sullivan endorsed him.

This was an extraordinary thing. Even Howarth was surprised, and no one found it more unaccountable than Dilling, himself.

The constituency of Morroway was divided on the Reciprocity issue, but the preponderance of sentiment was favourable. This involved a little difficulty for the Hon. Member, who did not approve it although he was confident that in securing the measure, the Borden Government would in no way imperil the existence of Canadian Federation. On the contrary, Mr. Sullivan was secretly—oh, very secretly!—of the opinion that unrestricted Reciprocity with the United States would be the most effective antidote to the disintegration sentiment with which our National wells are being poisoned. He believed that it would mean peace, plenty, and a renewed ambition amongst a class of people in whom hope had almost died; that its immediate result would be employment in lieu of discontented idleness, and an instantaneous circulation of money. He saw clearly the advantage that would accrue to the fishermen of British Columbia and the Maritime

Provinces, were they able to dispose of their perishable merchandise quickly in the American market at a maximum price and a minimum cost for transportation. He saw also that the Quebec and Ontario farmers could sell to the Middle States at an advanced profit, while the grain speculators of the Prairies could offer their wheat in the Chicago pit before it was harvested and at the lowest possible figure for haulage. Moreover, Mr. Sullivan realised that there would be no congestion at the freight terminals, because cars would be moving north and south as well as east and west; and, furthermore, the railways of both countries would be co-operating.

Nor did he overlook the fact that the prairie farmers could buy their implements at fifty per cent less than present prices for Canadian manufactures—a Utopian condition for which every man with large holdings ardently prayed according to the particular doctrine he professed.

But Mr. Sullivan opposed Reciprocity. For years he had opposed it. He held a considerable number of bonds issued by the Grand Trunk Pacific, which though guaranteed by the Government of Canada must inevitably depreciate if the silver stream continued to be diverted from the National coffers in to the channels fashioned by Eastlake and Donahue—those enterprising exponents of the cult whose treasure lies in earthen vessels. He also happened to be heavily invested in Eastern industrial corporations. Long ago, Mr. Sullivan had decided that anything less than an impregnable tariff barrier between the United States and Canada would spell his financial obliteration.

Therefore, although it irked him to lift a finger towards Dilling's political advancement, and although he found it extremely difficult to justify his support in the face of his traditional opposition to Eastlake and Donahue, Mr. Sullivan threw the weight of his influence against Howarth, who expected it, and Gilbert, who hoped for it, in order that Dilling might obtain the portfolio.

"In him we have a specimen of a genuine twentieth century man," he argued, "one who actually believes there is such a thing as a British Constitution. He prints it in CAPITALS, (God save us all!) and he loves it with as much veneration as the younger Pitt. Furthermore, he believes that the incredible utterance of Pitt, in 1784, is true to-day and forever—'The British Constitution,' he said, 'is equally free from the distractions of democracy and the tyranny of monarchy. It is the envy of the world . . .'

"For myself," the Hon. Member continued, "I think that Dilling is the best debater we have had in the Commons since Confederation. He eclipses Cartwright—the best of his day—because when that strict economist fell a victim to his own high temper, he swapped logic for vituperation and lost the ear of the Big Men of the House; he is a match for

Denby, who too often talks to Hansard and the Galleries, and too seldom comes to grips with his antagonists on the floor of the Chamber. When, I ask you, gentlemen, has Sir Eric ever influenced a vote on a Division?

"Dilling, on the other hand, captures both parties by his earnestness, and his logic is as irrefragable as his temper is cold. Although I have heard him declare that he despises rhetoric, yet we all know his ability to draw deep from the pure wells of English undefiled. What Horace Walpole said of the youthful Fox as a debater, could be as aptly applied to Dilling . . . . 'Cicero's laboured orations are puerile in comparison with this boy's manly reason'."

The Hon. Member brought his remarks to a climax by terming Gilbert a traitor, charging Borden with political locomotor ataxia for making no effort to stem the tide of Western opinion towards the Reciprocity movement, and pronounced it treason against the Imperial Crown—thus serving at one and the same time, his ambition and his pocket-book.

The contest was short and sharp. It was universally recognised—even by those who held divergent political opinions and were personally antipathetic—that Dilling was the man for the Cabinet, and Sullivan's speech left them no alternative but to support him.

Howarth and Turner rattled the handle of the door and demanded admission. Sullivan complied jauntily, giving no sign of the mental struggle in which he had been engaged. Indeed, at the moment of their entrance, he recalled the gilt mirror that hung opposite his desk, the drawer marked "Unfinished Business" and the fact that a little manicurist was disconsolately awaiting him.

With an admirable gesture of preoccupation, he concerned himself with the telephone.

"Is that my dearie?" he questioned into the instrument. "Forgotten? 'Pon my soul, I hadn't! Simply couldn't break away . . . eh? Yes, in my office, certainly . . . No, there was no thought of another party. . . . Well, I won't come if you are going to be cross . . . Promise? All right . . . within five minutes . . ."

The business that was never finished while the three of them lived, was placed upon the desk and uncorked. Sullenly, two men drank, while the third tossed off his portion and then consulted his reflection with meticulous care.

"Sorry," he said, "but I must rush off. Exacting little devils—these women. *Très exigèante*, as our French friends say. But help yourselves, boys, and lock the drawer when you leave—that is if you have the grace to leave anything!"

His flair met with no response.

"Damned if I can understand you, Sullivan," Howarth burst out. "Here, for months, we've been trying to freeze Dilling to death, and keep the E. D. Co. from establishing a firmer foothold in Parliament, and now you turn right round and boost him into the Cabinet. Surely, one of us is crazy!"

"Only under stress, old man! Ordinarily, you are merely peculiar," returned Sullivan, with a smile.

"Gilbert's a much safer man," Howarth went on, "to say nothing of any qualification *I* may possess."

"Yes," Turner cut in, "what the devil were you thinking of, Rufus? Didn't Bill, here, deserve your support?"

"Neither of you would believe me if I were to tell you my reason for backing Dilling's claims," said the Hon. Member for Morroway, feeling that he must make some sort of explanation.

"Let's have it, anyway," said Howarth.

"Well—er—" confessed the other man, pulling on his gloves, "I acted according to my best judgment in the interest of the whole country."

"Oh, hell!" remarked Mr. Turner, M.P.

"I've been asked to swallow many a big mouthful," cried Howarth, "but this one chokes me."

"And granting this noble patriotism—this alarmingly noble patriotism, I might say—" sneered Turner "why such sudden interest in the welfare of our fair Dominion?"

"By God!" breathed Howarth. "I believe in my soul that that little baby-faced simpleton has put one over on you, Rufus! She's got you halter-broke and working for her husband!"

"Mrs. Dilling?" echoed Turner, incredulously.

"No fool like an old fool," quoted his friend. "I've become accustomed to seeing him lose his heart over a fine pair of shoulders and a well-turned ankle, but I'm damned if I ever thought he would lose his head!"

Sullivan paused with his hand on the door.

"It strikes me, Billy," he said, "that disappointment makes you rather coarse. Forgive my seeming inhospitality, gentlemen, but I dare not keep a lady waiting."

As he turned from the bright thoroughfare into a shadowy street, Mr. Sullivan was not free from disturbing reflections. This was a big game he played, and one that admitted of miscalculations. He tried to keep before him its analogy to Chess, when a man sees ultimate gain developing out of a temporary triumph won by his opponent. He tried to assure himself that he had been wise in helping Dilling to victory as a means whereby to accomplish his swifter defeat. Only the short-sighted player tries to vanquish his foe at every turn.

There was nothing small about Rufus Sullivan. Even his defamers granted him a largeness that extended to his very vices. He sinned, but he sinned grandly, with a *joie de vivre* that was lacking in the righteous deeds of confessed Christians. He loved readily and hated magnificently, but he did not begrudge the object of his hatred a modicum of pleasure. So, in this matter, he could look with equanimity upon Dilling's attainment of the Ministership and feel no envy at his brief success.

For it *must* be brief . . . and yet . . .

As he swung along, his eyes fixed on a window where a balloon of rose light swayed out into the darkness, the Hon. Member for Morroway realised that such schemes had been known to fail. By some totally unforeseen miracle, the anticipated downfall had not occurred, and men had lived to bite the hand that so calculatingly fed them. Would Dilling prove to be one of these exceptions? Would he survive to frustrate Rufus Sullivan's ambitions?

These and other cogent problems engaged the Hon. Member throughout the ensuing hours. The taffy-haired manicurist found him abstracted and singularly unresponsive.

CHAPTER 18.

*T*he new Minister wore his honours with such an utter absence of hauteur, that, to many persons his manner was wanting in the dignity they had been taught to associate with the position.

Never cordial and rarely responsive, Dilling now made the unfortunate error of trying to be both, and few there were possessed of sufficient astuteness to recognise in his changed attitude, a sincerity as native to him as it was embarrassing. Most people saw only the insinuating affability of the professional politician and added another black mark to his already heavy score.

Marjorie, on the other hand, half-convinced that by following the advice of Lady Denby and Azalea, her "stiffness" had been a factor in securing Dilling the appointment, redoubled her efforts to appear ungracious—with the result that the indifference of many acquaintances crystallised into active dislike.

"They're experimenting with *receets* for popularity," remarked Mrs. Pratt to her social rival, Mrs. Prendergast. "I don't mind anybody being popular," she graciously conceded, "if I don't have to see how they go about it. But this business," she jerked her head towards the Dillings, "is, in my opinion, perfeckly disgusting!"

The ladies sat in a corner of the Royal Ottawa Golf Club, and although they had just partaken of a dinner given in honour of Raymond Dilling, their mien was far from congratulatory. They had made astonishing progress in their ascent towards Society's Parnassian Heights, and once a week, at least, their names appeared in the local calendar of fame.

Mrs. Pratt employed the methods of a battering ram, charging through obstructions with ruthless vigour, and indifferent alike to wounds inflicted or received. She spent her money shrewdly, squeezing double its worth from every dime. Even her victims respected her.

Mrs. Prendergast adopted the opposite course. She slithered through the barriers lying in her path sublimely unaware that they were supposed to be barriers. It was related of her that one morning, happening to shop in a store sanctified by the immediate presence of a party from Government House, she preceded the Governor's lady down a cleared passage, passed first through the door held open by an apoplectic Aide-de-Camp, and bestowed upon that young gentleman a gracious, if bovine, smile. She spent the proceeds from Prendergast's ANTI-AGONY ALIMENT lavishly, using two dollars to accomplish the work of one, with regal unconcern. Slowly, she was buying her way onward and upward.

Both she and Mrs. Pratt entertained—if one may be permitted so euphemistic a word—with resolute frequency. Mrs. Pratt rarely received anyone less important than a Senator, now, and Mrs. Prendergast had recently dined a lady, honourable in her own right. The fact was chronicled in the Montreal papers and also in SATURDAY NIGHT.

Both ladies saw the advantage of making their homes a rendezvous for the young, and using their children's friends as a bridge, however precarious, to that happy land where Society dwelt. Moreover, both expressed the resentment of their class against one who, in their judgment, had been exalted above her station, and from that altitude demanded homage from people not only just as good but far better, i.e., themselves. There was no limit to the servility they would offer an unworthy aristocrat, but a deserving member of the bourgeoisie—never!

"How do you mean 'experimenting'?" asked Mrs. Prendergast, referring to her friend's remark.

"Well, it's hard to explain," said Mrs. Pratt, "in so many words, that is." The implication here was somewhat veiled. How many words legitimately belonged to an explanation, Mrs. Pratt didn't know. But Mrs. Prendergast was not embarrassingly curious, so she continued.

"When they first came, *he* was the disagreeable one, so superior and grumpy you couldn't get a word out of him."

"Yes," assented the other. "I remember saying to the Dawkter that it must be very trying to be married to a mute."

"On the other hand, *she* was just the opposite—apparently trying to cover up his grouchiness and bad manners. I don't know whether you understand me, Mrs. Prendergast?"

"Oh, yes! Oh, certainly," cried Mrs. Prendergast, emphatic in defence of her intelligence. "I understand exactly. Indeed, I remember saying to the Dawkter that I found her quite a pleasant little thing."

"Well, she's fur from pleasant, now! Heaven knows I try to see good in everybody, but rully, Mrs. Prendergast, I think I may be purdoned for saying that by the airs she puts on, you'd think she was a member of the Royal family! And now that *he* has been given such a prominent position in the Party—can you blame me for asking what is politics coming to?"

Mrs. Prendergast hastened to assure her that such a question was blameless. She was not vitally interested in politics nor the intrigues that grew out of Party differences, and it concerned her very little who occupied the positions of prominence. That they should appreciate her and those belonging to her was a matter of far greater importance.

She cherished an ambition to be associated with the "Old Families" of the Capital—those who regarded the ever-changing political element with disfavour. Substantial clubs appealed to her—the Rideau for her husband, the Minto for her children, the Laurentian Chapter, I.O.D.E., for herself, and the Royal Ottawa for them all. As a matter of fact, she and the Doctor had just been admitted as Life Members of the latter. In the ordinary course of procedure, they might have waited twenty-years.

A banging of doors and loud commotion in the hallway prevented further conversation, and Hebe Barrington, surrounded by a group of Naughty Niners, danced breezily into the room. Seeing Dilling, she ran forward and caught him by both arms.

"Congratulations, Raymond!" she cried. "I've been out of town or you would have had them sooner. Aren't you very proud and happy? Your friends are, for you! Whose funeral is this?" she demanded looking with gay impudence over the group. "Ugh! I can guess. One of these deadly Party affairs, given—of course—in your honour! How do you do, Mrs. Dilling? Why, hello, Mr. Pratt . . . *and* Doctor Prendergast!" She extended a naked left arm and shook hands across the enraged head of Lady Denby. "Come along with us, Raymond. We're going to dance. Mona Carmichael will teach us some new convolutions, so to speak. Come!"

In a low, embarrassed voice, Dilling demurred.

"Oh, stuff and nonsense! They won't miss you. And, besides, a Minister must acquire a bagful of lightsome parlour tricks, otherwise he'll be monstrously heavy wheeling. Gaze upon this company, Raymond, and take warning!"

She laughed gaily, ignoring the tensity with which the atmosphere was charged.

"Seize him!" she cried. "Lay violent hands upon him, and if he struggles, smother him—with affection."

Half a dozen boys and girls rushed forward and dragged Dilling away. As Hebe moved off after them, Pratt called out to her.

"Won't you take me, Mrs. Barrington? I may be a Minister some day—you never can tell." He bravely avoided his wife's eyes.

"You shall be my particular charge," retorted Hebe with well-feigned delight. Mr. Pratt bored her inexpressibly. He was rapidly acquiring the manner of the professional politician, who looks upon every individual as a vote and who conducts himself as though life were a perpetual election campaign. He had the air of one who thinks he is the soul of the very party, moving about from group to group, telling ancient political stories as having happened to himself, and releasing at set and stated intervals, borrowed and well-worn epigrams.

Certainly, Hebe did not find the companionship of Augustus Pratt inspiring, but just now it pleased her to pretend the contrary and bear him off beneath the battery of angry eyes the women trained upon her.

As they moved towards the door and his rather moist hand caressed her unclad elbow, she said in a loud voice,

"None but the immediate relatives of the deceased followed the body to the grave . . . I don't wonder people have wakes, do you, dear Mr. Pratt? Solemnity in massive doses is so depressing. Have you tried the Argentine? It's enchanting! You take three steps to the right . . ."

A brief silence followed their exit. The women glowered at Mrs. Pratt and Marjorie Dilling as though they were personally responsible for their husbands' defection. The men fidgetted and offered one another fresh cigarettes.

Lady Denby drew her lips into a thin line and remarked to Madame Valleau who was choking back a yawn,

"I do wish that woman would wear some clothes! It simply infuriates me to see her going abroad like that!"

The Frenchwoman smiled.

"Perhaps that is why she does it."

"I don't know what you mean, and I don't see anything funny," Lady Denby retorted.

"One observes so much! For myself, I think it very funny you do not realise that instead of dressing to please men, as most people think, women dress to annoy other women. Consider yourself, *par example* and this gay Madame Barrington! There, you see?"

The gay Madame Barrington presented a violently contrasting appearance the following morning, as she lay on the Eyrie Chesterfield and consumed a box of Russian cigarettes.

Her eyes were heavy and dull. Her complexion, wearing the make-up of the night previous, looked thick and dead. Over her citron-tinted sleeping robe she had flung an inadequate *batik* garment that required continuous adjustment or reclaiming from the floor.

Sharp spears of light thrust themselves between the close-drawn mulberry curtains, and sought out the vulnerable spots in Hebe's housekeeping. A thin film of dust lay on a teakwood table; flakes of ash and tobacco strewed the floor. A stale odour combining scent, cigarettes and anise-seed hung in the still air.

Mr. Sullivan, correct in new spring tweeds, lay back in an easy chair and absently caressed the glass he held in his hand. Beside him on the table, stood a decanter and syphon.

He sniffed, with disapproving discernment.

"Do you find absinthe a satisfying beverage, my dear?"

"Oh, as satisfying as any other."

"Well, tastes differ . . . and stomachs. For my part, I'm afraid of the stuff. The less subtle and more reliable Scotch is good enough for me, although there are occasions, it goes without saying, when the bouquet of a fine wine is somewhat more acceptable. I am fond of a high grade of Burgundy, and am unique, I believe, in fancying a glass of old Madeira, which, by the way, is not adequately appreciated among the English people."

Hebe watched him sullenly, but said nothing.

"It was during the French war that our soldiers made the discovery of this delectable drink, and it was they who carried the taste for it back to England, where, I admit, its flavour deteriorates. Climate probably, though there are some who maintain that Englishmen don't know how to keep it."

"Why did you come to see me?" Hebe asked the Hon. Member, bluntly.

She lit a fresh cigarette and dragged her negligée from the floor, knowing that Mr. Sullivan had not called upon her to discuss the virtues of various intoxicants. She suspected that the real object of his visit would be even less agreeable as a topic of conversation. Her feeling towards Mr. Sullivan could never be accurately described as blind adoration, but this morning she unqualifiedly hated him.

"Why *did* you come here at such an hour, Uncle Rufus? You know how I loathe to be disturbed early in the day. I'm never human till noon."

"The artistic temperament is interesting in all its phases," murmured Mr. Sullivan, suavely.

"Don't be funny!"

"Nothing is further from my intention. With perfect gravity I assert that a woman is infinitely appealing to me in her gentler moods. Her fragility, her beautiful feminine weakness ... She inspires me with overwhelming tenderness ... And how doubly charming when her verve returns." He smiled, reflectively, at the tip of his boots.

"Oh, drop that nonsense and tell me what brings you here!"

"Well, my dear Hebe, I must plead a stupid man's irresistible desire to discuss a somewhat delicate situation—albeit of his own making—with the cleverest woman of his acquaintance."

"Bosh!"

"The unadulterated truth, I assure you. I am paying you no idle compliment, my child."

"Thanks," said Hebe, shortly. "Go on."

"I succumbed to the imperious need for feminine companionship, sympathy, understanding."

"Eliminate the first two."

"Charming naïveté! Delicious frankness! Hebe, you enchant me!" The Hon. Member drained his glass, touched his lips with a lavender handkerchief and beamed upon his sulky hostess. "But, tell me, what do you think of our new Minister?"

"You know what I think. Not that my opinion matters a damn!"

"A mistake, my dear. If you approve of the appointment, then your opinion coincides with my own, and that, in itself, lends it some importance. I feel that Dilling is the very man for the post ..."

"... which is the very best reason in the world for your opposition to his securing it."

Sullivan laughed, indulgently. He raised his cuff and consulted the face of his watch.

"In ten minutes," said he, "you will be human. Meanwhile, may I help myself?"

The hiss of a syphon filled the room and Hebe stretched out her hand for the glass. For a space neither of them spoke, and then the midday gun sounded its message over the city.

"Now," said the Hon. Member for Morroway, "what about this business with Dilling?"

"I can't do anything. I've tried."

Mr. Sullivan protested that she hardly did herself justice. "A woman of your age—er—experience," he tactfully amended, "*and* talents . . ." He smiled benignly at her. "Now is your golden opportunity. The more prominent his position, the more conspicuous he becomes, and every act is subject to criticism."

"I tell you I can't do it."

"Don't be so childish. The world talks of men compromising women, but that's a difficult task compared with the ease with which women compromise men. What's the matter? Are your weapons rusty with disuse? It seems to me that only just before you came up here I heard rumours of . . . Oh, but let that pass! The point is now, that there must be no further dallying. Before's there's any possibility of his obtaining any hold on the country, Dilling must go, must hang himself, must dig his own grave and bury himself! It's up to you!"

Hebe avoided his glance, and, as he regarded her, a change came over him. His suavity vanished, his smile disappeared, as his lips set themselves into firmer lines. In his eyes, tiny hot sparks gleamed like pinpoints of fire. There awoke in Mr. Sullivan's breast a disturbing suspicion.

"What's the matter?" he repeated. "Why don't you drag him through the streets at your chariot wheels—as is your playful wont? Let people see that this zealous prophet who preaches righteousness and a higher idealism, is bitten no deeper by his fine doctrine than is the average disciple of orthodoxy. Get busy, girl; get busy!"

"He won't respond," muttered Hebe. "He's different."

"Bah! *You're* different—that's the trouble. I'm half inclined to believe you've fallen for this aesthetic milk-veined Parliamentarian—that you've become the victim instead of the victor—that you have allowed your undisciplined emotions to play you tricks. But by God! you shan't play any on me! I'm a bad man to double cross, Hebe, and don't lose sight of that for an instant. You undertook to see this thing through . . . now, go to it!"

"I tell you it can't be done! I've worked like a dog, and anyhow, there's nothing in it for me—nothing but humiliation . . . Besides," she added, with seeming irrelevance, "I can't live on Toddles' salary!"

Mr. Sullivan laughed as he made his way to the door. With the knob in his hand he turned, and observed,

"I know you can't! Moreover, I know you *don't* . . . my dear!"

CHAPTER 19.

*E*verybody now called upon Marjorie. Even the A.D.C.'s from Government House were to be found at her receptions on Monday afternoons. Invitations poured in upon her. She was an integral part of Canada's official life, and her presence was deemed necessary at all public assemblages. Socially, she was accounted of importance, and her attendance at private affairs lent to them that subtle odour of distinction which—with a fine disregard for principle—democracy loves to inhale. Tradespeople solicited her custom, agents waited upon her pleasure and her patronage was sought for a bewildering variety of functions.

She found herself in the hands of exploiters, who called at all hours, with slight excuse or no excuse, to crave favours or heap them upon her, with high hope that she would liquidate the debt in social currency, and Marjorie never learned to deny herself to these people. She was more embarrassed than flattered by their ambiguous attentions, and was positively distressed at having to take precedence over those who, but yesterday, had snubbed her.

Life became a round of perplexing complications, and she yearned for the peace and quiet that used to be hers at home.

Then, too, she was worried by the fierce light of publicity that played upon her. Interviewers distorted her timid utterances in half a dozen metropolitan papers. Illustrated weeklies requested her photograph for publication. Local reporters took a sudden and absorbing interest in her gowns, and the gatherings at which she was expected to wear them— gatherings, which, under other conditions, would not have attracted the Press by so much as a line.

"The Sweet Arbutus Club enjoyed the distinction of entertaining Mrs. Raymond Dilling at its annual supper on Thursday evening. The President of the Club, Mrs. Horatio Gullep, received the members, and little Miss Ermyntrude Polduggan presented the distinguished guest with a shower bouquet of white carnations. The Secretary, Mrs. (Dr.) Deitrich, and the Treasurer, Miss Emmeline Crogganthorpe, presided at the supper table, while the following young ladies assisted . . . Throughout the evening several delightful selections were rendered by the Club Orchestra, consisting of the Messrs. . . . and the Misses . . . Mrs. (Rev.) Muldoon charmed her audience with three recitations, and the programme was brought to a close with a chorus sung by seven dainty little maidens all under the age of seven . . ."

This was the sort of thing that Mrs. Long claimed not to have read and that drove Lady Denby to a state closely akin to frenzy.

"I never saw anyone so intractable," she cried to Azalea. "You would think that she actually preferred those awful people!"

"I believe they are ardent workers in the church," murmured Azalea.

"Even so! Church work should be encouraged, and I admire her for undertaking so much of it. But you know as well as I do, Azalea, that a Minister's wife has her own peculiar duties to perform, and they are not fundamentally concerned with—"

"Church workers," suggested the girl.

"Well, I mean to say that she needn't be afraid we will contaminate her. There *are* Christians outside the Church."

"I'm glad to hear you say so, Lady Denby! There certainly aren't many in it."

"Child! How can you think of such things?"

"You flatter me," returned Azalea. "It's not original. Nietzsche gave me the idea. He said there was but one Christian, and Him they crucified."

Lady Denby was outraged by this blasphemy. She was not the only person who thought Azalea Deane had developed an unpleasant emancipation since the death of her father, and she took this occasion to mention her feeling in the matter.

"I have nothing to say against the Civil Service," she concluded, "but I have noticed that so many of the women who enter it acquire an air of independence that is unbecoming to a lady. I am speaking as a friend, and for your own good, my dear, so I trust that you will give heed to what I say."

"Thank you, Lady Denby," murmured Azalea. "Now to return to the Dillings—"

"You *must* make her see that these parochial affairs should not claim her attention."

"I have tried to make her see that, but it is difficult. You will remember that her creed is a literal acceptance of the golden rule. Indeed, she is literal in everything."

Lady Denby sighed. "Well, keep on trying. Upon my word, I think the world is turning upside down! Where *are* the nice young people, nowadays? Why couldn't she have been like Helena Chesley or Eva Leeds, or the Angus-McCallums, or—er—even you? You would have made him a very good wife, Azalea!"

Azalea turned a painful scarlet, but Lady Denby was too deeply immersed in her own trend of thought to notice her companion's confusion or to read its meaning.

"There seem to be but two types of young woman," she complained, "hers, and the one represented by that terrible Barrington person. Of the two I almost incline towards the latter. At least, she would give some tone to the Party."

"I grant it."

"Don't misunderstand me, Azalea! You know well enough what I mean. She has a manner . . . On the other hand, here is a young couple, qualified in many respects to adorn not only the Party but the Dominion. Heaven knows we need his brains. Except for a few of the older men, notably my husband, the country can't muster enough to fill a good-sized thimble! But what do they make of their gifts! Nothing! Less than nothing! They ignore advice, scorn convention and, unless they suffer a radical change of heart, they will undermine the foundations of the very structure which has made them, by refusing to adapt themselves to the exigencies of their official position. Can you imagine him a Prime Minister, representing Canada abroad—for example, at an Imperial Conference?"

"Yes, I can!" flared Azalea. "And furthermore, I can imagine that in a broader field, associating with bigger people, Raymond Dilling would be accepted at his genuine worth. Proportions would be adjusted, and the gifts he undoubtedly possesses would shine with a brilliance undimmed by the shadow of his humble origin. I mean to say," she went on, "a shadow that is formed, locally, by petty insistence upon a matter that is of no importance. Here, in this trivial atmosphere, heavy with a spurious culture, most of us regard the position as less significant than the man. We expect him to adorn his office, and the manner in which he wears his mantle means more to us than the manner in which he administers his public duty."

"Fine feathers . . ." began Lady Denby.

"Moreover," continued Azalea, unheeding the interruption, "we are impressed with his personality first and his political integrity later. People of a different calibre would relegate the mantle to its proper place, and Dilling, the orator, the statesman, would come into his own. Do you suppose," she cried, with more heat than she realised, "that the men who mould our Imperial policies are influenced in their estimate of Raymond Dilling's usefulness to Canada—to the Empire, indeed—by considerations of his talents and inflexibility of purpose, or by his adherence to custom in wearing a black tie or a white?"

"Now you are being stupid, Azalea," pronounced Lady Denby. "Conventions cannot be broken without harming both the offender and the cause he represents. There never has been a telling argument in favour of conventionality, yet it persists. My charwoman may be *gauche* and amuse me, but similar behavior on the part of Lady Elton, for example, would disgust me and kill my respect."

"But the Dillings are *not gauche*," Azalea defended. "I know few words that could be more inaptly applied to them. Mrs. Pratt is *gauche*, for if she followed her instincts she would do the clumsy, cruel and vulgar thing. The Dillings, on the other hand, do the orderly, kind and decent thing. They make no pretence, use no lacquer or veneer. If they err at all, it is not due to *gaucherie*, but utter simplicity. They do not think that it becomes them to ape or assume the manner of the great. They even go so far as to be *logical*, which is the last attribute that one should have to be socially presentable. Oh, why, Lady Denby," she cried, "*why* can't people let them alone, stop this carping criticism, and applaud, if they won't follow, the fine example that is being set them? As a man thinketh . . ."

They parted in some constraint, Lady Denby unpleasantly stirred by the truth behind Azalea's championship, and Azalea quivering with indignation at the unreasonableness of such attacks upon the Dillings. Never had she hated her townsfolk more bitterly than at this moment. "They are like a swarm of vicious wasps," was her thought, as she raced along through the mild spring night, "stinging a lovely and unoffending body until its sweetness is absorbed and its beauty marred."

And Azalea was alive to another sensation. Above the clamour of her directed thinking, Lady Denby's words rushed unbidden into her mind, and would not be dislodged.

"You would have made him a good wife, Azalea!"

"God," she thought, "why must life be so cruel? Why is it that some of us are denied not only the privilege of having, but even that of giving? I could give him so much . . . so much . . ."

A verse filtered through her memory. It was the cry of Ibsen's *Agnes*, and it spoke to her own heavy heart:

"Through the hours that drag so leaden,

Think of me shut out of sight

Of the struggle's beacon-light;

Think of me who cannot ask

Aught beyond my petty task;

Think of me beside the ember

Of a silent hearthstone set,

Where I dare not all remember

And I cannot all forget . .."

CHAPTER 20.

Sleep eluded her. Wide awake, she lay on her back, staring into the tepid darkness and listening to the whisper of a thin, spring rain. Her thoughts were of Raymond Dilling.

Only at night, beyond the reach of prying eyes, did Azalea dare to open the doors of her soul's concealment. Only then did she allow herself the freedom of the emotion that possessed her, and enjoy the warmth of a communion that no one could suspect. Her thoughts were like perfumed caresses ... tender, delicate, and as they held him in sweet contact, she glowed with the reflection of their radiance, conscious that her entire being was suffused with a light—an ectoplasm—visible to the naked eye.

To-night, however, her thoughts were poisoned with acute bitterness. The world, as Lady Denby had said, was upside down. Clamouring for justice, it offered high reward for iniquity, nepotism and refined knavery of every colour.

"Give us Honour and Idealism," cried the voice of the People, "but give them to us garbed in the motley of hypocrisy and alluring vice. If you must be good, disguise yourself, so that you are still a knave and a rattling good fellow!"

Would the Public—that vague, vast body, of which none of us acknowledges himself a member—never come to the realisation that in Raymond Dilling the country had the man for whom it sought, a man of magnificent honesty, courage and fidelity to high purpose; a man whose talents were devoted to more lasting matters than the wearing of a morning coat, and the sequence of forks at a dinner-table? Would the Public never see that to him these things were non-essentials? Beau Brummel, she reminded herself with angry vehemence, spent several hours daily conferring with his tailor, and doubtless both found the association profitable. A pilot, on the other hand, has time—during the pursuit of his calling—for no such recreation. That he guide his ship through shoal and reef, fog and other dangers of the sea, is all that is required of him. Nor is he adjudged a less worthy pilot because he appears unshaven to steer his vessel into port.

Which did Canada need—a Beau Brummel to lend her picturesqueness in the Council of the Nations, or a pilot to guide the destiny of her Ship of State through the reefs of ready disaster?

Into her mind came the story of a young man who climbing in the Alps, lost his footing and was hurled to his death in the glacier hundreds of feet below. One of his companions, a scientist, computed that at the end of so many years, the body would reappear as the glacier moved towards a certain outlet. On the date specified, a group of the youth's friends gathered at the spot signified, to see if the computation would prove correct.

It did. There, before the company of old men, battered and scarred in their struggles against life, lay the body of the boy—fair and unsullied as on the day he had left them.

Azalea wondered whether Raymond Dilling, having climbed so far along the treacherous crags of politics, must lose his foothold and plunge into a glacier of oblivion; and she wondered, passionately, if such had to be, would he emerge after a lapse of years, beautiful and fair, to reproach the country that had rejected him.

Azalea was, perhaps, the only person who saw Dilling's reaction to Public Opinion. Universally, he was supposed to be indifferent, a man of stone, impervious alike to enmity and friendship. But she could recall half a dozen instances when the lack of sympathy—more difficult to endure than active opposition—from men whose warm approbation he richly deserved, filled him with corroding discouragement. She knew that he felt his isolation keenly, and was depressed by it.

Her thoughts turned to this new appointment, and her happiness for him was dulled by the manner in which Ottawa had received it. There had been noticeably lacking the warmth of genuine congratulation that made formal expression of it acceptable. The Press of the Dominion and many foreign countries commented enthusiastically upon the Government's action, and paid a worthy tribute to the young Minister, but the people amongst whom the Dillings lived, were lukewarm and perfunctory. Azalea knew that to Raymond, the honour—the cloak—was cold, and that he shivered as he wore it.

She wondered what he thought about the attitude of Rufus Sullivan. There was something altogether extraordinary in the support of the Hon. Member for Morroway. Azalea did not agree with certain organs of the Press that credited him with sinking private considerations in the interest of public weal. She did not believe in the sincerity of Mr. Sullivan's vaunted Imperialism. Unable to find any proof for her suspicions, yet she came very near the truth in listening to the warning of her instinct.

Of Mr. Sullivan's private affairs, she knew nothing. Nor of his ambitions. Amongst his friends—and he had friends!—he was not adjudged an ambitious man. He kept modestly out of the Press, and appeared in Hansard only often enough to satisfy his rather easygoing constituents. He never gave interviews. Interviews, he had observed, had an unpleasant way of rising to condemn one. It was safer not to espouse a cause, for then one could not be accused of inconstancy when one disavowed it.

This reticence on the part of Mr. Sullivan was variously regarded as humility towards those of superior wisdom, and an almost extinct distaste for publicity. There were many who thought that save for a certain moral obliquity, Mr. Sullivan was a very fine man!

But Azalea distrusted him. With the feminine shrewdness that is really a manifestation of Bergsonian intuition, she saw his modesty as caution, and naturally inferred that caution is only necessary when one has something to conceal. The fact that he never declared himself definitely upon any stand, made her suspicious of his enthusiastic support of Dilling. Azalea sensed treachery behind it.

Scattered bits of gossip, an odd suggestion dropped here and there, unremarked at the time, rose now to the surface of her mind, and strengthened her case against Rufus Sullivan. Besides, had not Lady Denby hinted that Sir Eric was not unqualifiedly pleased at the championship of the Hon. Member for Morroway? That, in itself, was cause for apprehension.

So far as Azalea knew, Mr. Sullivan had never denounced Eastlake and Donahue, nor had he uttered any anti-Imperialistic shibboleths, but she simply could not bring herself to accept his attitude as sincere, and something warned her that this sudden flare of patriotism served an ignoble end.

What, she asked herself, could he gain by putting Dilling in a position of honour and importance?

Bribery was unthinkable, but might it not be that he sought some higher honour for himself, some post which could be more easily acquired by a friend at court than by personal application?

"That's stupid," thought Azalea, "for the man has hosts of influential friends, who, though hesitating to introduce him to their wives and daughters, would exert no end of energy to gratify a political whim. There must be something else . . ."

She drew in her breath sharply.

What if animosity towards Dilling, and not friendship, or even self-interest, had prompted this extraordinary act of Mr. Sullivan's!

Was it possible, she asked herself, that he had built his policy on the theory that Dilling would be self-defeated by the deficiencies which Lady

Denby so persistently deplored? Did he rely on the Capital's beguilement by a Beau Brummell, and its rejection of a pilot who placed the substance before the shadow? Sullivan was astute enough to aim at Dilling's most vulnerable spot, realising that it was scarcely probable for him to be overthrown by a political misadventure.

A motive was not far to seek ... Marjorie! Did Mr. Sullivan wish to cripple his antagonist beyond the chance of giving battle, and then himself reap the spoils? He was, she decided, quite capable of such infamy.

She required no complaints from Lady Denby to remind her of the Dillings' social short-comings. Times without number, she had tried to convince Marjorie that in Ottawa—in any Capital, probably—Success demands that aspect of good breeding which may be described as a superficial adaptability to others. But neither Marjorie nor her husband would conform to the standards set by other people, when those standards were opposed to the principles on which they had been nurtured.

"It's deceit," said Marjorie.

"It's duplicity," said Raymond.

Success was not worth attaining unless it accompanied a cleanly heart.

In such small matters did they transgress against the rules of that great governing body called Society. In such stupid little things! It was immaterial to Dilling whether he appeared in black shoes or tan. Marjorie developed a perfect genius for wearing the wrong clothes. At a luncheon given to some distinguished visitor, she could see no reason for "dressing up", while for an affair confined to the humbler members of the Sunday School, she would wear the best that her wardrobe afforded. Similarly, in entertaining, she would provide the simplest repast for a guest of high degree, and spread before the officers of the Sweet Arbutus Club, a dinner that was elaborate by comparison.

"People like Lady Sommerville and the Countess of Lynwood," she argued, "have so much better than I could give them, they wouldn't even notice any effort I could make. But with the others ... it means something to them to be entertained in a Minister's house. When I have them here, I am giving somebody real pleasure. Don't you think it is worth a good deal of trouble?"

The caparisons of greatness would always remain for them non-essentials. All externalities were vain pomp and inglorious display. The things that counted lay within—within the heart and mind and soul of man, and these they pursued and cultivated ardently.

Azalea began to fear that without a drastic shifting of ideals, life would soon become quite insupportable for them in their Land of Afternoon.

The birds were stirring, and a sullen dawn was taking possession of the sky before she fell into a troubled doze. She was conscious of a disturbing dissonance, a harsh thumping that beat against her brain, and she awoke to the sound of Lady Denby's voice crying,

"You would have made him a good wife, Azalea!"

Heavy-eyed, she entered the office in the morning.

"Hello," cried Dilling. "You're here, at last! I'd begun to fear that you were ill."

The eagerness in his manner enraptured her. She drew it into her being, and was refreshed as from a draught of wine. She was conscious of a lifting of the weight that lay upon her spirit. He had been watching for her . . . he had been anxious . . . afraid that she was ill . . .

She looked at him, standing in the doorway, vibrant with unusual health and vigour, scarcely able to keep the glory of her happiness from shining through her eyes. "Here you are, at last," he had said. It was wonderful but it was true.

Dilling relapsed into his accustomed matter-of-factness. He was utterly unconscious of his dependence upon this girl. At least, he was unconscious of the extent of his reliance. During the time he was waiting here, when his thoughts were definitely concerned with her, he was by no means wholly aware that she stood for him as an absorbing problem, intensifying mysteries and contrasts, pricking strange and sensitive spots in the sheath of his imagination. He only dimly suspected how much he owed her for the enlargement of his world and the discovery of new regions of thought and feeling.

He had looked at the clock, trying to summon a sense of irritation. Azalea had never been late before. Instead, he succumbed to anxiety. She must be ill . . . He tried to recall her appearance, yesterday, and failed. He was stupid, that way . . . intensely stupid. He never noticed people . . . Marjorie was very clever. She could have seen in an instant whether Azalea Deane was ill . . .

A curious thought cut athwart the woof of his reflection, a thought that had disturbed him more than once. Might she be tiring of her work? Did she find it—him—too exacting? Perhaps she wasn't coming back at all!

He rose, opened the door and looked out into the corridor. She was not coming. Tired out, probably . . . sick of her job! How could he make the work more interesting, he wondered? How could he show her greater consideration?

He found it difficult not to drive Azalea. She encouraged him to overtax her strength. "If she'd only tell me when she's had enough," he thought guiltily. "But she won't stop . . . won't take advantage of the scheduled periods of rest!"

Dilling felt that he must put a stop to this sort of thing. For example, the girl must go out for lunch. He must see that she went. Anticipation of proposed tyranny sent an agreeable warmth over him. There were many Members who took their secretaries out to lunch . . . why should he not take Azalea?

A very sensible solution, so far as it went. He would see that she ate a proper meal in the middle of the day. He might take her at noon . . . if she would only come.

The sequence of his thoughts was shattered, and Dilling caught himself speculating upon a hitherto unconsidered problem—Azalea's relations with other men. What were they? Had she any close friends? If so, which were the men, and if not, why? Had she ever been in love, and why had she not married?

Hastily, he discarded all the men he knew as unworthy of such a relationship, and then he fell to wondering how much she liked him. Was she capable of any depth of feeling, or was a sort of consistent cordiality, the expression of an intellectual glow that substituted for emotion?

But he made little headway. He found that the clear, cold reason that ate like an acid through the metal of ordinary barriers, was impotent to solve this subtler question . . . that he was slow and clumsy in considering the psychology of Romance.

Not that Dilling scented the least romantic element in his relationship with Azalea Deane. On the contrary! Never had he consciously admitted her femininity; never was he aware of the slightest exoteric appeal. Truly, did women say of him, "He's a cold fish!" Azalea was, to him, a fine mind, a sort of disembodied intelligence, upon whose judgment he unconsciously leaned, and whose approbation he keenly desired.

As he drew the telephone towards him to put an end to his impatience, the door opened and she entered the room.

"One might judge from your cheerful aspect, that the House would prorogue before lunch," she smiled at him.

"No such luck! Although, as a matter of fact, I believe the end's in sight. The Budget should be down this week. There won't be much more after that."

"This week?" Azalea bent diligently over her desk, "Then it won't be long before you start West, again."

"Marjorie and the kids will probably go home. But I have no intention of accompanying them."

"Well, what will you do?" asked Azalea, in surprise.

"I shall stay around Ottawa and become a golf addict. I played eighteen holes yesterday afternoon."

Above the mad singing of her heart, she caught a strange note in his voice, a note she was at a loss to diagnose. "I shall stay in Ottawa . . ." he said calmly, but in a peculiar way.

She dared not trust herself to look at him. Eyes are responsible for more betrayals than are the lips. She wondered, nervously, whether he was looking at her. "I shall stay in Ottawa . . ." Surely, he had not meant . . . No, no! The thing was impossible! Never, by so much as a fleeting glance, had Raymond Dilling expressed anything more than friendliness towards her, and at that, it was the friendliness that man offers man. Had he not deplored the fact that she was born a woman? Hope that was as dear as it was unfounded, died under one smart blow of Reason and Azalea called herself a weak fool. She was ashamed.

"You are singularly uninterested in the affairs pertaining to your Minister," Dilling teased. "Why don't you ask me some intelligent questions?"

He looked at her with a sudden softening in his glance that was almost warm enough to be affectionate.

"Very well. Why are you going to stay in Ottawa?" she asked, looking squarely at him.

"Ah, that's the wrong question. I can't tell you at this moment. But you may make a note and refer to it, again." The same curious sombreness crept into his voice. A new intensity shone in his face. "Later, I will remind you that I *had* a reason! But ask another . . ."

"With whom did you play golf?"

"None other than His Royal Highness. Are you impressed?"

"Not a whit! I'm not even surprised."

"What?"

"No! I've already seen it in the papers."

"You're joking!"

"Really! It's the first item in the Social Column. Only the reporter neglected to mention the score."

Dilling thanked heaven for that. The Duke, he thought, must be one of the best players in the United Kingdom. "He beat me", he added. "Indeed, Pratt, who followed us round with fatuous insistence, called it a wallop."

"Do you know," said Azalea, "I can scarcely picture you being beaten. Somehow, one feels that you ought to do everything well."

"Heaven forfend! You don't understand me, Miss Deane! You think me always and inevitably serious—that my disposition will not permit me to do things by halves. Nothing is further from the truth."

"But you don't agree with Horace, do you? Remember, he said that it is pleasant to play the fool deliberately, and be silly now and then."

"I do not! No one who recognises the thin line that divides sanity from its awful opposite, can ever willingly approach that line. On the other hand, however, I believe that it is an expedient of great psychonomic value to do things which one knows he does badly—or let us say inartistically—at times."

"Golf certainly offers rare opportunities to many persons," murmured Azalea.

"And dancing! Look at me ... I dance as badly as I play golf, but candidly, I don't *want* to do either of them well. My mind rests itself in the conviction that I am doing badly, and so I am refreshed."

"What harm do you see in doing them well?"

"Speaking for myself—and myself alone, you understand—I should be ashamed of excelling in either of these arts, because excellence spells much long and arduous labour in acquiring perfection. You remember Herbert Spencer's rebuke to the young man who beat him handily at billiards ... 'Your exceedingly great skill argues a mis-spent youth', he said. That's just it! Skill in trivial things is not worth while unless you are earning your bread thereby. For example, were I a golf pro. or a dancing master ... No, Miss Deane, I despise the crack amateur."

"Oh!"

"It's true, and having said so much, you will be prepared to hear me add that I dispute the sonorous counsel, 'Whatsoever thy hand findeth to do, do it with all thy might'. Utter nonsense, I call it!"

"Alack, alack!" cried Azalea. "What shall we do for copybook mottoes?"

"I'll give you a better one . . . 'What's only worth doing once in a while, should be forgotten until the next time!' Now for the foreign papers. This parcel? Thank you."

He glanced rapidly through half a dozen of them—English, French and German. Azalea, watching him, saw his expression darken into apprehension, the meaning of which she could not fathom. Nor was she able to interpret his increasing preoccupation until one August morning he called her to the telephone.

"I can tell you now why I stayed in Ottawa," he said. "Despatches have just arrived . . . England has declared war on Germany . . . Canada will have to fight!"

PART THREE
They Conquered

CHAPTER 21.

*D*estiny seemed to be setting the stage for Armageddon, the last tragic scene in the play of human life. Pandora's box had been opened and every mortal ill loosed to the bonds of hate. For more than three years, the sword of War had maimed the body of civilisation. It was a time when the vision of young men was carnage, and the dream of old men, despair. Prussian frightfulness was still exacting dreadful tribute from Celt and Anglo-Saxon battlefields that had lost all trace of old-time chivalry. The virtue of sheer sacrifice was confined to the English-speaking Dominions, the flower of whose youth had gone forth against a foe that had not directly challenged them; gone forth with joy to build their splendid bodies into ramparts that might be shattered but never stormed.

The Blond Beast was shaking the blood from his eyes and looking anxiously across the Atlantic. But America had not yet decided to step into the breach.

Thus with the men. Nor was the mettle of our women lacking in the hour of trial. Spartan mothers never sent their sons into battle with finer renunciation than did the mothers of the unconscripted youths who crowded the transports in the first two years of conflict. Women stepped into the gaping ranks of industry at home—into the farms and fields, and into factories originally designed for making ploughshares and pruning hooks, but now converted into plants for fashioning the panoplies of war. Thousands of these women clad themselves in the overalls of labour, and hundreds put on the uniform of the Red Cross. Life so lived was hard but it was intense, and "Carry on", came to express one of the spiritual values of the ages.

This was one picture of the activities of women during the grim tourney of Might against Right. There was another, not so inspiring. It revealed the cocotte and the flapper. Birds of beautiful plumage, these, who thronged London, Paris, Ostend—God knows where they were not—and sang their siren songs into masculine ears echoing with the shriek of shot and shell . . . songs that offered forgetfulness, Nirvana, to men who came out of a stinking Hell where the form of Death stalked grinning at their side. These were they who filled the theatres, cabarets, and tea shops, providing fat profits for jewellers, modistes, motor liveries; the hotels and inconspicuous road-houses.

How swiftly in our own land came the changes wrought by war! One grew inured to bobbed hair, knee-length skirts, universal smoking, Einstein, trousered women, camouflage, expensive economy and economical extravagance, unashamed macquillage, weddings à la volée, War Babies, and appetency for divorce.

The social limousine, as it sped on the road of Hysteria, was not alone in its responsiveness to the influences of the time. The car of politics was jolted from its accustomed track. Union Government was formed under the leadership of Sir Robert Borden, and both the great parties lost their distinctiveness, not so much from the deliberate fusion as from the departure of the pick of capable men from each. To complete the debacle of the Liberal Party, Sir Wilfrid Laurier—the thaumaturge of Canada's peaceful days of growth—passed away, stupefied by the alarms of war. The nation lost its beautiful Parliament House by fire, set it was generally thought, by the myrmidons of the Kaiser.

In the Dillings' home, changes had also made their way. Marjorie found the top floor convenient as a meeting place for the dozen and one organisations over which she was asked to preside. Dilling had an office on the ground floor as well as at the Victoria Museum—whither the burnt-out Members of Parliament had been driven for refuge, and Azalea practically lived at the house.

Mr. Sullivan was by no means an infrequent visitor and Lord Ronald Melville, the A.D.C., found a curious respite from Society's kaleidoscopic demands upon him in the prim ugliness of Marjorie's drawing-room.

"I like him better than any man I ever knew," she confided to Azalea, one evening as they sat waiting for the children to return from a masquerade at Government House. "He's so old-fashioned."

Azalea laughed. "In what way?"

"Ever so many ways! He doesn't like women who smoke or swear, and he's so fond of children."

"That *is* old-fashioned!"

Marjorie nodded. "I don't think he likes Ottawa very much. He said that the Society here was like a blurred and microscopic reflection of London life. Wasn't that pretty strong, Azalea?"

"Well, it certainly is a definite view."

"I find it easy to get on with him," Marjorie continued. "All the things I like to talk about seem interesting to him. With other people, no matter what I say, it doesn't sound quite right, but with Their Excellencies and Lord Ronald, there is such a different feeling!"

She sighed. Long ago, she had observed that famous people whose names she used to revere in Pinto Plains, neither talked nor acted like the sons of God; gradually, she discovered that age was not to be confused with sapience or high life with respectability. She realised that to succeed she must say daring things to people from whom she shrunk, and repeat the latest gossip freshened by a spraying of her own invention. She divined that in being kind to men and allowing them to talk frankly with her, she earned the enmity of their wives, and that if she held herself aloof, these same women considered her a stick and a fool. She could acquire neither the smart badinage of people of parts, nor the air of those who used ponderosity to cloak their native insipidities.

"You should be very grateful for being clever," Marjorie said. "If I were only a little bit cleverer, I shouldn't have found Ottawa half so—so—difficult." She blushed. "Do you know, Azalea, I used to think that everybody here would be like Lord Ronald, good and kind and friendly. I used to think Society was exactly like *that!*"

Azalea's mouth grew hard. She knew, without being told, that some one had inflicted a hurt upon Marjorie's tender spirit, and all her love rose up in revolt.

"Society!" she cried. "Can't you see that what we dignify by that name is merely a mechanism devised to give a certain class of climbers and parasites the power to lead a comfortably otiose existence at the expense of the shrinking and the credulous?"

"I'm afraid I don't understand quite all of that," confessed Marjorie. "But I know it's clever. There are so many clever people, here. That is what makes me seem stupider than I really am, by comparison."

"They are not clever," contradicted Azalea. "They are simply experts in the art of pretence. They succeed by bluff."

"You have to be clever to do that," argued Marjorie. Then suddenly, "I hope you won't mind my saying so, Azalea, but you know I've often thought how much better everything would have been for everybody if you had been married to Raymond!"

Azalea raised startled eyes to see Dilling standing in the doorway. That he had overheard Marjorie's words was obvious. He stood regarding her with a strange interest as if studying her in the light of a sudden revelation. With an onrush of knowledge, he became conscious of his soul, for the first time. He knew its needs and how Azalea had met them during the months they had worked together. He saw Azalea as a woman . . . as the luminous source of all his inspiration.

A moment passed . . . a moment that held an eternity of understanding. Soul met soul, disdaining the barriers of sense. The room was filled with the sound of Marjorie's knitting needles. The clock began to chime . . .

The pell-mell entrance of the children shattered the spell that gripped them. Baby, drunk with excitement, staggered to Marjorie and climbed, a crumpled heap of tarltan and tinsel, into her lap. Besser, proudly wearing a jester's cap over one ear, retrieved from his pocket, three sticky lumps that had once been cake, and laid them on the table. Althea, infected by the snobbery in which she had so lately been a participant, flipped up her skirts at the back, and wriggled decorously upon a chair.

"Well, my treasures, and was the party boo-ti-fool?" demanded Marjorie.

A torrent of speech answered her.

"And were you dear, good children?" she asked. "What of my tomboy, Althea?"

"I was the goodest one at the party," replied that young person. "Mind you, Mummie, I was the *only child* what folded up my napkin!"

CHAPTER 22.

Dilling and Azalea met on the following morning, in all outward respects, exactly as they had met for nearly five years.

A third person watching them would have detected no change in their manner, no relaxing in their poise, no studied indifference. Neither was there discernible the strained control proclaiming a furtive curiosity—a hunger—to see how the other would behave.

"Good morning," said Dilling, finding her engrossed with the mail. "I hope you are well."

Azalea echoed this cliché and observed that their correspondence seemed to increase daily. It was the sort of thing they often said.

"I'll be ready in just a moment," he told her, and passed quickly behind the green baize door that gave into his private office.

All this was as it had been many times before.

Azalea caught her breath in two fluttering little sighs. That was over; and without any of the embarrassments she had dreaded. It had been quite easy—almost disappointingly easy—but altogether fine. That was what she had prayed that Dilling should remain; it was what she knew he would always remain—fine!

At the same time, she wondered how he felt, exactly what minute little thoughts had come to him since he stood between the dull, fringed portieres and stared at her, stunned, yet with the light of a sublime revelation dawning in his eyes. She wondered with a hot stab of pain, if he felt himself duped, humbugged, betrayed.

She visualised the brief and pregnant scene again, imagining—or was it divining?—the thought that must have come to him as his eyes held hers in that sudden bond of understanding. "This is a piece of staggering news to me," he must have said. "I am taken at a disadvantage ... emotionally naked ... but you knew ... you knew ..."

And she saw herself mutely admitting the accusation, but with sadness, as a mother might have felt when some disturbing information could no longer be withheld from the child she loved. And she wondered if he suffered at losing the false serenity in which he had been living.

Did he resent the age-old wisdom that enabled her to see, while he groped and stumbled, fatuous in his blindness? Did he feel humiliation?

On her desk the buzzer sounded. His summons. For a moment, Azalea sat quite still, looking at the little instrument that had called her in exactly the same way countless times before. And yet, not quite the same. To-day, there was something different. No, it would never be the same again.

As she gathered up her notebook, pencil and a sheaf of papers, her heart ached for him.

"Why," she asked herself, rebelliously, "why must the cup of knowledge be so bitter? Why must the coming of truth be so difficult and hard to bear?"

He did not raise his eyes when she entered the room, but presently, he seemed to know that she was seated and ready.

"Taking up the matter of the Quebec Bridge," he began, "is the report down from Council, yet?" Then, without waiting for an answer, "But first, are there any Imperial despatches?"

The routine of the morning progressed as usual. Reports to Council, petitions from small centres demanding votes from the Public Treasury out of all proportion to their possible returns, eternal complaints and criticisms from malcontents, applications for pensions from War Widows, enquiries from distracted mothers—all the departmental *acta-diurna* of a ministerial incumbency that had to be cleared away before he was free to undertake the pressing matters that fell to his especial talents to perform.

And he compelled his brain to function along its accustomed channels, while some inner chamber of his mind carried on a separate trend of thought—separate, and, at the same time, veiled, like the thinking that is part of a dream.

He wondered how Azalea felt, sitting there so composedly; and beautiful, like Lamb's divinely plain *Miss Kelly*. Was there an element of pity, even contempt beneath her consistent consideration, for the man who was insentient to the message of his own heart? Dilling recoiled from the mawkish flavour of the phrase. He despised all sentimentality, and had he been called upon to debate the subject would have denied the heart the conspicuous place universally accorded it, in emotional relations between the sexes. Imbeciles and sensualists "fell in love", because the world refuses to countenance the cruder, if more honest, passion. Dilling had never been in love—neither with Marjorie nor any other woman. Even now he refused to connect the term with Azalea. He had suddenly become aware of joy in her companionship, of his dependence upon the mental stimulation she provided, of a hitherto unsuspected peace in their spiritual communion. In her, he had found the priceless thing for which men seek throughout their lives—Understanding.

"I couldn't get along without her," he said to himself. "She understands me." And having thus spoken, he could say no more. It was the highest tribute he could pay—the highest tribute any man can pay to woman.

With Azalea, he felt himself the man he wished to be; not smug and stodgily content, but rejoicing in the struggle towards an ideal which he believed was one that she approved.

Sitting opposite her, apparently engrossed in matters of a widely divergent nature, Dilling examined himself, detachedly. He had no desire to touch her ... to cry to her, "I love you!" But the thought of losing her companionship, mental contact with her, produced a pain so intolerable that it dismayed him.

And in that flash of utter wretchedness, he saw how completely he was wedded to Azalea; how sublime was this cold, pure marriage of the spirit. With Marjorie, mental companionship was absolutely non-existent. They were bound together by duty, habit, and the intimacies permitted those who have accepted man-made ritual as final ... and Divine. They had no need of one another. Fondness expressed the extent of his emotion, and for several years, he had realised that a fierce maternalism on her part was substitute for the rarer ecstasy of love.

He was as free from connubial fetters as it is given man to be. Marjorie was never exacting, but even so, Dilling was conscious of restriction, bondage. He wanted to be free!

He thought of other married men, and saw for the first time how their wives crowded into their lives; they were like two snails trying to crowd into the same shell. Through no fault of hers, Marjorie often crowded him. Then his mind turned to Azalea, who never had provoked that sensation in all the years of their association. On the contrary, she always seemed to liberate his mind, to give him light and space and air. She was his mate, not his keeper or his charge.

He wondered when she first began to love him, and whether the knowledge had brought her pleasure or unrest. Had she felt humiliation at his unresponsiveness, perhaps? Had he ever hurt her? What a contrast between Azalea and Hebe Barrington! A gentle perspiration broke out on his brow, and he lost the trend of his thought for an instant. One was suggestive of the hot breath of the jungle; the other, the cool freshness of the open sea. Mentally, Dilling removed his sandals as he looked across the crowded desk, and reverently kneeled at Azalea's feet.

"I'm glad I know ..." he said to himself. "Not that it will make the slightest difference. We will go on exactly as before. Thank God, she is sensible—not like other women!"

It did not occur to him, however, that he was like other men—in one respect, at least; that this was a matter differing from any problem that had entered into his career. It would not be settled once and for all. It would not be laid away beyond the need of further consideration. He was soon to find that he could not ignore the insistency of this strange emotion that caught him at most unexpected, inconvenient moments. At first, such unaccustomed tyranny annoyed him. But gradually, he grew to like it, to seek the refreshment of it, as one who finds refreshment in the perfume of a flower.

Mechanically, he selected a letter from the wire basket under his hand, and dictated,

"Dear Mr. Jackson,

"(The Jackson case again. I'll finish it this morning!) . . . I have just had your letter, dated 22nd ultimo—now a week overdue, here—by this morning's mail. It does not occur to me that carelessness caused your delay in sending it off. I note that it was posted only four days ago.

"I am inclined to think that it was some evocation of your better judgment, I will even go so far as to say conscience, in this extremely unpleasant affair, that provoked a debate within yourself as to whether the letter should be mailed to me, at all.

"It is necessary at times to speak plainly to one's friends, and a moment's reflection will convince you, I am sure, that this is such a time. Frankly, your letter and its suggestion that I should use my political influence to forward the project of the Moccasin Realty Co. Ltd., which is only the business name cloaking that of yourself and your son-in-law, to sell the jerry-built Cameron Terrace to the Dominion Government at five times the price for which you built it two years since, is a stark offence to me. I will have no part or lot in such an unpleasant—I speak euphemistically— transaction, and I ask you to consider this answer final.

"The Terrace has twice been reported against by the Inspector of the Indian Department as quite unfit for the purpose of an Indian School. You, sir, are perfectly well aware that it is ill-drained and impossible to heat without being veneered, or stuccoed, at great additional cost.

"I shall say no more about the matter, but if my refusal to aid your attempt upon the Treasury of this overburdened country costs me the loss of your support—if it should cost me the loss of my entire constituency—I shall accept the situation in the knowledge that, at least, I have done my duty. It is only upon such a footing that I can remain in public life . . ."

He raised his eyes, hard and cold with anger, and asked,

"Do you think he'll believe I'm sincere?"

Azalea shook her head. "He'll complain, as so many of them do."

"How's that?"

"He will say when in power the Liberals forget their principles and the Conservatives, their friends."

They both sighed.

The banging of doors and quivering of beaver-board partitions that had converted the spaciousness of the Victoria Memorial Museum into cubicles wherein Canada's Parliamentarians might be temporarily housed, the scurrying along corridors and clang of the elevator gate, told Azalea that noon had come. When immersed in work, Dilling was utterly oblivious to the flight of time.

"What about lunch?" she asked, as soon as he paused. "The gun sounded some time ago."

How often had she said exactly the same thing!

"Are you so hungry?" he asked, astonished to miss the playful effect he had intended to convey. Dropping into the still room, the silly words had almost a nervous note.

"Starving," lied Azalea, easily, and knowing his unadmitted dependence upon food.

"Very well. I'll go, too. But I'm coming back early, to-day. We must unearth that Hansard before I go to Council. It will never do to let Bedford get away with his want-of-confidence Motion on the British Preference, in this high-handed fashion! We must make him eat his words . . . and while I think of it. Miss Deane, please don't let anyone—*anyone*—disturb me."

CHAPTER 23.

Azalea lunched lightly, and then found herself an inconspicuous bench in the little park off Lewis Street. The sun was warm and golden; the air soft with the promise of approaching summer. The trees had already burst into leaf. Careless children had left their toys about on the moist walks. Gardeners, taking advantage of the dinner hour, had deserted the wire-fenced enclosures that would presently break into a melody of colour.

But Azalea saw none of these things. She was at variance with spring. More autumnal was her mood. She sat quite still, unfidgetting, yet with the air of one who is tense, who is waiting for the storm that is bound to break.

"How long can this go on?" she was thinking. "He won't continue the pretence that things are the same. He is too honest. But what will he do, then?"

A wave of exultation surged over her. It wouldn't be easy for him to find another secretary, she said. He would miss her in the office, to say the least. And not only in the office. His eyes had betrayed so much. Why could they not go on, she asked herself, with passionate vehemence?

They could. The whole thing rested upon her. The type of relationship that exists between men and women, always rests upon the determination of the woman. In this case, Azalea knew that she must keep Dilling from being too conscious of her. She must make none of the unspoken demands that even the least exacting woman makes upon the man who has confessed himself in love. Neither must she allow him to feel that a secret bond was held between them. Above all, she must keep his emotional temperature at its accustomed low ebb. Any suggestion of coquetry on her part, now, would disturb his tranquility, and remind him that he had violated the spirit of the narrow law governing his moral code.

Could she do all this? If so, she knew they could go on.

Azalea believed that love could exist between a man and a woman without emotional gratification and without expression save in the terms of friendship. She believed that it can be fed freely, by the mind and by the spirit, just as the body can be fed sanely without the bizarre concoctions demanded by self-encouraged neurasthenics. The secret lies in a woman's power, and wish, to keep the association free from the tempering of passion. It is not enough to control it, argued Azalea. It must never be aroused. And this is rare, but not impossible.

She was not a vain woman. There was no conceit in her, and illusions had long since flown on the wings of dreams that were unfulfilled. She knew that she was plain, unlovely, unmagnetic; that never since adolescence had she awakened the readily distinguishable expression in man's eyes that proclaims his discovery of the femaleness in his companion. But it was because she hadn't tried!

According to her theory, the physical envelope matters comparatively little. The mysterious force that is called attraction, magnetism, passion, what you will, exists in plain and beautiful alike, and can be projected at will. Therefore, she possessed the female's instinctual power to project this force—this beam that is like a shaft of light, and blinds the man upon whom it is thrown. He beholds the woman in a flame of radiance, unmindful of her lack of pulchritude. And not only is his physical sight impaired, but his mental eye loses its clarity of vision, and he invests this uncompanionable female with every quality he thinks desirable. He wants her. He starves for her. He will not be denied. And after marrying her, what happens?

The woman, having acquired the man upon whom she has fixed her choice, grows careless, indifferent, lazy. She no longer lights the shaft that dazzled him; she no longer projects it in his direction. He blinks, looks, and rubs his eyes; half the time, he doesn't understand . . . Where is the woman he loved and married? Who is this creature, this unattractive stranger who pushes herself into his life, and tries to dominate, absorb it? There has been some hideous mistake . . . Steeped in the delusion that man is the determining factor in the mockery of emotional marriage, he takes the blame upon himself, persuaded that the fault is his. At first, he tries to hide his disenchantment. He says nothing . . . He determines to do nothing . . . just go on . . . They both go on . . . spiritually too far apart, physically too close together . . . bound by Church and State, and accustoming themselves to the functioning of two persons who live in that abominable intimacy— ironically termed the bonds of Holy Wedlock!

Azalea believed that the bond of wedlock could only be holy when it is not artificially constructed by predative females in search of economic ease, with a possible thrill or two, to boot. She agreed with the cynicism that marriage is man's after-thought and woman's first intention. She further believed that by continuing the rigid control of herself—control that neutralised and de-natured her—she and Dilling could maintain a relationship that not only was free from irregularity, but embarrassment.

Mingling with the stream of Civil Servants that flowed in and out of the Museum, Azalea's mind was still concerned with the relationships between men and women, married and single. She thought of her sisters with something very like disgust; of Lady Elton, Eva Leeds, Mrs. Pratt, Mrs. Blaine, Mrs. Hudson, Mme. Valleau ... what real comradeship did they offer their husbands? Swift's words came to her as being especially applicable. "There would be fewer unhappy marriages in the world," he said, "if women thought less of making nets, and more of making cages."

She had never tried to make a net, not even for Raymond Dilling. She loved him too deeply to trap—to ensnare him. And if she longed to make a cage for him, it was as a means of protection, safety, refuge; not the terrible gilt-barred thing in which he would feel a sense of shame at his imprisonment.

She could hear him pacing about his little room, muttering fragmentary sentences now and then. The sound disturbed her. He was not, as a rule, stimulated to intensive thought by prowling. Was she already responsible for disorganising the methodical workings of his mind?

Poise, control, fell from her. She turned the pages of Hansard feverishly and without intelligence. She longed to go to him, to take his frail body in her arms, to soothe him in her self-effacing renunciatory way. She longed to whisper to him, "There, my dear, you needn't dread me. You needn't be afraid."

Instead, she sat at her desk and fluttered the leaves of Hansard, and suffered the anguish of one who cannot take on the suffering of that beloved other . . .

A knock on the door startled her. She turned to see Hebe Barrington advancing into the room.

"Oh! *You* are still here?" was her greeting.

"I find the work congenial," returned Azalea.

The two women faced one another, understood one another. Neither made a pretence of concealing the animosity that had always existed between them. Azalea resented Hebe's habit of establishing herself, taking complete possession of situations and people, and ordering the destiny of all with whom she came in contact. Hebe hated Azalea for the calm tenacity and cold superiority that had thwarted her so many times in the past. She had just returned from England, whither patriotic fervour and the personal attractions of a certain fulgid major had drawn her. The zest with which she had undertaken a particular form of War Work had strained even Toddles' indulgence, until the only way they could live together was to live apart.

Hebe had abandoned her pursuit of Dilling, and renounced all complicity in Sullivan's plans after a stormy interview with that gentleman. What she demanded, grandly, were his nugatory projects compared with the clarion call of Empire? He felt very bitterly towards her, blaming her for the miscarriage of his schemes. Had he foreseen the outbreak of the War, or Hebe's defection, he never in the world would have assisted Dilling to a position of prominence where his public record commanded respectful admiration and where his private life was above reproach.

"Isn't this a killing little hole?" Hebe observed, alert to every detail. "Sordid, undignified. You should see the quarters of the British politicians . . . and the War Offices . . ."

Tiny flames of anger gathered in Azalea's eyes. There was something in the insolence of the other woman that suggested a personal criticism—as though she could have arranged the room more fittingly, prevented its sordidness, its displeasing atmosphere.

"A few flowers would make a difference," she went on, appraising Azalea's coat and hat that hung near the door.

"We don't spend much money on flowers, now, merely for decorative purposes," answered the other.

"What a pity! I always think that's what they're for. Is Raymond—Mr. Dilling—in there?"

"Yes, but he's too busy to be disturbed."

Their eyes met in open hostility.

"I object to the word 'disturbed'," said Hebe. "My visit is supposed to have exactly the opposite effect." She smiled, a brilliantly ugly smile.

Azalea lifted her shoulders almost imperceptibly. "Mr. Dilling gave me definite instructions to allow no one to see him. I'm sorry, but I can't make an exception, even in your favour."

"What fidelity to duty," mocked Hebe.

"You are very kind," bowed Azalea, as though receiving a compliment.

"You know very well that your employer would not refuse to admit me," cried Hebe. "Don't you think I can see the vicious pleasure behind this rigid adherence to your instructions? Let me pass!"

"You are making a ridiculous scene," said Azalea, white to the lips. "I am treating you just as I would treat anybody else—the Prime Minister, himself. You are not going to disturb—interrupt—Mr. Dilling!"

"How are you going to prevent me?" taunted Hebe. "Lay violent hands upon me and fling me to the floor?"

"I shan't touch you," retorted Azalea, her voice trembling with cold anger. "But I shall regard intrusion upon Mr. Dilling as a personal attack, and shall not have the slightest hesitation in ordering the policeman to protect his privacy."

She stretched out her hand towards the telephone and held it ready for use.

Hebe burst into a peal of derisive laughter. She advanced with an air of high daring. Then an expression of cunning crept into her fire-shot eyes. Azalea had threatened to call a policeman. He would lay restraining hands upon her. She would struggle upon the very threshold of the young Minister's office. She would scream. People would rush from their rooms into the corridor to see ...

A splendid scene! Magnificent! There would be a glorious scandal ... "Two women fight over the Hon. Mr. Dilling. Shocking episode in the temporary House of Parliament." She laughed again. Uncle Rufus would be not only placated; he would be grateful.

"I've warned you," said Azalea.

"You won't dare!"

"Stop!"

"I'm going in, I tell you!"

Raising her hand to push open the door, Hebe found Azalea directly in her path. But it was too late to change her intention, and she struck the girl a smart blow in the face. Exactly at that moment, Dilling stepped into the room.

There was a painful silence. Of the three, the Minister felt the greatest embarrassment. He could readily guess what had happened.

Hebe spoke,

"In another moment, we should have been almost angry, Raymond," she cried. "I couldn't make this dear girl see that I was an exception to your iron-bound rule covering the ordinary visitor."

"When did you come back?" asked Dilling, allowing his hand to lie limply between hers for an instant.

"Only this morning. Half past twelve, from Montreal. Landed yesterday, and here I am to pay my respects. And your faithful secretary wanted to turn me out. Scold her, Raymond," she cried, archly. "Please do!"

"I'm afraid I haven't time, just now," replied Dilling. Then, as he passed the desk to which Azalea had returned with a fine show of absorption in Hansard, he said, "Can you stay after five? We must consult together as to my future policy following to-day's eventful meeting."

"We?" echoed Hebe, with a noticeable touch of derision. "La, la! *Que c'est charmant!* I've heard that a successful politician is merely a matter of having a clever secretary, but I never credited the statement until now." She turned directly to Dilling. "You are going out?"

"Yes."

"I will come with you—as far as you go."

"Thank you," said Dilling. "We meet in this building."

He opened the door, started to pass through, then, remembering the conventions, waited for Hebe to precede him. Azalea did not raise her eyes, but she knew without looking that he did not glance behind him.

She sat motionless after they had gone, while her heart stilled its wild plunging, and the air cleared of crimson-hot vibrations. She did not think of herself or review the part she had played in the absurd drama of Hebe's making. She did not ask herself whether her attitude had been convincing or ridiculous. Strangely enough, she did not think, "I might have said . . ." Her concern was for Raymond Dilling.

She knew that he did not, never could, love Hebe Barrington. Jealousy was far removed from her considerations. But a slow, cold fear crawled through her as she thought of another contingency. Dilling's balance had shifted. He had become conscious of new and disturbing emotions. He was like an instrument tuned by a gentle hand and therefore prepared to respond even to the coarsest touch. Would not the very fact of his awakened love for her, make him an easier victim of Hebe's seductive beleaguerment?

The thought racked her throughout the afternoon. She could not keep her mind on her work. She spent herself in a sort of helpless passion of protection, feeling that she would give her very life to save him from the toils of the other woman. She had set him on a lofty pedestal, high above the ruck of mud and slime. Her pride in him was renunciatory, fiercely maternal. She wanted to keep him fair and pure for himself . . . not in the slightest sense for her.

She had grown strong in a fanatical belief that one of the chief elements of Britain's power is the moral weight behind it; that her statesmen are clean, straight-forward and honourable, on the whole, and that intrigue and deception are alien to their nature. Furthermore, she felt that now, in the Empire's hour of supreme trial, it was upon the power and pressure of this conviction throughout the world, that the future of England must depend.

CHAPTER 24.

*T*he Premier's health had been sadly broken by the War. This pandemic scourge had come into being while Canada was still in her nonage, and what she needed most in leadership throughout the conflict, was what he had most to give, namely, a fine obstinacy of purpose. Possessing this, the lack of dramatic picturesqueness was forgiven him by a spectacle-loving people.

But inflexibility is always a target and a challenge for assault, and when not engaged in repelling his foes on Mr. Speaker's Left, Sir Robert was called upon to reckon with the mutiny of his colleagues whose sense of honour was not inconveniently high. Throughout the actual ordeal of battle, the edge of the weapons of menace found him adamant. But towards the end of the four years' darkness, the strain became too heavy, and several months before the world settled to enjoy the hostility of peace, rumours of his impending resignation drifted along the currents of the House.

The break came later—after he had gone to France to sign the Treaty of Versailles on our behalf—a glorious mission, truly, and significant of Canada's entry into the Council of the Nations. It was then that the burden of his great labour and achievement levied a heavier toll than he could pay. Atropos threatened him with her shears. He sank into the relaxation of a profound collapse, and offered his resignation as Prime Minister. Holding the Rudder of the Ship of State with a world in arms, had broken him, as it broke the great Commoner, Pitt. That the parallel was not completed by his death, was a matter of national rejoicing, and he lived to know that his purity of conduct, his strength of purpose and his courage in the supreme crisis of civilisation, marked him as one of the real forces in history.

And so it happened that in Canada there was no man like Lloyd George who held his position unchallenged throughout the duration of the War. Political and military scandals had their ugly day. Heroes were exalted and overthrown almost within the same hour.

Dilling offered the closest analogy, perhaps, to the great British statesman. He retained not only his own portfolio, but undertook the directing of several others, while an interregnum occurred and there had been discovered no incumbent to fill the office. He had "acted" as Prime Minister on more than one occasion, and when these resignation rumours began to float about, his name was mentioned as a possible successor.

Public Works were paralyzed. The gargantuan ambitions of Eastlake and Donahue hung in abeyance. They dared not intrude their demands for further subsidies while war taxes bled the country white. Dilling turned his eyes from the elevators, and saw only the Empire's present need. Grain moved heavily eastward, but the great driving power of the West was crippled. The hand that rocked her cradle was engaged in destroying the very manhood she had suckled at her prairie breast. Capable of producing food for more than half the world, she was starving for sustenance to keep herself alive.

Never had the Hon. Member for Morroway been so deeply engrossed in the business of politics. Never had he applied himself so sedulously to the successful culmination of his vast schemes and secret projects, or neglected for so lengthy a period the gentler pursuits that so intrigued him. It was rumoured in some quarters that he had reformed. The rumour was not received with universal satisfaction, for the penitent has only the applause of the devotee who reclaims him.

Howarth and Turner watched him with mingled concern and respect, and wondered as to the nature of his game. After the entry of the United States into the War, and when the outcome was a foregone conclusion, these two gentlemen became somewhat apprehensive as to the future of the Party (and incidentally their own place in the political sun). The rumours of Sir Robert's resignation moved them profoundly.

"Of course," said Turner, as the three sat in Mr. Sullivan's cheerful office, "Sir Adrian Grant will be a candidate, but I don't believe he has the ghost of a chance. It looks to me like a walk-over for Dilling. He'll march to the seat of honour, terrible as an army with banners."

"Yes," agreed Howarth. "I don't know who's going to stop him. That damned silly boost of yours, Sullivan, has done us in the eye, if you ask me."

Mr. Sullivan examined the contents of his glass against the pale spring twilight, and remarked that he was always glad to hear the opinions of his friends, even though he had not asked for them. In the present instance, however, he seemed to detect some thing monstrous and repetitive.

"Sure, I've said it before, and I'll say it again," announced Howarth, warmly. "What's going to keep him from stepping into the P. M.'s shoes, if we have to go to the country? Hasn't he made good! Don't the people think he's a little tin god? Hasn't he got a lot of useful experience out of the last few years?"

"All because of this Minister business," supplemented Turner. "Except for that, we could have kept him down. He wouldn't have had a chance."

"But now, as matters stand, he'll walk in, put over the Elevator project, and . . ."

". . . the E. D. Company will flourish like a green bay tree, and where will our little plans come in?" demanded Turner, bitterly. "If you want to eat honey in peace, say the Russians, you must first kill all the bees."

Mr. Sullivan nodded, but preserved an inscrutable silence.

"Have you got something up your sleeve, old man?" asked Howarth, in a foolish, coaxing tone. "There's no denying you're a pretty shrewd lad in your own way, Rufus, and you don't often make mistakes. Personally, I rely absolutely upon your judgment, and am ready to follow—oh, *absolutely*," he insisted, conscious of a slight twitching at the corners of Mr. Sullivan's full lips. "At the same time, there are occasions recorded in history, when the most astute persons have been misled, when the best-laid schemes have taken a most unprecedented and disastrous twist. If you have a plan, why not take us into your confidence, Rufus? Why not discuss your ideas . . . three heads, you know . . ."

"Reminiscent of Cerberus", cut in Turner. "Pretty good watch dog, eh?"

"Sure," assented Howarth. "Three heads . . . as I say. And besides, I'm just restless in my desire to help."

But it was Marjorie who was the Hon. Member's first confidante. She neither realised the importance of this, nor appreciated the honour that he did her.

He had begged for an uninterrupted moment—a moment clipped from her over-full days, when appointment followed appointment in a continuous, dizzying succession—and, because he had said it was urgent, she agreed to receive him one night at ten o'clock. An earlier release was impossible from the pandemonium advertised as a Patriotic Bazaar.

"The dear little woman looks tired," he said, taking her hand. "Isn't she trying to push a great heavy Mercedes up a very steep hill, with a Ford engine? Aren't you doing far too much of this hysterical War Work, little Marjorie?"

"Wednesday is my worst day," she told him, and tried to withdraw her hand . . . "not the actual work, but going to things. You see," she explained, "it makes such a difference . . . I can't understand it, really . . . If we go to these patriotic things . . . the Ministers' wives, I mean. We don't do anything but walk around, and have people introduced to us, and it's *so* useless and tiring!"

"My dear . . . my dear!" murmured the sympathetic Member.

"I don't mind the work, a bit," Marjorie continued, trying to force a note of weariness out of her voice. "The sewing and sorting of donations and that kind of thing. I feel as though—as though, well, I feel that I am really doing something for our boys over there, whereas walking around these bazaars and sitting idle at Executive meetings—" she shook her head and left the sentence unfinished. "But you wanted to see me about something in particular, you said."

The Hon. Member for Morroway assumed his most charmingly avuncular air. Little by little, he overcame Marjorie's instinctive resistance. She was always so eager to like people, to believe in them and find them good. He asked if she could keep a secret—even from her husband, and gaining a somewhat hesitant answer, whispered,

"How would you like to see him Prime Minister, my dear?"

Marjorie's tired brain reeled. She couldn't grasp the thought, at all. Prime Minister . . . Raymond . . . so soon to see the fulfilment of his heart's desire? No, no! She shrunk away from the idea. There must be some mistake. They were so young, so inexperienced. They were not properly prepared, not sufficiently worthy. She felt an overwhelming pity for all those women whose lives were broken, and whose hearts were torn by the War. It shadowed the satisfaction, the joyousness she might have taken for herself. Prime Minister!

Sullivan sat quiet, watching her, and the changing expressions that sped across her haggard face. He read them as easily as though they had been printed there, and he waited.

"Do you want Raymond to be Prime Minister?" Marjorie finally whispered. "Do you think he *ought* to be?"

"There is little doubt on either score." Mr. Sullivan was soothing, reassuring. "As you know, I am only an inconspicuous cog in the political machine, but even the smallest cog can control the working of the whole. Just as it can obstruct," he added, lightly. "Without meaning to boast, I believe that my influence is sufficient to secure him the Premiership—just as I was somewhat instrumental in putting him into the Cabinet."

"Oh, Mr. Sullivan—Uncle Rufus, do you really mean to help?"

"With all my heart, little woman," he replied, "and so must you."

"I?" Her confused mind translated the assistance he suggested into a need for increasing "stiffness".

"Of course! Why not?"

"What must I do?"

Mr. Sullivan became affectionately confidential. The most important thing, he assured her, was persuading Dilling how ardently she wanted him to accept the position.

"But he won't refuse . . . will he?"

"There is just that little possibility . . . yes, it is conceivable that he might. I mustn't tire you with an exposition of the complicated question," he went on, "but to secure the support he needs, would require a slight change of policy . . . not quite superficially, either. I might go so far as to say *ab imo pectore*, if you know what I mean."

He watched the strained bewilderment in her eyes with something akin to brutal pleasure.

"Raymond is a strong man, determined almost to stubbornness, may I say? He is guided—er misguided, many of the older parliamentarians think—by an idée fixe. If I know him as I think I do, it will be hard to convince him that relinquishing it will be a sign not of weakness, but of strength."

"I'm afraid I don't understand all of this . . ."

"Don't bother your lovely head with it! I did not come here to worry you with tedious politics, but I do want you to understand me . . . so that we can work together in this most momentous matter. Raymond must be made to see that all previous measures now require adjustment to the changed times. The end of War is in sight, thank God, but we can't delude ourselves with the thought that the world will find immediate peace, that it will pick up its burdens and its pleasures where it left them off, and that the policies we followed prior to 1914 are those to take us forward to-day. He must change. Can't you persuade him?"

"I never interfere," said Marjorie, in a low voice. "He would think I was crazy to suggest anything about politics. I'm so stupid, you know."

"But you can plead your own cause—convince him of the happiness this promotion would mean to you . . . and," he hurried on, "you realise what it would mean for him, for the children, for the country! Why, he would be the youngest, the most brilliant Prime Minister in the world! Think of it, little Marjorie . . . our own splendid Raymond, of Pinto Plains!"

He rose to take his leave. Marjorie got rather dizzily to her feet. The room heaved in gentle waves, and the harsh lights suddenly went dim. An awful sickness attacked her, and out of the curious amethyst fog, the face of Mr. Sullivan advanced upon her, huge, satyric, terrible.

"What is it?" she whispered. "Oh, dear, what is the matter?"

"Aren't you going to kiss me?" he asked, in a voice that scorched her.

"Oh . . . please . . ."

Marjorie escaped from the hand that came towards her. She slipped behind the table. Mr. Sullivan followed. She ran to the Morris chair and took refuge on the other side of it, for a moment. Her knees would scarcely support her. This cloud threatened to blind her. The room was filled with a noise as of some one's heavy breathing. It occurred to her that Althea must be sobbing, upstairs.

"Come on, child! Don't be silly!" The voice of the Hon. Member sounded husky, but very loud. It thumped against her consciousness. "Aren't you going to give me one little kiss in return for the help I'm giving Raymond?"

"No, no! Please . . ." She circled unsteadily around the table, again.

"Well, by God, you will, then!" cried Mr. Sullivan. "I've had just about enough of this catch-as-catch-can. You come here!"

"No . . . oh, no . . ."

Marjorie crumpled in a heap on the floor, and burst into wild sobbing. She was beside herself with terror. Never again in his gentlest moments, would the Hon. Member deceive her with his avuncular air. Always, she would see him as a beast of prey, his eyes flaming, his hands searching for her.

Quite unconsciously, she began to pray.

"Oh, God, please . . . Dear God . . ."

Mr. Sullivan paused in his advance. He looked at the disordered heap on the floor. A revulsion of feeling came over him, and he turned away.

"Bah!" he said, angrily. "*Women!*" and, seizing his hat, he left the house.

CHAPTER 25.

*T*he Cathedral was palpitant with Fashion. For the moment, its dim religious light was lost in the flamboyance of smart Society's glare. Its serene atmosphere was fractured by cross-currents that blew in from an impious world. The Flesh and the Devil walked on the feet that pressed the red carpet to save from pollution the soles of those who were bidden to the Sloane-Carmichael wedding. And there were many, for Mona Carmichael was a Minister's daughter and the moving spirit of the Naughty Nine. Also, she was a bride extremely good to look upon. She possessed the slender body of the *jeune fils*, and an age-old wisdom in the advantageous exhibition of it. When not engaged in devising spectacular "stunts" for her eight disciples, she was usually enjoying masculine approbation expressed in terms that described the speaker as being simply crazy about her. She had reached the point when a modest man was the most boresome thing on earth.

No sermon that was ever preached from the pulpit of the sacred fane would have exposed the mephistophelean cynicism of the present day in its attitude towards the Solemnization of Matrimony by the Church, as did this particular wedding. It might have been a deliberate revival of some medieval mystery play, staged for the purpose of provoking a recreant world to repentance. Men in youth and age were there, whose thoughts throughout the ceremony were never lifted above the level of lubricity. Their presence at any of the matrimonial pageants of that gallant Defender of the Faith, Henry the Eighth, would have lent a distinct flavour to the atmosphere.

The younger married women among the guests recalled their own weddings, and endeavoured to convey the impression that they had relinquished themselves to their husbands with protest, if not martyrdom. They wore an unconvincingly pensive air.

The spinsters betrayed a touch of malice, although they tried to look as though feeling that any woman who married was a fool. Bitterly, they realised the transparency of their attitude, and that here and there, people were saying,

"Oh, there's So-and-so. Isn't it a pity *she* never married?"

Over all the Church, there was a restlessness, a strange suppression, louder and more definite than the syllabub of broken conversation.

Ushers, khaki-clad, passed ceaselessly up and down the aisles, wearing a manner of mixed hauteur and nervousness. They showed the effect of too much prenuptial and anti-prohibition entertainment. Groups of guests gathered, argued, accepted the places provided with scantily veiled distaste, and became part of the general unrest. Few there were who regarded marriage in the light of a spiritual concept, nor was it easy to see in these exotic social episodes any striving towards an æsthetic ideal. On the contrary, two young people came together, drained the moment of its last dram of pleasure, and separated—if not in a physical sense, certainly in a spiritual one, seeking amusement elsewhere, and with hectic sedulousness.

The family of the bride persistently referred to the spectacle as "simple", and endeavoured to preserve the illusion of economy throughout. This was a War Wedding.

A jungle of palms crowded the chancel and reared their feathered heads against the pillars of the Church. Masses of yellow tulips and daffodils suggested the simplicity of spring. Some twenty pews on either side of the centre aisle were barricaded against intrusion by plain silken cords instead of the richer bands of ribbon that ordinarily would have been used to separate those who had presented gifts in ridiculous excess of their means and affection, from those who had blessed the happy pair with sugar spoons and bon-bon dishes. Even the gowns of the women—according to their own description—harmonised with the note of rigid simplicity that prevailed. Mrs. Long, securely imprisoned by the yellow silken cord, smiled as she watched the procession, for she had seen—by the merest accident—Miss Caplin's advance copy on the function. Miss Caplin was the Society editress of THE CHRONICLE. "The mother of the bride wore a rich but simple creation of dove-grey radium satin, panelled with bands of solid grey pearls. The sleeves were formed of wings that fell to the hem of the gown and were made of dyed rose point. Mrs. Carmichael's hat was of grey tulle with no trimming save a simple bird of Paradise."

That was the sort of thing she had been instructed to say.

Mrs. Blaine passed in review. She was gowned in a black crepe meteor, with bands of rhinestones forming the corsage, and she wore a hat of uncurled ostrich feathers.

Mrs. Pratt's idea of economy was expressed by a royal purple chiffon velvet, trimmed with ornaments of amethyst and pearl.

Lady Elton had managed to pick up an imported creation at a figure that was reduced no more than her own, but she called it a "simple frock" of Delft georgette over silver cloth. Owing to some unfortunate confusion in the composing room, a few lines reporting work on the Civic

Playgrounds crept into the account of the wedding, and the following extraordinary announcement appeared:

> "Lady Elton looked exceptionally charming in a dull blue chiffon over three lavatories and two swimming baths."

A trembling usher, green-white from fatigue and dissipation, bowed Mr. and Mrs. Hudson into the pew. Mrs. Long's practised eye noted that the latter wore a sapphire charmeuse, relieved by old Honiton and showing a motif of fleur-de-lys done in hand embroidery.

"I don't know whether I'm all here or not," panted Mrs. Hudson. "Such a scramble at the last minute!"

"There doesn't seem to be any of you missing," murmured Mrs. Long.

"Oh, how do you do?" she bowed, as Sir Eric and Lady Denby crowded in.

Commonplaces were exchanged.

"I haven't seen you for some time," observed Lady Denby, leaning across the Hudsons.

"I've been keeping very quiet," returned Mrs. Long. "In fact, I'm going into the hospital to-morrow for rather a beastly operation."

Vague expressions of sympathy were dropped into the subdued noise about them. "I'm so sorry ... No, you don't look well ... Oh, there's Mrs. . . . . I hope it's nothing serious ... What *has* Eva Leeds got on?"

"That's the dress Haywood made for Lady Elton and she wouldn't accept," volunteered Mrs. Hudson. "They say he gave it to her. . . ."

Lady Denby interrupted. "What hospital have you chosen?" she asked, making a mental note of the fact that the event called for floral recognition.

"St. Christopher's."

"Oh, how perfect!" breathed Mrs. Hudson, indifferently. "You'll love it, there. The nurses are *so* good to your flowers!"

The recently-created knight, Sir Enoch Cunningham, lumbered up the aisle in the wake of his wife. Sir Enoch had established a record for patriotic service by charging the Government only four times a reasonable profit on the output of his mill. He was prominently listed in the Birthday Honours and on this, his first public appearance, was profoundly self-conscious.

"There go the Cunninghams," whispered Lady Elton from the pew behind Mrs. Long. "Aren't they sickening?"

"When Knighthood was in Flour," murmured Lady Denby, over her shoulder.

"He always reminds me of a piece of underdone pastry," said Mrs. Long.

"Well," remarked Mrs. Hudson, with a giggle, "they'll be pie for everyone now."

Across the aisle, Pamela de Latour was agitating herself over the fact that Major and Mrs. Beverley were sitting amongst the intimate friends of the groom.

"Why, in heaven's name, do you suppose *they* have been put *there?*" she demanded of Miss Tyrrell and the Angus-McCallums, who shared her pew.

"Didn't he and Sloane fly together?" suggested one of the latter. "Or did he save his life . . . or something?"

"I don't know. But it seems odd to put them away up there. I heard he'd lost his job," said Miss de Latour.

"I heard that, too," agreed Miss Mabel Angus-McCallum.

Miss Tyrrell couldn't believe it. She urged her companions to recall everything that looked like corroborative evidence, and even then cried skeptically,

"But are you *sure?* May he not have taken on something else?"

Miss Latour didn't think so. She had the news on pretty good authority. She regretted, however, to have caused Miss Tyrrell such acute distress, and hoped the report might be incorrect.

"Although I doubt it," she said. "Colonel Mayhew told me that they were going back to England."

"I had no idea they were such great friends of yours, Lily," whispered Miss Mabel Angus-McCallum. "In most quarters they were not very popular."

"Friends?" echoed Miss Tyrrell, indignantly. "They were no friends of mine, I assure you!"

"Then why—" began the other three "—why are you so upset by hearing that he's lost his job?"

"Because," answered Miss Tyrrell. "I was afraid it wasn't so!"

Several rows behind them, Azalea Deane sat crushed against the ample folds of Miss Leila Brant. She had refused to accompany Marjorie Dilling, despite the latter's threat that she would stay at home rather than go alone.

"I know you are not serious," returned Azalea, in her gently insistent way, "for, of course, you should be there. A special seat will be reserved for you, and you must pretend to enjoy hob-snobbing with the notables."

Miss Brant fidgetted, fretting at her failure to impress Azalea with a sense of her importance. Like Mr. Sullivan, her activities were conducted largely and with a certain grandeur that was pleasing even to those who recognised its intense untruth. She adorned the cheap and commonplace, and had really a shrewd eye for transforming simple articles into pieces of expensive and decorative uselessness. Furthermore, she shared with Dilling a perfect genius for discovering clever assistants—artisans—whose ideas were better than her own, and whom she never tried to lead, but was content to follow. Moreover, she learned long ago to cultivate none but the wealthiest of patrons. Her shop, her wares, even she, herself, exuded an atmosphere of opulent exclusiveness. To be a regular patron of the Ancient Chattellarium was to attain a certain social eminence, to share the air breathed by Millionaires, Knights and Ladies—by Government House. One never stepped into the shop without meeting somebody of importance.

At the moment, however, she was not entirely happy. She had a vast respect for Azalea, but didn't like her. Azalea always made her uncomfortable. She was conscious of secret amusement, perhaps a tinge of contempt behind the enigmatic expression in her etiolated eyes. Whereas Dilling, in Azalea's presence, felt himself the man he wished to be, Miss Brant recognised a very inferior person hiding behind the arras of her very superior manner, and she felt that Azalea saw this creature plainly, penetrating its insincerity, its petty ambitions; in short, that she perceived all the weaknesses that Miss Brant hoped none would suspect.

"There's So-and-So," she cried, incessantly. "In strict confidence, I will tell you that they have just given me rather a nice commission to do their— Oh, and there's So-and-So! Where in the world, *do* you suppose they will seat all these people?"

Azalea smiled and shrugged. Miss Brant felt snubbed, as though her companion had said, "Why bother? It's not your affair. You always take such delight in meddling in other people's business."

She took refuge in that too-little used harbour, Silence. But briefly. She left it to remark,

"Oh, there go the Prendergasts! How do you do?" she bowed, with extreme affability, catching Mrs. Prendergast's eye. Then she flushed. Azalea was regarding her with a smile that seemed to strip every particle of cordiality from her salutation and reduce it to a medium of barter exchanged for the extremely expensive gift Mrs. Prendergast had been cajoled into buying for the bridal pair. Miss Brant felt somehow that Azalea was thinking,

"If she hadn't made a satisfactory purchase, you wouldn't even bother to nod your head. You never used to."

"You may not believe it, Azalea," she said, as though moved to self-justification, "but Mrs. Prendergast is *really* rather a dear. It sounds stupid, but one can't help seeing that her intentions are good."

"Really! Aristotle said that Nature's intentions were always good. The trouble was that she couldn't carry them out."

"But they really *are* getting on," protested Miss Brant, watching the ostentatious progress of her patron down the aisle. "Don't you think they are acquiring *quite* an air?"

"I think the Dawkter is acquiring quite a pragmatic walk. And it's especially conspicuous in church."

"Yes, isn't it?" assented Miss Brant, hastily, and wondering if Azalea referred to some physical disability that had resisted the effects of ANTI-AGONY. "There! They've been put with the Pratts. Confidentially, I'll tell you that *she* bought rather a good bit, too . . . didn't want to be eclipsed by the Prendergasts, you know. *Isn't* their rivalry amusing?"

"And lucrative, I should say."

Miss Brant veered away from the sordid business angle. "Look at them, now," she cried. "Mrs. Pratt has the floor. She doesn't even pause for breath. Azalea, what *can* she be saying?"

"Words—words—words! I'm afraid Mr. Pratt frequently regrets ignoring Nietzsche's advice."

"Whose?"

"Nietzsche's. Don't you remember, he said, 'Before marriage this question should be put—Will you continue to be satisfied with this woman's conversation until old age? Everything else in marriage is transitory'."

Miss Brant cast an inward glance upon her own conversational powers, and wondered if there was anything personal behind Azalea's remark. Aloud, she said,

"How clever of you to remember all those quotations, my dear! I always wish—Oh, there goes Mrs. Dilling! Heavens, doesn't she look like a ghost?"

Azalea had already noted the haggardness of Marjorie's appearance, and, knowing nothing of her encounter with Mr. Sullivan, attributed it solely to the over-strain of War Work.

"She doesn't know how to save herself," she said.

"Yes, she really has been rather splendid, hasn't she?" assented Miss Brant. "*Everyone* says so ... I remember the first time I ever saw her. She wanted a terrible what-not-thing repaired. Little did I imagine, then, that some day she would be the wife of a Minister of the Crown. And have you heard a rumour about the Premiership? It makes me feel *quite* weepy. Only—only—I *wish* she wouldn't wear such *awful* hats!"

"What do people say?" asked Azalea, ignoring the latter remark.

"Oh, *you* know the sort of thing—that she has done so much more than lend her name to patriotic functions and sit on platforms; that she has actually worked in the War Gardens, packed boxes, sewed, cooked and visited the soldiers' wives. You know, it *is* rather splendid!"

Azalea nodded and raised her eyes to the stained glass window memorialising another Gentle Spirit who found His happiness in ministering to the needs of the humbler folk. "It *is* rather splendid," she agreed.

"It must be very late," said Miss Brant. "I wonder if that little minx, Mona, has been up to some of her tricks. By the way, have you heard about the Trevelyans?"

"Mercy, no! Not already?"

"Positively!"

"Why, it seems only last week since we were watching them get married. Is it a boy or a girl?"

"Both! And the screaming part of it is that the instant Mona heard the news, she *had herself insured against twins!*"

"You're joking!"

"It's a fact. Lloyd's took her on. I say, Azalea, doesn't Mrs. Dilling look ghastly?"

Marjorie sat next Mrs. Blaine and Lady Fanshawe, feeling more ghastly than she looked. She had never been ill in her life, save when the babies came and that, of course, didn't count. One just naturally had babies and made no fuss about it. But this was different. She had no particular pain. She wasn't quite sure that her head ached. But she felt strangely weak and uncertain of herself.

Lady Fanshawe and Mrs. Blaine were complaining of their servants. Neither would admit the other's supremacy in having the worst the Dominion afforded.

"But you have a very good cook," Mrs. Blaine protested.

"My dear, how *can* you say so?" cried Lady Fanshawe. "Twice, she has nearly poisoned us!"

"Well, the dinner I ate last Thursday at your house couldn't have been better."

"A happy exception, I assure you."

"Why don't you get rid of her?" asked Mrs. Blaine.

"I shall ... but not at once—not until I have some one else in view. However, if you need a cook, dear," she went on, "why not try Mrs. Hudson's Minnie? *She* is really an excellent woman, and can always be tempted with higher wages."

Mrs. Blaine turned away with a fine assumption of indifference, and Marjorie ventured a sympathetic word in Lady Fanshawe's ear.

"It's very bothersome, isn't it?" she murmured, "especially when one does so much entertaining. You always seem to have such bad luck with your servants. I believe I could send you a cook."

The older woman flung a peculiar look at her, and whispered, "You dear, simple soul! I've a perfect *treasure*! But I don't dare say so; every one of my friends would try to take her from me!"

Outside, the handsome departmental car drew smartly to a standstill, and the Hon. Peter Carmichael assisted his daughter to alight. She tripped up the carpeted stairs with no more concern than though she were going to a Golf Club Tea.

The trembling, green-white usher came forward to meet her. A group of bridesmaids stood near the door.

"Well, old thing," cried Mona, "how's the silly show, anyway?"

"Full house," returned the usher. "S.R.O. as the theatres say. At five dollars a head, you'd have quite a tidy nest egg, y'know!"

"Rotten business—ushing," cried Mona. "You look all in, young fella me lad."

"I am. A company of duds, I call 'em. Balky as mules. Nobody wants to sit with anybody else."

"Do you blame them?"

"My God, no! As the poet sang, 'I'd rather live in vain than live in Ottawa'!"

"Come, daughter," said the Hon. Peter, fussily crooking his elbow.

"The lovely bride entered the church on the arm of her father," simpered Mona, pinching his ear. "Forward, everybody. We're off!"

Four little flower girls led the way, four being a simple number, much less intricate than forty-four or ninety-four and a fraction. Their costumes were beautifully simple—flesh-coloured tights and a pair of wings, in cunning imitation of Dan Cupid. They carried bows and a quiver full of arrows, the latter tipped with yellow daffodils.

They were followed by the six bridesmaids, who also carried out this note of extreme simplicity. Their costumes were composed of yellow tulle, sprinkled with a profusion of brilliants, and were supposed to suggest early morning dew upon a field of tulips. In place of flowers, they carried simple parasols of chiffon, and each wore the gift of the groom—a gold vanity box bearing a simple monogram in platinum.

The bride was gowned in plainest ivory satin. She had dispensed with the conventional wreath of orange blossoms, and her brow was crowned with a simple rose-point cap, whose billowy streamers fell to the tip of her slender train. She wore no ornaments save the gift of the groom—a simple bar of platinum supporting thirty-two plain diamonds.

At the sight of her, a ripple of admiration ran through the crowd. She felt it and was pleased in her youthfully insolent fashion. She bore herself with none of the modesty that characterised the bride of fifty years ago. Rather was she suggestive of the mannequin on parade.

The bridal party was just turning from the altar to the inspiriting strains from Mendelssohn, when Hebe Barrington entered the church with Mr. Sullivan.

"Oh, Lord, we're late," she muttered, pulling him quickly along the aisle. "We'll have to find seats somewhere before the parade reaches us."

"Not so far forward," protested the Hon. Rufus, trying to hang back.

"Don't be so bashful," returned Hebe. "We're creating quite a sensation and stealing some of the limelight from the bride. '*La vice appuyé sur la bras de crime*,'" she whispered, enjoying herself enormously.

"This is a damned awkward mess," growled Mr. Sullivan, under his breath. "I can't see a seat, anywhere."

"Nor I, and they're nearly upon us. We'll have to stop here."

The location selected for the enforced halt was not a happy one for Lady Denby—nor, indeed, for any of the occupants of that pew. In order to prevent confusion and a disarrangement of the procession, Mrs. Barrington and her escort were obliged to disregard the silken cord and squeeze in beside Sir Eric, and thus cut off quite successfully the view of the spectacle from his diminutive and enraged wife.

She accepted their apologies frostily, and made an obvious effort to escape from the offending pair, but the density of the crowd frustrated her design. She found herself impinged upon Mrs. Barrington's scented shoulder, and absolutely unable to free herself. The colour mounted hotly to her delicate cheeks. Her eyes sparkled dangerously.

"You *must* come to some of my parties, dear Lady Denby," Hebe said, sweetly. "You, and Sir Eric . . . just simple affairs, you know, where we can snatch an hour's relaxation. A little drink . . . a cigarette, a game of cards—er—do you dance?"

"I do not," said Lady Denby.

"Ah! What a pity!"

"Nor do I smoke."

"What?"

"Nor drink, nor gamble."

"Perhaps you swear," suggested Hebe, with elaborate mischievousness. "One must have some vices."

"I don't agree with you," snapped Lady Denby, relieved to find that they had almost reached the door.

"Well, what *do* you do, then?" queried Hebe, in a tone that was louder than was at all necessary.

Lady Denby stepped into the vestibule. In a space momentarily cleared, she turned and faced her tormentor.

"What do I do?" she repeated. "I mind my own business . . . wear untransparent petticoats, and . . . sleep in my *own* husband's bed!"

CHAPTER 26.

*D*illing had refused to go to the wedding. Work was his excuse. He intended to clear up the accumulation of departmental business that lay massed in an orderly disarray upon his desk.

But he didn't work. Each attempt proved to be a failure. He was conscious of fatigue—or, if not precisely that—of the ennui one feels when work is universally suspended, as on a rainy, dispiriting holiday.

The outer office was hushed and empty. That Azalea's absence could so utterly bereave the atmosphere, struck him as preposterous, an incomprehensible thing. He struggled against it, but without success. He was lapped about by a feeling of isolation, of stark desolation. Staring at Azalea's vacant chair, it seemed as if he stood in the midst of a dead and frozen world. With an effort at pulling himself together, he closed the door and returned to his position by the window.

He looked with blind eyes towards the southern sky, where pennons of smoke followed the locomotive that crossed and re-crossed the little subway bridge. Winter had been industrious during the past months and seemed loath, even now, to relinquish her supremacy to Spring. Tall pyramids of snow still clung to the corners of the Museum where abutments of the building shut off the warmth of a pale gold sun. The ground was black and spongy, and in every gutter, rivulets of water stirred the urge of the sea in the minds of swarms of children.

But Dilling saw none of these things. He was fighting the oppression of this curious lassitude and striving to recapture his ardour for work. The effect was not noticeably successful. He felt tired, stupid, drugged, as though some vital part of him was imprisoned and inert. He longed to be free, to abandon himself to a riot of emotion, to feel as acutely with his body as with his mind. He longed to overcome this numbness, this nostalgia of the senses, and to taste the fruits that gave to life its pungent tang and flavour. For the first time he saw himself emotionally shrivelled, inappetent of joy, and he veered away from the knowledge, wishing that he could remodel himself to love and suffer and hunger like other men.

He forced himself to a perception of the panorama at which he had been staring, the clumps of bushes heavy with uncurled buds, the gay costumes of the children playing in the icy gutters opposite, a sharp red tulip bravely facing the frosty air. He knew now that never had he taken into account the vital force behind living objects—cattle, flowers, trees, even the wheat itself, and he began to feel that all these and even inanimate things, such as the chair and desk in the desolate outer office, were instinct with life; Azalea's life! How pitiful his limitations!

He loved her. He wanted her. He needed her. Life was without form and void lacking the stimulation, the inspiration of her presence. She was his *alter ego*, upon whom his mind and spirit depended as did his frail body upon food. Thinking upon her made him free of the hitherto remote pleasance of comradeship between the sexes.

"What torment," he muttered, repeatedly. "What torment to know this joy and be unable to possess it!"

The telephone rang. He turned impatiently to the instrument.

"Sullivan?" he echoed. "No—not too busy. I'll be up there shortly."

During the week preceding his conversation with Marjorie, the Hon. Member for Morroway had busied himself in a cautious testing of the extent of his influence. He found that a majority of the Western Members needed no incentive from him to support Raymond Dilling, and from them he withheld all mention of the proposed change in policy he had suggested to Dilling's wife. With the Maritime Members, however, he employed slightly different tactics, approaching them as one entrusted with confidential information, and hinting that in exchange for the premiership, Dilling would be willing to foreswear his platform, betray his original sponsors, and stand forth as a defender of Eastern interests, with especial emphasis upon those concerned in the annihilation of the Freight Bill, the abandonment of the Elevator project, and the indefinite postponement of the Eastlake and Donahue railway measures.

With but an odd exception or two, his self-imposed mission was entirely successful. He called on Marjorie. He arranged for an interview with Dilling.

Five men rose as the youthful Minister entered the room: Howarth, Turner, young Gilbert, the Radical, the Hon. Gordon Blaine, who administered his Ministerial office—without portfolio—with unbroken suavity and bonhomie, and Mr. Sullivan, himself.

"Good afternoon, gentlemen," said Dilling. "No, I won't drink, if you will excuse me."

He accepted the chair that Howarth offered, and waited for some one to speak.

What a scene it was, and what an episode for the Muse of History . . . Over in France, the flower of Canada's youth—the heirs of the ages—were freely offering their splendid bodies upon the altar of War in testimony of the eternal need of human sacrifice for things that transcend all human values. Over there, the spirit of the young nation was responding magnificently to a supreme test of its fineness. Here at home, within the very walls of the buildings dedicated to the purpose of moulding and directing the welfare of the nation, men of mature years were not ashamed, by plot and intrigue, to make of Canada a scorn and a byword. A man of the highest instincts for public service was being tempted by his political associates to foreswear his ideals by a sordid bargaining for power.

The Hon. Member for Morroway was the first to break the silence.

"Mr. Dilling," he began, "we are all men of plain speech, here, and there is nothing to be gained by euphemisms or beating about the bush. In a word, then, we wish to sound you on this question of the Premiership, and to offer you an option—let us call it—on the post."

So, and in this wise, the supreme moment of his career had come to Raymond Dilling.

The shock was such that his mind refused for a moment to function. The Premiership! The goal for which he had striven! The pinnacle of his ambition! And to be reached so soon!

What would Azalea say? . . . and poor little Marjorie?

"You—er—take me at a disadvantage, gentlemen," he said. "I am unprepared for this . . ." and he turned again to the spokesman.

Mr. Sullivan felt his way after the manner of a cautious pachyderm,

"This offer," he said, "is contingent upon a slight change of policy. You would, no doubt, be willing to reverse your attitude on what I may describe as the Wheat and Railway proposals. I need not say," he continued, smoothly, "that this can be done without any forfeiture of your honesty of purpose, or any reflection upon your acumen as a statesman. Understand that we approach you in the true and best interest of the Canadian people. Once understand that, Mr. Dilling, and I am convinced that you will allow no consideration of personal disadvantage to weigh against your compliance with our wishes."

Dilling made no reply, but a pungent French phrase that he had read somewhere, welled up to him curiously from the subconscious . . . "*Il faut faire tout le rebours de ce qu'il dit.*" This gave him pause, the instinct for caution was touched. Was this his cue for the answer he should ultimately give? Did this not warn him to take the very opposite course to that pointed out to him? He must have no illusions as to the right of the matter.

Then temptation gripped him. His soul was in tumult. Principle cried out, "Abhor that which is evil," while the Will to Power smote him with the reminder that "Opportunity knocks but once at the door of kings". What could he not accomplish for his beloved country with sovereign power in his hands and his talents in the very flower of their prime! How subtle was the lure.

Must he not recognise in this offer the call of destiny to complete the work of nation-building begun by those fathers of Confederation—Macdonald, and Cartier and Tupper? These were names never to be erased from the scroll of Fame, and why should not he be numbered of their immortal company?

The torch of constructive patriotism lighted by them, had burned low. Let it be his to revive the waning flame. Was this not the vision that had inspired him, that had drawn him from the Last Great West?

That Dilling was powerfully moved was patent to those who had come to tempt him. His frail body quivered with the strain, and Sullivan was too astute a politician to neglect this fleeting advantage. He pressed for an answer before sober second-thought could evoke for Dilling a suspicion of the duplicity underlying the offer.

"What do you think of the idea, Dilling?"

This challenge to a swift decision served to impress him with the danger of the situation, and Dilling's mind reacted with fine discernment. No matter how he decided, he would not be swayed by impulse.

"What do I think of the idea? I think your proposal is most generous in its implication of my fitness for so tremendous a post. I am overwhelmed by the honour you would do me, deeply grateful to you and your influential friends for this frank appreciation of my efforts in public life. But I fear you estimate them too highly."

"Nothing of the kind," the Hon. Gordon Blaine interrupted, amiably.

"The only man for the job," muttered Turner.

"Be that as it may," Dilling continued, "I must take time to consider. For you, as well as for the country and myself, my decision must not be arrived at on the low plane of personal advantage. But I shall not delay you longer than to-morrow morning, gentlemen. There is need, I see, for prompt decision. Meanwhile, accept my assurance of obligation, and allow me to bid you good afternoon."

CHAPTER 27.

*I*t was only natural perhaps, that Dilling should suffer the full and terrible force of Sullivan's temptation after he thought he had conquered it, for it was only then that he permitted himself the dangerous pleasure of examining its possibilities. In his silent office, surrounded by the hush of a building deserted now save by the Dominion Police who never relaxed their vigilance, he considered the might-have-beens, and wrestled with beasts that threatened to rise up and devour him.

Sullivan's implications recurred in their most convincing aspect. Sullivan was so nearly right. Must not a statesman possess flexibility of mind as well as rigidity of principle? Must not he be able to adapt himself to the exigencies of the time? Dilling required none to remind him that the whole fabric of Canada's political life was changed, that the policy in ante-bellum days was, in many cases, inimical to the public good, to-day. He saw, clearly, that concentration of the Dominion's resources upon Returned Soldiers and their re-establishment was an inevitable consequence of War. He knew that Freight, Elevator and Railway projects must be postponed. And he was in favour of postponing them. But Sullivan asked more. He asked that the very principles that had inspired his support be abandoned in exchange for a post of power.

Ambition's seductive voice whispered of compromise. What else is diplomacy, indeed? Supreme issues have been won by a trick; statesmanship is permitted greater latitude than is allowed the private individual.

He had learned that a sensitive conscience is a disability in political life. If a man is revolted by the corruptness of his Party, he can not lead it with spirit, nor can he justify it as a medium for serving the State. It is sadly true that rather to his imperfections than to the fineness of his qualities is the success of the statesman due.

On the other hand, public men of genius, in these days, are not excused for their *dulcia vitia* as they used to be. "I would be damned," he reflected, "for the frailties that seemed to endear Pitt to the populace. So long as a leader is chaste and sober, he may be unscrupulous with impunity."

His spirit cried out in anguish, and he was tortured by the whirling orb of thought that compels great minds to suffer the perturbation of a common life-time in the space of a moment. He raised his eyes to the window, unconsciously seeking strength from the glory framed there. Suddenly, his soul was quickened; he became alive to the wonder of God in Nature ... the sun was setting in amber dust ... pale greenish streaks stretched overhead and dissolved in a pansy mist. Upon the horizon, masses of heavy cloud lay banked like a mountain range bathed in violet rain.

The words of the psalmist flashed across Dilling's mind and he murmured, " 'I will lift up mine eyes unto the hills, from whence cometh my help.' If God can pour strength into a frail vessel, may He pour it generously into me."

There was a light tap on the door, and Azalea entered the room.

Dilling stared at her without speaking. He had never attached much importance to coincidences. They were, he thought, significant only in the world of fiction. When they occurred in reality, they only emphasised the incoherency of the substance. But Azalea's coming was like an answer to prayer. He could think of nothing to say.

"Marjorie told me you had not come home," she began, "and I thought that perhaps the work—Why, what is it?" Her tone changed. "What is the matter?"

Briefly, he told her. "They have given me until to-morrow morning to make up my mind."

"Perhaps I'd better go," she said.

"No, no! Stay and help me. I don't feel as if I could fight this thing out alone."

Heavily, he threw himself into a chair. His thinness, his pallor, his general air of frailness, made Azalea faint with pity for him. Sitting in the half-tone of departing daylight, his hair seemed silvered with frost, his face was drawn, his body sagged like that of an old man.

"What do you think I should do?" he asked her.

"What you know is right."

"But if I don't know what is right?"

"Ah, but you must! None knows it better. Education is only a matter of knowing what is right and then having the courage to do it."

He objected almost petulantly, supposing that he lacked the necessary courage. Azalea smiled, and there was pride behind the gesture.

"That, above all others, is the virtue you possess. It is the foundation upon which all the rest are built. It is that which helps them to endure . . ."

Dilling listened to the quiet confident voice with an emotion so profound that it was like a deep-bosomed bell ringing in his soul. He was conscious of a curious sensation, as though his spirit had escaped a crushing weight—(a weight that still cramped his body)—as though it had been set free.

In a low voice, and in phrases that were disjointed and but half spoken, he began to talk about himself, his ambitions, his career; and Azalea listened feeling that part of him had died, and that she was hearing but the echo of his voice.

"It never occurred to me that my life was barren," she heard him say, "barren and grim . . . just a brain . . . a machine that, given direction, could drive on with peculiar force and vanquish those of different constitution . . . Never felt the need of friends . . . nor the lack of them . . . Alone and grim . . . But I loved Canada!" A suggestion of warmth stole into his voice. "I loved the West . . . I asked for nothing better than to serve my country—it may be that some men serve women that way . . . I wanted to get into the heart of it, to feel the throb, the life-waves beating out across the land . . . Then the Capital . . . so different . . . The men, the administration . . . Bewildering to find that I could take my place with those upon whom I had looked as gods . . . Poor Marjorie! This would mean much to her . . ."

"When the facts are known, you will go down in history," Azalea told him, "as a shining example of political integrity."

"I'm not so sure. More likely, I will be held up to illustrate the failure of Success. My God," he cried, suddenly, "why can't I live . . . why can't I live?"

His suffering was terrible for her to bear. Yet, she held herself in strict control. "Success has become an odious word to me," she said, "a juggernaut to which Truth and Justice are too often sacrificed. You have achieved . . . there is achievement even in failure . . ."

Her words filled him with bleak despair. He had hoped that she would argue his decision, try to persuade him to alter it, show him that he was wrong. For a fleeting second, he was guilty of resentment, doubting that she divined his pain at relinquishing his career. But he looked into her face and was ashamed.

"Azalea!"

"Raymond!"

A flame of delight ran through his being. It was as though his whole body had been transfused with the ultimate beauty of life. "Do you think I have achieved?"

"Yes ... the expression of a great spiritual truth," she answered. "No compromise, no diplomacy—another name for deceit. That you have been misunderstood and defamed was only to have been expected. It is the price men pay for putting forth the truth. But you, who have been so fearless— you are not weakening now?"

"No," he said. "I cannot weaken with you to help me. I will go back. There is no other way."

"Go back?" she echoed. "Go back to the West?"

"Life would be intolerable here—especially for Marjorie."

"You will leave Ottawa altogether?" The words were scarcely audible. She had not anticipated this.

"Not altogether. Part of me will remain. This is my soul's graveyard, Azalea ... They say a soul cannot die, but never was there a more soothing untruth spread abroad for the peace of the credulous. Mine died to-day— only a few hours after it was born."

"My dear, my dear," she whispered, trying to keep her voice free from the coldness of death that lay upon her own spirit.

They sat in silence a space, while waves of misery welled up about them. Then Azalea's control broke. She covered her face with her hands.

"Don't!" cried Dilling, sharply. "Don't! Tell me the truth—do you want me to stay?"

"No!"

Suddenly, he left his chair and knelt beside her, burying his face in the folds of her dress, and groping for her hand. For a time, he could not speak, could not tell how much he loved her, could not articulate the thought that hers was the power to make vocative his life's stern purpose. He could only cling to her and suffer.

"Azalea," he cried, at last, "how can I go? I can't live without you—I'm not even sure that I can die!"

She felt strangled and heard words falling from her lips without understanding how she spoke them. "Are you forgetting the needs of the West—the opportunity for your talents, there? Will you close your ears to the call of your ambition?"

He denied the existence of ambition. It had died when life was stricken from his soul.

She raised his head between her hands. They trembled and were cold.

"Raymond, do you love me?"

"You know it."

"Then pick up the standard once more! Carry on! Respond to that inner voice that presently will cry out to you. Ambition is inspired by emotion rather than intellect. If you love me, don't fling down the torch!"

"But I need you," he protested. "You are the fount, the source of all my power. You are my torch. Without you, the world is plunged in darkness. I can see to do nothing."

"There is an inextinguishable beam of friendship. More . . . When one achieves an understanding such as ours, one enters into a spiritual romance."

He bowed his head against her breast. Gently, she encircled his body with her arms. Twilight quivered in the still room.

Presently, he looked up.

"And what of you, my dear? Yours is the harder part . . . Will you suffer very much, Azalea?"

She closed her eyes to hide from him her agony. "Emotions, even the most happy ones, are shot with pain," she said.

"Yes, I'm learning that, myself, God pity me! But I don't want you to suffer through my love. Oh, Azalea . . . woman . . . you have been my white angel, my guiding star, that I took for granted as naturally as that one, in the sky! You have been for me the Truth and the Light, the balm for which I cried in all my agony and strife. You have accepted me as I am, nor asked a profession of my love in any way that was not *me*. And I leave you, never having served you. What is there of me that can hold a place in your life?"

She thought a moment, then,

"Listen," she whispered. "Here is my answer. I wrote it yesterday . . .

"Sometimes I wake and say, 'I love him!'

And sometimes, 'He loves me!'

But whichever way it is

The day is filled with a finer purpose."

"Azalea, let me kneel at your feet!"

"No, no! Kiss me . . . Oh, my dear love, kiss me . . ."

For a time, they clung to one another, and when at last she withdrew from him, the room was plunged in utter darkness.

CHAPTER 28.

Of the five men who were left in Mr. Sullivan's office, the Hon. Member for Morroway was not the least abashed. He had never confronted a moral quality like this in his whole experience. After all, he thought, recalling the sheer fineness of the man, men are something more than a mere merchantable commodity in the market of politics. Possibly, there are others who, like Dilling, disproved Walpole's *mot*, that every man has his price . . .

It was not, however, on the knees of the gods that Mr. Sullivan should be diverted from his purpose by considerations such as these. He felt that Dilling was the only man to play the lead in the interesting drama he desired to stage, that he must win him beyond all doubt, and soon. Nothing but a refusal could be expected if so lofty and withal so astute a mind had time for reflection.

Dilling had just finished a solitary dinner—Marjorie served in a canteen every Wednesday evening—when his visitor was announced. The Hon. Member for Morroway was conscious of a change in him; there was the rapture of a seer in his eyes, and a bearing of victory—a jocund note of heroism in him.

"Why did you follow me, Mr. Sullivan?" were his words of greeting. "I thought I said I needed time for my decision."

"Indeed, you did, Mr. Dilling. But it is important that I should have your answer at once, and besides, you gave me no chance to persuade you that you would be right in accepting the Premiership at this juncture in our history. Will you consent to hear what I would like to say?"

Dilling led the way into his study and motioned the Hon. Member to a chair. He stood.

"Proceed, Mr. Sullivan. I shall need much encouragement if I am to meet your views."

"Hang it all, Dilling, let's get off our high horses and down to brass tacks—if you will allow me to mix my metaphors! You left us before I had a chance to show you, as I had intended, that the interests of Canada imperatively demand that no more money be spent at this time in facilitating the marketing of wheat—for that is what your Elevator and Railway policy means in the last analysis. First and foremost the Returned Soldiers are to be considered if we are to shut off Bolshevism from rearing its ugly head here. Are you in accord with me, so far?"

"Quite," returned Dilling. "What then?"

"The inevitable. The Governmental money bags will be kept lean for some years in meeting the just demands of the returned men, and the sentiment of the whole community will be behind them. Not only will the bankers of Eastern Canada put a spoke in your wheel—for they are spiteful over losing so much money in the West—but you will find it difficult to borrow money in the States when the people recognise that an extension of Canadian railroads means hostility to the pet scheme of many of their financiers."

"Financiers are traditionally hostile," said Dilling.

"True, but the situation here is particularly acute, for these men to whom I refer have sought to obtain the sanction of this country to a greater utilisation of the Great Lakes and St. Lawrence waterways for transportation. They can scarcely be expected to lend money for a diverting project . . . and you can wring blood from a turnip as easily as you can borrow money in England!"

"I'm afraid your last observation is only too true, Mr. Sullivan."

"I'm sure of it. I don't think I need elaborate the national argument in favour of your change of front, I've said enough on that head. Coming to the more personal side of things, every statesman from Julius Cæsar to George Washington has had to compromise. You can't be stiff in your adherence to principle even in appointments to government posts! Sir John Macdonald, Laurier—all of them—have had to appoint incompetent persons to the Civil Service over the heads of men thoroughly qualified in ability and character to serve the State in the finest way . . . a matter of expediency . . . expediency . . ."

Dilling said nothing, so Sullivan went on.

"What's the use of quoting Lincoln as a model of probity in dispensing offices—Lincoln was the only man in the world who could be prophet, priest and king in politics at one and the same time—and *he* couldn't save his face, to-day!"

Somewhere, a door closed, and the treble of childish voices blended in happy confusion.

"Think of your wife and children, Dilling . . . Marjorie . . . I use her Christian name by right of a deep and esteemed friendship . . . Marjorie has suffered greatly from the snobocracy of Ottawa. She has confided much to me, that out of respect for your busy life, has been withheld from—er—her natural confidant, and it is only to be expected that you should seize the opportunity to furnish her the pleasure of playing a supreme stellar role in the social life of the nation. Moreover . . ."

"Stop, Mr. Sullivan! You have said enough . . . more than enough! You have offended me by the casuistry of your argument on behalf of the public need for my desertion of the policies I have proclaimed. Your appeal on the personal side is a gross insult to me. However I may have seemed to waver until this moment, I now unhesitatingly and absolutely decline to accept your overtures. More than that, you have persuaded me that I must leave public life. No, I beg of you, say nothing further! Let me bid you good night, Mr. Sullivan—but do not leave me without the conviction that you have done me a real service."

Sullivan lowered his head as he left the room. A curious aching had taken possession of his throat. He had been accustomed to swear after unsuccessful interviews with politicians . . . Just now, profanity refused to rise at his command.

Marjorie's tired voice roused him.

"It's very late, dearie," she said. "Won't you try to get some rest?"

"Presently. I've something to tell you, first. Will you come in and sit down?"

With unaccustomed gentleness, he arranged a chair for her. She dropped into it as though suddenly bereft of the power to stand. Her eyes were feverishly bright, and fixed upon him with apprehension that amounted almost to fear.

Dilling was conscious of intense pity for her. How unequal she was to the demand he—his life—imposed! How gamely she had borne the strain!

He hated her appearance to-night. Evidently, she had returned from the canteen only in time to dress for some more brilliant function. She wore a peach-coloured satin, covered with a sort of iridescent lace—a hideously sophisticated dress, too low and too light; it bedizened her, overlaid all her native simplicity. Dilling was, as a rule, oblivious to the details of women's clothes, but to-night his perceptions were sharpened, and he examined his wife critically.

As he did so, a horrid thought took possession of his mind. He saw her dress, her manner—her barricade of behavior—as something degrading, detestable, utterly foreign to her. A more imaginative man would have fallen back upon the fancy that the pure gold of her nature was being covered with the whitewash of social pretense. So deeply did it offend him.

"I have been offered the Premiership," he announced.

"Oh!"

That was all she could say. Months ago she had arrived at the point where she stood on guard over every act and utterance, fearing to proceed lest she should violate some sacred creed and call forth criticism and disdain. And now, when she wanted to speak, she could not. Inarticulate and frightened, she sat, like a person paralysed by nightmare.

"Yes, this afternoon," Dilling continued, and then as he had told Azalea, "they have given me until to-morrow morning to decide."

"It's splendid," said Marjorie. "It's wonderful . . . but then you deserve it, dearie. You've worked so hard!"

"So have you, Marjorie!"

"Exactly what will it mean?" she questioned, timidly. "Will we have to move again, and do more entertaining?"

"You take it for granted that I'll accept?"

"Oh! You *can't* refuse?"

"Why not?"

"Well—well—" Mr. Sullivan's promptings eluded her entirely. "The premiership? . . . Oh, Raymond, you mustn't refuse!"

She began to argue, falteringly, but with a desperate earnestness that betrayed her own lack of conviction. And as he listened, an odious suspicion crept into Dilling's mind.

"Who's been putting you up to this?" he demanded. "You are voicing arguments that are not your own. Tell me, Marjorie, who has been putting words into your mouth?"

Marjorie refused to meet his eyes, but her lips framed the name "Sullivan".

It was her manner more than her speech that caused the dawn of a slow horror. Dilling recalled evidences of the man's frequent visits—books, flowers, chocolates, games for the children—Yes, he remembered now, that the children called him "Uncle Rufus" . . . and hadn't Sullivan, himself, hinted at an unsuspected intimacy? Had he not boasted of being Marjorie's close confidant?

"How long has this been going on?" he asked, pursuing his own line of thought.

"Ever since we first came," whispered his wife, failing wholly to follow him.

"You don't mean *years?*"

She bowed her head.

"Why did I never know?" He put the query more to himself than to her.

"I never tried to keep it from you, Raymond!" she was stung into making a defence. "The very first night . . . you were right in the house. No, not this house—the other one. I should think you would have heard us coming downstairs . . . Always, I have tried not to bother you!"

"Coming downstairs?" he echoed. "My God . . . my God!"

A sudden blackness enshrouded him. He was swallowed up in the wreckage of a too-long life, lived in too short a span. His career had been swept away his love was denied him, and now he had lost his wife . . .

"My God," he said again—elemental words wrung by elemental anguish.

A cry, low and terrible, penetrated his misery. Marjorie flung herself at his feet, and gasped,

"No—no—not *that*, Raymond . . . Are you listening to me? Not *that!*"

"What, then?" he muttered.

"Oh, how could you, Raymond? You couldn't think I would do a thing like that?"

"Then what do you mean?"

The story of her association with the Hon. Member for Morroway fell in broken sentences, often misleading, by reason of the very shame she felt in its avowal. As he listened to the innocent little tale, Dilling's heart was torn with pity, and more clearly than before he saw the futility of attempting to mould their simplicity to the form of conduct required by their position. He thought of the West—his West—of a rugged people who were still alive to the practical advancement of idealism, divorced from stultifying subservience to convention. He felt an overpowering urge to return, to identify himself once again with those sturdy people, whom, he believed, would answer the guidance of his hand. He was theirs. They were his. The West was his kingdom, and there he would be content to reign.

A crushing weight seemed lifted from his spirit. Shackles fell away.

"Would you like to go home," he asked Marjorie, "to go home for good and all, I mean?"

The light in her face answered him. It is abundantly true that experiences realised, are a glorified incarnation of dead wishes. The promised return to Pinto Plains was, for Marjorie, a dream that was coming true. She knew the exquisite pain of seeing the complete fulfilment of a passionate desire. No words could translate her feeling.

And so, with gratulation that was void of all regret, they went back to happy mediocrity, far from The Land of Afternoon.

THE END

Lightning Source UK Ltd.
Milton Keynes UK
UKHW010806071022
410089UK00004B/274